PRAISE FOR THE NOVELS OF
#1 NEW YORK TIMES BESTSELLING AUTHOR
BARBARA FREETHY

"I love *The Callaways*! Heartwarming romance, intriguing suspense and sexy alpha heroes. What more could you want?"
-- *NYT Bestselling Author* **Bella Andre**

"I adore *The Callaways*, a family we'd all love to have. Each new book is a deft combination of emotion, suspense and family dynamics. A remarkable, compelling series!"
-- *USA Today Bestselling Author* **Barbara O'Neal**

"Once I start reading a Callaway novel, I can't put it down. Fast-paced action, a poignant love story and a tantalizing mystery in every book!"
-- *USA Today Bestselling Author* **Christie Ridgway**

"In the tradition of LaVyrle Spencer, gifted author Barbara Freethy creates an irresistible tale of family secrets, riveting adventure and heart-touching romance."
-- *NYT Bestselling Author* **Susan Wiggs**
on Summer Secrets

"This book has it all: heart, community, and characters who will remain with you long after the book has ended. A wonderful story."
-- *NYT Bestselling Author* **Debbie Macomber**
on Suddenly One Summer

"Freethy has a gift for creating complex characters."
-- *Library Journal*

Also By Barbara Freethy

To my amazing and talented daughter Kristen.
I love sharing this journey with you!

ON A NIGHT LIKE THIS

The Callaways

BARBARA FREETHY

HYDE
STREET
—PRESS—

HYDE STREET PRESS
Published by Hyde Street Press
1819 Polk Street, Suite 113, San Francisco, California 94109

© Copyright 2015 by Hyde Street Press

Printed in the United States of America

Cover design by Damonza.com
Interior book design by KLF Publishing

ISBN 978-0-9906951-0-3

One

-➤➤➤◄◄◄◄‐

As a teenager, seeing her father's car in the driveway when she came home from school had always made Sara Davidson uneasy. She would steel herself for the evening to come, never quite sure why she felt afraid. Stephen Davidson had never physically abused her, but he had been demanding, and his words cut like a knife. It wasn't always what he said that was the worst part; it was the rejection in his gaze, and the cold quiet that usually followed his disappointment in her.

It would be different now, Sara told herself as she got out of her rental car. She was twenty-nine years old, a successful lawyer, and she hadn't lived at home in ten years. So why did she feel trepidation?

Because her relationship with her father had never been quite right.

They were biologically connected, but emotionally they were as distant as two people could be. Her mother, Valerie, had been the buffer between them, but her mom had died when Sara was nineteen years old. For the past decade it had been just her and her dad. Actually, it had mostly been just her.

While her father had paid for her education and living expenses, he hadn't come to her graduations—not from college or from law school. The last time she'd seen him in person had been five years ago when they'd both attended the funeral of her grandmother, her father's mother.

She walked up the path, pausing at the bottom of the stairs, her hand tightening around the bottle of wine she'd brought for her dad's sixty-fifth birthday on Sunday. She'd tried her best to get him something a wine connoisseur would appreciate – a bottle of 1989 Chateau Mouton Rothschild Bordeaux. The wine had cost as much as her monthly car payment; she hoped it would be worth it. Her father was her only living relative, and she still, probably foolishly, wanted to believe they could find a way to connect with each other.

Her nerves tightened, and she had to fight back the urge to flee. She'd flown all the way across the country to see him; she couldn't back down. Trying to calm her racing heart, she looked around, reminding herself that this had once been home.

Her father's two-story house with the white paint and dark brown trim was located in the middle of the block in a San Francisco neighborhood known as St. Francis Wood. Not far from the ocean, the houses in this part of the city were detached and had yards, unlike much of the city where the homes shared common walls.

Her family had moved into this house when she was nine years old, and one of her favorite places to be was sitting in the swing on the front porch. She'd spent many hours reading or watching the kids who lived next door. The Callaways were a big, Irish-Catholic blended family. Jack Callaway, a widower with four boys, had married Lynda Kane, a divorcee with two girls. Together, they'd had fraternal twins, a boy and a girl, rounding out the family at eight kids.

As an only child, Sara had been fascinated by the Callaways and a little envious. Jack Callaway was a gregarious Irishman who told great stories and had never met a stranger. Jack was a San Francisco firefighter, following in his father's and grandfather's footsteps. The Callaways had been born to serve and protect, and all of the kids had been encouraged to follow the family tradition. At least two of the boys had become firefighters, and last she'd heard her friend Emma had done the same, but she hadn't spoken to Emma in a long time.

A wave of nostalgia hit her as her gaze drifted down the block. She'd let her childhood friends go—not that there had been that many, but she could still hear the sounds of the past, kids laughing and playing. The Callaway boys had run the neighborhood, taking over the street on summer nights to play baseball, football, or any other game they'd invent. She'd occasionally been part of those games, but not often.

She might have grown up next door to the Callaways, but she'd lived in an entirely different world—a world of quiet structure and discipline, a world where expectations for grades and achievement were high, and having fun didn't factor into any equation.

Sighing, she pushed the past back where it belonged and walked up the stairs. Time to stop procrastinating.

She rang the bell, and a moment later the front door swung open. She drew in a quick breath as she met her father's dark gaze. At six foot four, Stephen Davidson was a foot taller than she was, and had always scared the hell out of her. He had dark brown hair, brown eyes, and wiry frame. Today, he wore black slacks and a white button-down shirt that had always been his uniform during the week. He seemed thinner than she remembered, although he'd always been fit. His sense of discipline extended to every part of his life.

"Surprise!" she said, forcing a smile on her face.

"What are you doing here, Sara?"

"It's your birthday on Sunday."

"You should have called."

"You would have told me not to come."

"Yes, I would have done that," he agreed. "It's not a good time."

It hadn't been a good time in over a decade. "Can I come in?" she asked.

He hesitated for a long moment, then gave a resigned nod.

She crossed the threshold, feeling as if she'd just gotten over the first hurdle. There would be more coming, but at least she'd made it through the door. Pausing in the entry, she glanced toward the living room on her right. It was a formal room, with white couches, glass tables, and expensive artwork. They'd never spent any time in that room as a family, and it didn't appear that that had changed. Turning her head to the left, she could see the long mahogany table in the dining room and the same dried flower arrangement that had always been the centerpiece.

The fact that the house hadn't changed in ten years was probably a sign that her father hadn't changed either.

"You shouldn't have come without calling, Sara," her father repeated, drawing her attention back to him.

"Well, I'm here, and I brought you a present." She handed him the wine.

He reluctantly took the bottle, barely glancing at the label. "Thank you."

"It's very rare," she said, wishing for a bigger reaction.

"I'm sure it is." He set the bottle down on a side table.

She squared her shoulders, irritated by his lack of enthusiasm. But she knew it would take more than a bottle of wine to crack the iceberg between them. "I'd like to stay for the weekend."

"You want to stay here?" he asked, dismay in his eyes.

"Why not? You have the room." She headed up the stairs, figuring it would be best not to give her father time to argue. He was an excellent attorney who knew how to win an argument. But she was pretty good, too.

When she reached the upstairs landing, her gaze caught on the only two family pictures that had ever hung in the house. On the left was a family shot of the three of them, taken when she was about eleven years old. She remembered quite clearly how desperately her mother had wanted a professional family picture and how hard her father had fought against it, but it was one of the few battles that Valerie had won.

The other photo was of her and her mother taken at her high school graduation. Her mother had a proud smile on her face. They looked a lot alike, sharing many of the same features: an oval-shaped face, long, thick light brown hair that fell past their shoulders, and wide-set dark brown eyes. A wave of sadness ran through her as she realized this was the last photo of her and her mother. Valerie had died two years later.

Turning away from the memories, she moved down the hall. Her room was at the far end of the corridor. It had been stripped down to the basics: a mattress and box spring, her old desk on one wall, her dresser on the other. The bookshelves were empty and so were the drawers. Only a few nails revealed that there had once been pictures on the wall. There was absolutely no trace of her childhood.

She shouldn't be surprised. Her father had shipped her several boxes a couple of years ago, but it still felt a little sad to see how her early life had been completely erased.

Moving to the window, she looked out at a familiar view – the Callaways' backyard. The large wooden play structure that was built like a fort with slides and tunnels was empty now. Like herself, the Callaways had grown up. She wondered if any of them still lived at home.

"As you can see, I'm not set up for guests," her dad said, interrupting her thoughts.

She turned to see him standing in the doorway. "I'm sure there are some extra sheets in the linen closet. I don't need much."

He stared back at her, his eyes dark and unreadable. "Why are you here, Sara?"

"I wanted to be here for your birthday. It's been a long time since we've shared more than an email. We should talk, catch up with each other."

"Why on earth would you want to talk to me?"

The confusion in his eyes made her realize just how far apart they'd drifted. "Because you're my father. You're my family. We're the only ones left."

"Do you need money?"

"This isn't about money. Mom would not have wanted us to end up like strangers. We need to try to improve our relationship."

He stared back at her for a long moment, then said, "There's nothing left for you here, Sara. I wish you well, but we both need to move on. If you stay, it won't go well. We'll only disappoint each other."

Her chest tightened, the finality of his words bringing pain as well as anger. Her father was like a brick wall. She kept throwing herself at him, trying to break through his resistance, but all she ever achieved was a new batch of emotional bruises.

"You're a grown woman now," he added. "You don't need a father."

"Not that I ever really had one," she countered, surprising herself a little with the words. She was used to holding her tongue when it came to her dad, because talking usually made things worse.

"I did my best," he said.

"Did you?" she challenged.

A tickle caught at her throat and her eyes blurred with

unwanted tears. She had not come here to cry. She sniffed, wondering why the air felt so thick. It took a minute to register that it was not her emotions that were making her eyes water, but smoke.

The same awareness flashed in her father's eyes. "Damn," he swore. "The kitchen—I was cooking—"

He ran out of the room, and she followed him down the stairs, shocked by how thick the smoke was in the entry.

She was on her dad's heels when he entered the kitchen. The scene was unbelievable. Flames shot two feet in the air off a sizzling pot on the stove. The fire had found more fuel in a stack of newspapers on the counter that had been left too close to the burner, those sparks leaping to the nearby curtains.

Her father grabbed a towel and tried to beat out some of the flames, but his efforts only seemed to make things worse. Embers flew everywhere, finding new places to burn, the heat growing more and more intense. Moving to the sink, she turned on the faucet and filled up a pitcher, but it was taking too long to get enough water. She threw some of it at the fire, but it made no difference.

"Move aside," her dad shouted, grabbing two hot pads.

"What are you doing?" she asked in confusion.

He tried to grab the pot and move it to the sink, but she was in the way, and he stumbled, dropping the pot in the garbage. She jumped back from an explosion of new fire.

"We have to call 911," she said frantically. But there was no phone in the kitchen, and her cell phone was in her bag by the entry. "Let's get out of here."

Her father was still trying to put out the fire, but he was getting nowhere.

"Dad, please."

"Get out, Sara," he said forcefully, then ran into the adjacent laundry room.

"Wait! Where are you going?"

"I have to get something important," he yelled back at her.

"Dad. We need to get out of the house." She coughed out the words, but she might as well have remained silent because her dad had vanished through the laundry room and down the back stairs to the basement. She couldn't imagine what he had to get. There was nothing but gardening tools and cleaning supplies down there.

She started to follow him, then jumped back as the fire caught the wallpaper next to her head, sizzling and leaping towards her clothing.

"Dad," she screamed. "We need to get out of the house."

A crash echoed through the house. Then all she could hear was the crackling of the fire.

Two

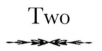

Sara ran through the fire and down the stairs into the basement. A single light bulb dangled from a wire over the stairs, showing her father in a crumpled heap on the cement floor.

She dropped to her knees next to his still body. He was unconscious, blood under his head, and his right leg was twisted in an odd position. She put a hand on his chest. His heart was still beating.

"Dad," she said. "Wake up."

He blinked groggily. "Sara?" he asked in confusion. "What are you doing here?"

"The kitchen is on fire. We need to get out of the house." A glance back over her shoulder revealed smoke pouring through the open door at the top of the stairs. There was no way out of the basement without going through the kitchen.

Her father tried to sit up, but quickly fell back, groaning with pain. "My leg is broken. You go."

"I can't leave you here. That's not an option."

"You can't carry me. Go. Get help."

"I'll be right back," she promised.

She ran up the stairs, shocked and terrified when she saw how much worse the fire had gotten in literally minutes. The heat was intense. She could barely breathe, and there was a wall of flames between her and the only way out. She couldn't afford to be scared. Grabbing a towel off the top of the nearby washing machine, she covered her nose and mouth, and prepared to make a dash for it.

Before she could move, a figure appeared on the other side of the flames—a man.

A wave of relief swept through her. Help had arrived.

He barreled through the fire and smoke, batting away the flames as if they were troublesome bees. When he stopped in front of her, her heart jumped again.

"Aiden?" She lowered the towel from her face. He was the last Callaway she wanted to see.

"Sara?" he asked, shock in his eyes.

"My dad is in the basement. He's hurt." She waved her hand toward the open door in the laundry room. "I think he broke his leg. You have to help him."

"First you, then him," he said decisively.

"But—"

"The longer you stand here arguing—"

"Fine." She took his hand, put the towel over her mouth and nose and let him lead her through the flames.

It was a terrifying pass through fire. She felt as if any minute her hair would go up in flames. She was glad she'd put it up, fewer tendrils to catch the sparks. Her eyes streamed with tears, and each smoky breath seared her lungs. She could barely see the furniture now, and she was more than grateful to have Aiden by her side. He moved with decisive confidence as if daring the fire to touch them.

When they reached the hall, he patted some lingering sparks out of her hair and off of her clothes, giving the rest of her body a quick look before saying, "Go outside. The fire department is on its way." And with that, he disappeared back into the fire.

The sound of sirens made it easier for her to leave the

house.

She grabbed her purse off the hall table and saw the front door hanging off its hinges. Aiden must have broken it down to get inside. The reality of what was happening hit her again. A few more minutes and neither she nor her father might have made it out of the house.

She ran down to the sidewalk just as the first fire engine came around the corner, followed by two more trucks and an ambulance.

She met the first firefighter as soon as his feet hit the sidewalk. "My father is trapped in the basement," she said. "The door is off the laundry room by the kitchen. Aiden Callaway went to get him, but they haven't come out yet."

"Aiden?" the guy echoed.

She nodded, not really surprised that the firefighter seemed to know Aiden since so many of the Callaways worked in the department.

"Wait here," he told her.

She crossed her arms in front of her waist as the firefighters entered the house. Everything would be okay, she told herself. Aiden was with her father, and they were both going to be fine.

Aiden must have seen the flames from next door and in typical Aiden fashion, he'd run straight into the house without waiting for backup. The Callaways had never been short on courage; sometimes on good sense, but not on guts. And Aiden didn't just end up in trouble; he often went looking for it. At least, he had when he'd been younger.

It had been more than ten years since she'd seen the very attractive guy-next-door, who had been the object of the most intense crush she had ever had in her life. Aiden had been a bad boy and she'd been a very good girl. But one reckless night had taken their relationship to a new level. Then Aiden had brought it all crashing down.

Her gut clenched at the memory of what had been the best and worst night of her life. She'd put Aiden out of her mind for a long time, but now he was back, and so was she.

Only temporarily, she reminded herself. This wasn't her home anymore and never would be.

"Sara?"

She turned to see Lynda Callaway, Aiden's stepmother, crossing the lawn at a brisk pace. A tall, willowy blonde, Lynda Callaway moved gracefully, like the dancer she'd once been.

"Are you all right, Sara? I couldn't believe my eyes when I drove around the corner and saw the fire engines and the smoke. What happened? Where's your father?"

"He's inside. So is Aiden," she added.

Lynda paled at that piece of news, her gaze flying to the house. "Aiden? Aiden's here?"

"Yes. I guess he saw the smoke. He broke down the front door." She glanced back at the house. Smoke was pouring through the front door, flames still visible through the windows in the dining room. What was taking them so long? "Aiden went to get my father. He fell down the basement stairs. I didn't want to leave him, but I couldn't move him."

Lynda put a reassuring hand on her arm. "You did the right thing."

"I think he broke his leg."

"Your father is a strong man. He'll come through this.

She'd always thought he was strong, but when she'd seen him on the floor, he'd looked surprisingly fragile and suddenly very human.

"How did the fire start?" Lynda asked.

"He was cooking. I distracted him when I showed up. We were upstairs arguing, and we didn't smell the smoke right away. What is taking them so long?"

"They'll want to be careful moving him," Lynda said,

putting her arm around Sara's shoulders.

It had been a long time since Sara had felt such a motherly touch, and the emotion of it brought tears to her eyes. She'd been a strong, independent woman for a long time, but right now she felt like an uncertain girl who was really, really happy not to be alone.

They stood in quiet for a few moments, watching firefighters attack the fire from both inside and outside of the house. She saw two men up on the roof, using axes to make some sort of a vent. Their work was efficient and apparently done without any sense of fear. She'd been inside that heat, and she couldn't imagine volunteering to go back in.

"How do they do it?" she muttered. "How do you do it, Lynda? The fire was so terrifying, so out of control, and it was only in the kitchen. How do you not worry every time your husband or sons leave the house?"

Lynda smiled. "I've had a lot of practice. I trust in my husband, my children, their fellow firefighters and their training. That gets me through." She paused, her smile fading away, her gaze turning back toward the house. "I can't believe Aiden is here. He's been impossible to reach the last few weeks. I wasn't sure when or if we'd see him again."

"Really? Why?"

"He's had some trouble in his life."

"Isn't that usually the case with Aiden?"

"This time is different."

Before Lynda could explain, Aiden came out on the porch, carrying her father over his shoulders. They crossed the lawn and then, with the help of another firefighter, her dad was placed on the gurney and attended to by the waiting paramedics.

Sara moved as close as she could get, relieved to see that her father was awake and able to answer questions, but it was clear he was in a lot of pain. Once they had him stabilized on the stretcher, he was loaded into an ambulance.

"I'll meet you at the hospital," she told him.

"No, I need you to stay here, Sara. Keep an eye on my house."

"I'll take care of everything," she promised. "Then I'll come to see you."

The ambulance doors closed. A moment later, he was on his way to the hospital.

"Do you need a ride?" Lynda asked her.

"Uh, no," she said, trying to pull herself together. Everything was happening so fast her head was spinning. "I have a car. I'll wait until the fire is out, and then I'll go."

"You've grown up into a beautiful, capable woman, Sara," Lynda said with an approving gleam in her eyes. "Your mom would be proud."

"I hope so. I still miss her."

"So do I. And so does your father."

"That's not easy to believe."

Lynda gave her a knowing look. "Your father is a difficult, complicated man. I've lived next door to him for twenty years, and I don't feel like I know him any better now than when he first moved in. Since your mom died, he's become even more reclusive."

She nodded, her attention distracted by Aiden's approach. Now that they were outside, she could see him more clearly. As his gaze met hers, she felt a familiar rush of adrenaline. He'd always had the ability to unsettle her, to make her feel off balance, dizzy, her heart beating too fast, her words getting choked in her throat. It was silly to feel that way now. Her teenage crush had ended long ago. She certainly didn't intend to go back there.

Unfortunately, Aiden was still a very good-looking man, even with ash in his brown hair, sweat on his brow, a three-day growth of beard on his face and tired blue eyes. Add in the faded jeans with a rip at the knee and a T-shirt that clung to his broad chest and strong shoulders, and Aiden was still as hot and sexy as ever, maybe more so.

Sara drew in a breath, trying to dampen down her physical response. She could handle it now. She didn't need to get all worked up about a man who had only once seen her as more than his sister's best friend and the girl next door, and that one time had ended in regret on his part.

Fortunately, Lynda broke the awkward tension between them.

"Aiden," Lynda said. "I can't believe you're home. Why didn't you call me back?"

"I figured you'd see me soon enough." He paused. "Are you okay, Sara?"

"I'm fine. Thank you for saving my father."

He shrugged, as if what he had done had been of little consequence.

"I've been leaving messages for you for three weeks, Aiden," Lynda said.

"I needed some time to clear my head," he replied.

"Well, I'm glad you're finally home. I've been so worried about you since—"

"I'm fine," Aiden said, cutting Lynda off. "I'll be over to the house in a minute."

"All right," Lynda said, obviously sensing that this wasn't the time to grill her son. "Sara, please stop by later and let me know how your father is doing. In fact, come for dinner. We eat around seven, but any time you get back is fine. I'll save you a plate."

"That isn't necessary."

"You won't be cooking in that kitchen tonight. Just come by," Lynda insisted. "There's always room for one more at our house."

"Okay, thanks."

With Lynda gone, she shifted her weight, crossing her arms, then uncrossing them, wishing that Aiden would stop looking at her with those incredible blue eyes.

"So, is the fire almost out?" she asked.

"Looks that way, but you won't be able to go inside until the fire inspector signs off."

"When do you think that will be?"

"Depends," he said. "Could be an hour or more."

"I'm lucky my dad lives right next door to firefighters. Although it doesn't sound like you live at home anymore."

"Not in a long time," he said shortly, his gaze drifting toward his childhood home.

She stared at his profile. In his early thirties now, Aiden's features had become better defined, his jaw stronger, his blue eyes harder and more cynical than she remembered.

His gaze returned to hers, and she couldn't help wishing she looked a little better. She knew she was more attractive than she'd been in high school, because once she'd left her father's house, she'd discovered makeup and hair products, short skirts and high heels. Unfortunately, she'd dressed herself down to visit her father, pulling her hair back in a knot and wearing gray slacks and a button-down blouse that did little to show off her shape. The fire had made her sweat, and she could feel her hair falling out of her bun, so it wasn't her best moment.

Not that she cared, she reminded herself. There had been plenty of men in her life since high school, since Aiden. She was no longer his adoring fan.

She searched for something to say, something smart, witty, casual, but nothing seemed right. There had been a time in her life when she'd lived to catch a glimpse of Aiden, and another time when she'd hoped never to see him again, but now here he was, here they were, and she couldn't think of a damn thing to say.

She tucked her hair behind her ear. "So…"

"So," he echoed. "It's been a long time."

"Yes," she agreed, feeling irritated with her awkwardness.

"How did you set the kitchen on fire?"

"I wasn't the one who was cooking," she said.

Aiden gave her a doubtful look. "You're saying your father did that? Your father who lives by a rulebook and never ever takes a misstep? The man who can do no wrong and cannot tolerate failure in others?"

"Yes. Apparently, he is human," she replied, not surprised that Aiden's assessment of her dad was so spot on. He'd grown up next door, and her father had yelled at the Callaway boys on more than a few occasions.

"Are you living here now?" Aiden asked.

"No, just visiting. What about you?"

A shadow crossed his eyes. "I'm not sure of my plans."

Before she could press for more information, one of the firefighters joined them. "Callaway? What are you doing here?"

"Helping out," Aiden said shortly.

Something sparked between the two men, something intense and angry. Sara felt like she'd just landed back in the middle of another fire. Aiden had always had a million friends and he'd been a guy's guy. To see someone who obviously hated his guts was surprising.

"Quite the hero. You always land on your feet, don't you?" the other man sneered.

"If you say so," Aiden said evenly.

Fury burned in the other man's eyes a split second before he pulled back his arm and punched Aiden in the face.

Aiden stumbled backward, his hand flying to his right eye.

Sara gasped in surprise, startled by the unexpected

attack. "What's happening?" she asked, but no one was listening to her.

"That was for Kyle," the man said. "And this—"

Before he could finish his statement, one of the other firefighters intervened, grabbing his pal's arm. "That's enough, Hawkins. Get in the truck."

Hawkins looked like he wanted to argue, but after giving Aiden another scathing look, he reluctantly followed orders.

"What just happened?" Sara asked.

Neither man seemed inclined to answer her. After exchanging a long look with Aiden, the firefighter gave her his attention. "The inspector just arrived. He'll let you know the damage and when you can go inside."

"Thanks," she said.

The firefighter gave Aiden a hard look and then headed to the truck.

"Okay, what was that all about?" she asked Aiden.

He rubbed his rapidly swelling cheekbone. "Nothing."

"That man didn't hit you for nothing, Aiden. He said it was for Kyle. Was he talking about Kyle Dunne?"

"Leave it alone, Sara."

"What happened to Kyle?"

Aiden's jaw tightened. "He died, and it's my fault."

His blunt words shook her to the core. Kyle Dunne was the same age as Aiden. They'd been friends since kindergarten. Now he was dead? Why? How?

It was clear Aiden had no interest in giving her more details; he was already moving down the sidewalk.

"Aiden, wait," she called, but he didn't turn his head.

As he walked toward his truck, she noticed a limp in his stride. He'd suffered an injury of some sort. At the same time that Kyle had died?

Why would anyone blame Aiden for his best friend's death? There was no way Aiden would have let Kyle die without trying to save him. Aiden was a born protector. She'd just witnessed him in action when he'd rescued her father, a man he didn't even like. Aiden would have put his own life on the line for Kyle.

Memories of Aiden and Kyle together flashed through her mind. She could see them playing catch in the street until well after dark, hosting poker games in the room over the garage for all their high school friends, getting dressed up in suits for their senior prom. Kyle was dead? He'd always been so much fun, a joker and a prankster. Kyle and Aiden had caused a lot of trouble together, and they'd been closer than brothers. Aiden had to be reeling. No wonder there had been so much worry in Lynda's eyes when she'd mentioned Aiden.

As Aiden pulled his bags out of his truck, she was torn between wanting to ask him more questions and wanting to put some distance between them.

He was the one guy she'd never been able to forget, the one guy who still haunted her dreams. The last thing she needed to do was talk to him. She had enough problems to deal with. She turned her back on Aiden and headed across the lawn to talk to the fire inspector.

Three

Aiden was relieved to get to his truck, to get away from Sara's compelling gaze. When he'd decided to return to San Francisco, he hadn't counted on seeing her again. She was a complication he didn't need.

But damn, she was pretty. His gut tightened as he sneaked another look at her, watching her move across the lawn. She'd always been cute in a girl-next-door kind of way, but she'd grown up to be a beautiful woman. He liked the way her sun-streaked light brown hair sparked with gold, the curve of her hips in her form-fitting slacks, and the soft swells of her breasts that had filled out in the decade since he'd last seen her.

She still dressed like a librarian, but he knew there was passion inside of her. He'd seen it firsthand. He just hadn't handled it very well back then. In those days, he hadn't handled a lot of things well in his life. Hell, not in these days either, he thought with a frown.

Forcing himself to look away from Sara, he headed up the driveway. He'd debated coming home for three long weeks. It could be either a great or a terrible decision. So far, it wasn't looking good.

The last thing he'd expected to run into was a fire. For a split second, he'd hesitated, the events of three weeks ago still fresh in his mind, but instinct had driven him forward. And this time no one had died.

Thinking about Kyle, he put a hand to his aching cheekbone. He should have seen that punch coming. It wasn't the first fist to the face he'd taken since Kyle had died, and he doubted it would be the last. But the physical pain he could handle. It was the one deep inside that seemed overwhelming and relentless. He'd tried to outrun it, to drown it in booze, but it was still with him, and he wondered if it would ever leave.

Opening the side door, he stepped into the house and set his bag down inside the door. He grabbed a kitchen towel, swiped some ice out of the freezer and then applied it to his face.

Lynda entered the kitchen a moment later, her brows pinching together as she took in the ice and the bruise on his face.

"I didn't realize you'd injured yourself," she said.

"It's fine," he said, not choosing to explain.

He sat down at the same large, rectangular table where he'd once done his schoolwork and let the feeling of being home run through him. The large country-style kitchen had oak cabinets and hardwood floors. His mother had had the kitchen redone when he was in high school, adding tons of cupboard space to accommodate the amount of food eight children could consume in any given day. There was also plenty of open counter space including a center island that had often served as ground central for his sisters' baking adventures. He'd usually tried to stay out of those, at least until the batter could be tasted. He smiled at the memories.

This house had always been a safe harbor, but he wasn't sure it would be now. Lynda might be cheerful and welcoming, but he suspected his father and older brother, Burke, would have a different attitude. He'd already received several phone and text messages from both of them, and they'd gone from initially being worried about his health to being extremely pissed off that he wasn't trying to counter some of the negative reports that were out there.

"Are you hungry, thirsty?" Lynda asked, worry in her eyes. "What do you need?"

What did he need? He couldn't begin to tell her.

"Just sit down," he said. "I don't need anything."

"Don't you?" she challenged as she took the chair across from him. "You're hurt, Aiden, and I'm not talking about that bruise on your face, although that looks more like the handiwork of someone's fist than a fire."

Lynda had always been perceptive, sometimes more than he'd appreciated. She'd been his stepmother since he was eight years old. It had taken him a while to connect with her; he'd been really close with his biological mom. But Lynda was the one who had been there for him when he needed a mother.

"Who hit you?" she asked. "And don't waste my time denying what happened."

"Ray Hawkins."

Her lips tightened. "Kyle's friend."

"Yeah. His cousin Dave was on my crew when Kyle died. He hadn't been jumping with us very long. He'd just transferred from Missoula. He wasn't a big fan of mine either."

"Can you tell me what happened to Kyle?"

Her words brought with them a flash of memory, the roaring forest fire, the whipping winds, and the fear on the faces of his fellow smokejumpers. Fire season was supposed to be over. It was the beginning of October. They'd been packing away their gear, preparing to move on to their off-season jobs. But a hundred unexpected lightning strikes in the Shasta-Trinity forest had changed their plans.

"Aiden?" Lynda's persistent voice brought him back to the present. "What happened to Kyle?"

"He died." The words felt as unreal now as they had three weeks earlier.

"How?"

"Does it matter?" He set down the ice pack. "It was my fault."

"I don't believe that."

"Everyone else does. I'm sure Dad or Burke or someone has already told you that I'm responsible."

"I want to hear what you have to say," she said.

"And you've heard it."

She stared back at him. "I've heard nothing. You're different, Aiden. Harder, edgier, angrier—I barely recognize you."

Sometimes he barely recognized himself.

"You're going to stay for a while," she said, as if daring him to argue. "You need to be home with your family. You need to heal."

"Is there room?" he asked, not sure which of his many siblings were staying in the house these days.

"There's always room for my children," she said.

"I'm thirty-two," he reminded her.

"When I look at you I can still remember the nine-year-old who wrapped up his lizard and gave it to me as a birthday present."

"You should have been honored. It was my favorite lizard," he said, relieved with the change of subject.

"You were testing me."

"Well, you passed. You weren't at all scared. I was impressed."

"Thank goodness it wasn't a snake. You can have your old room over the garage if you want. Shayla, Colton and Emma are in the other rooms right now."

"That's fine." He'd be happier out of the main house. There would be less chaos and hopefully fewer questions if his siblings or parents had to walk down the driveway and up the stairs to talk to him.

As he rose, the side door opened, and his sister Nicole walked in with her five-year-old son, Brandon. Nicole was exactly the same age as him. It had been weird at first to have his stepsister in the same grade, but Nicole was a fun-loving, optimistic sweetheart who always found the good in people, and he could usually count on her to see the bright side of life.

A blue-eyed blonde with a curvy build, Nicole had always been attractive, especially to his friends. He'd tried to keep them away from her and for the most part he'd succeeded, until Nicole met Ryan. They fell in love at nineteen, moved in together at age twenty, married at twenty-one and became parents at twenty-seven. Unfortunately, their son had been diagnosed with autism two years ago at age three.

Aiden hadn't seen his nephew in almost a year, and while Brandon had grown about two inches, his eyes were no longer curious and alive but rather dull and dark, his gaze filled with shadows from the world he had retreated to. Aiden had hoped there would have been improvement by now, but it didn't appear that way.

"Aiden," Nicole said, happy surprise lighting up her eyes. "You've finally surfaced."

"Had to come up for air sometime."

"I'm so glad. Brandon, do you remember your Uncle Aiden?"

Brandon didn't answer. He was tugging on her hand, trying to get away, his gaze fixed on the door leading out of the kitchen and into the dining room.

"Honey," she said again. "Look at your uncle."

Brandon pulled harder, his expression changing from dull to determined.

"It's okay," Aiden cut in. "We'll talk later."

"Good idea," she said, letting Brandon go.

"Where is he off to?" Aiden asked.

"He likes the fish in Dad's aquarium," she answered. "It's better than television to him. He loves coming over here to see the fish. And there aren't too many things that he loves."

He could see the strain in her eyes and got up to give her a hug. She was thinner than he remembered. "How are you doing with everything?"

"I'm good," she said, but the shadows under her eyes didn't support her answer.

"Really? You look tired."

"I am tired, but there's a lot to do. For the record, you don't look much better," she said as they both sat down. "Is that a black eye?"

"Long story," he said.

"They always are."

"So things with Brandon…"

"Are getting better," she said. "Not as much as we had hoped for by now, but there are small improvements in between the setbacks."

He admired her positive attitude. He couldn't imagine what she was going through. But she adored her son, and she'd fight for him to the last breath. "How's Ryan?"

Her smile faltered. "He's… I don't know how he is, to be honest. He works a lot, and he's not as optimistic as I am about Brandon's recovery, so we tend to frustrate each other. He mentioned the other day that maybe we should take a break."

"You're married. You can't take a break. I'll talk to him."

"I'm sure he'd love to see you, Aiden." Nicole turned to Lynda. "I came over to ask if you could watch Brandon tomorrow morning. I have to monitor the SAT testing. I'll be gone a little over three hours."

"Of course, honey," Lynda said. "I'd also be happy to watch Brandon so you and Ryan can get away together. Sometimes parents need to separate from their children and reconnect."

"I know you're right, but it's hard to leave Brandon overnight. He's not good when his routine changes. And I can't afford a setback. I should probably go see what he's up to."

"I'll go," Lynda said, waving her back into her seat. "You visit with Aiden."

"Okay."

"So what aren't you telling me, Nic?" Aiden asked when they were alone.

"What do you mean?"

"Your smile has a lot of cracks in it."

"It's been a rough couple of weeks, but it's going to be fine."

"How's the teaching job?"

"I'm job sharing this year, so it's just one day a week. That's pretty much all I can handle in between Brandon's school, doctor appointments and therapy sessions, but enough about me. How are you? I heard you were hurt."

Her gaze ran down his body, but she wouldn't be able to see his scars. They were on the inside.

"I tore some muscles in my leg, otherwise I'm fine."

"I doubt that. We've been worried about you, Aiden. You didn't come to Kyle's funeral. You didn't call anyone back. Mom and Dad went to the hospital in Redding to see you, and you had checked yourself out against doctor's orders."

"I had to get out of there."

"Where did you go?"

"I just drove around. I didn't come to the funeral because

Vicky asked me not to," he said, referring to Kyle's widow. "I figured the least I could do was honor her wishes."

"How could she not want you there? I don't get it. No one does. You and Kyle were best friends."

"She blames me for Kyle's death."

"But it was an accident, right?"

"That depends on who you talk to."

"You need to explain, Aiden, to tell everyone exactly what happened."

"I can't."

"Can't or won't?" his sister challenged.

"It doesn't matter. Result is the same. Kyle is dead. No explanation will bring him back."

"I hate to see you taking the heat."

"I can handle the heat." Changing the subject, he added, "Right now, I'm more concerned about you and Ryan. Things are worse than you're saying, aren't they?"

"Life is just harder now," she said. "I have to focus on Brandon. He's my child, and I have to make him better. I know that Ryan wants that, too. But he can be negative, and I can't listen to his doubts, so sometimes I don't listen to him at all," she confessed.

"You're in a tough situation, no doubt, but you have to get through it together."

"I hope we will, but there's a short window of time where we can really impact Brandon's diagnosis. That time is now. I have to put my energy there. And Ryan is just going to have to wait."

He nodded, thinking he definitely needed to hear Ryan's side of the story.

"So, how did you get the black eye?" Nicole asked. "That looks recent."

"It happened about thirty minutes ago. There was a fire next door at Sara's house."

"I know. I saw the fire engine on my way in. At first I thought it was just Dad or Burke stopping by our house to get something. Do you know what happened?"

"It started in the kitchen. I had just parked my car out front when I saw the flames. There was no one else around, so I broke down the door. I had to rescue Sara's father. He had tripped down the stairs and broken his leg."

"Seriously? Did he hit you while you were rescuing him?" she asked with a knowing gleam in her eye. "You were not one of his favorite people, especially after your paintball team sprayed the side of his house with purple paint."

He smiled. "I forgot about that."

"Well, I haven't forgotten. I helped you clean it up."

"You were a good sister that day. Mr. Davidson didn't punch me. It was someone else."

"Who?"

He shrugged off her question. "It doesn't matter."

She shook her head in wonder. "It's amazing how often trouble finds you. Is Mr. Davidson all right?"

"He should be fine in time."

"It's good you arrived home when you did. Who knows how long it would have been before someone found him?"

"Not that long. Sara was with him."

"Sara is back?" she asked in surprise. "I haven't seen her in years. She and Em were so close, I almost felt like I had another little sister. How is she?"

"Don't really know. She was worried about her father and upset about the fire." As he finished speaking, his mom and Brandon returned to the kitchen. Brandon ran immediately to Nicole's side, keeping his gaze on the floor, as if the last thing he wanted to do was make eye contact with Aiden.

"I have to go," Nicole said. "Can you say goodbye, Brandon?"

The little boy didn't say a word, but he did give a

negative shake of his head.

"At least I know he hears me," Nicole said. "I'll see you tomorrow, Mom. Aiden, don't be a stranger."

"I'll come by this weekend," he said.

After Nicole and Brandon left, Aiden looked over at Lynda. "How does she do it?"

Lynda shook her head, her eyes a little sad. "I have no idea. She has this deep well of strength and determination, but I worry about what happens if she doesn't get the results she wants so desperately. That little boy is everything to her, but I don't know if even her amazing will can bring him back."

"I wish I could help."

"Well, you're in town for a while anyway. Maybe you can spend some time with them."

"I will," he promised. He got to his feet, biting back a revealing groan, but his mother's sharp eyes didn't miss a thing.

"You're in pain," Lynda said.

"It's not that bad." His leg had been getting better, but his muscles were cramping from the weight he'd had to put on his leg while carrying Sara's father up the stairs. "I will take a rest, though."

"I'll call you when dinner is ready."

"Thanks, Lynda."

She smiled. "I'm glad you're home, Aiden."

He smiled back, but he had a feeling his father might not feel the same way.

Four

⟶⟫⟪⟵

Her family home was a mess. Three hours after the fire, Sara surveyed the damage in her father's kitchen. The room was completely destroyed by fire, smoke and water, and the adjacent rooms had also suffered. The entire downstairs would need work—new carpets, new paint, new flooring. The enormity of the devastation blew her away. She'd never imagined an unattended pot could ignite such a big fire. Her father was going to have a heart attack when he came home. His neat and tidy house was in complete disarray, much like the state of her life.

She'd had such high hopes for the weekend, imagining them finally reconnecting and breaking down the walls between them. But when he'd come out of surgery, he'd barely acknowledged her presence. He was in a lot of pain and groggy from the drugs, but really his behavior was no different than it had been before the fire.

Maybe she should just accept the fact that they were never going to be more than strangers to each other. In fact, maybe she should start the acceptance process now. She could go back to New York, to her apartment, to her job. But she'd never been a quitter, and while she'd taken a long break from her father, she was here now, and she wanted to make some kind of change.

Her father would be in the hospital for several days. Then

he would be off his feet for weeks after that. He would need help getting this house back together. Maybe she could get the process started.

"Sara?"

The sound of a familiar female voice drew her away from the devastation. She walked out of the kitchen and through the dining room to find her childhood friend, Emma Kane-Callaway, standing in the entry. Emma wore dark jeans tucked into black boots and a cream-colored sweater under a black leather jacket. A hazel-eyed blonde who barely reached five foot two, Emma was still a force to be reckoned with. An athlete, and a bit of a tomboy, Emma had always been brimming with courage, confidence and drive, making her more than capable of keeping up with her five brothers.

"Sorry for walking in, but the door is busted," Emma said, waving her hand to the door that was hanging off one hinge.

"Aiden kicked it in when he rescued us."

"I heard he arrived just in time. Aiden was never one for finesse."

"No, but he saved my father's life so I'm very grateful." She paused, a smile spreading across her face. "It's so good to see you, Emma."

Emma smiled back. "You, too. I wish it was under better circumstances." She opened her arms to give Sara a hug. "How are you doing?"

"I'm hanging in there."

"Tough day, huh?" Emma asked, sympathy in her gaze.

"It wasn't great."

"You won't want to stay here tonight, Sara. It stinks. Why don't you come next door? You can share my room the way we used to when we were kids."

"We're a little old for that, aren't we?"

"It will be fun, and my mom will love it. She's been

complaining that the house is too empty these days with only three of us kids living at home, although Aiden is back now, so that makes four." Emma paused, giving her a sharp look. "And if you're worried about Aiden, he's in his old room over the garage. So I doubt we'll see much of him."

"I'm not worried about Aiden," she said quickly. "Why would you think that?"

"Oh, maybe because something went down between you two a very long time ago and no one ever told me what it was," Emma complained, her sharp gaze resting on Sara's face.

"You always had a big imagination, Em. By the way, I like your short hair," she added. Emma's silky, straight blonde hair had been cut at an angle, the ends framing her face. "It brings out your eyes."

"Thanks. It's easier to wear under my helmet. And you just changed the subject," she said pointedly.

"I did, didn't I? How is it being a female firefighter?"

"Actually, I'm an arson investigator now."

"Really?"

"Yes. I always liked a good mystery, so it's the perfect job for me. What about you? You're a lawyer, right? Your dad must be proud you followed in his footsteps," Emma said.

She shrugged, doubtful he cared one way or the other.

Emma frowned. "You look exhausted, Sara. There's nothing more you can do here tonight. Let the house air out, and you can tackle things in the morning. My mom made lasagna, and she has a plate for you in the oven. What you need right now is a good meal and some peace and quiet."

Her stomach growled at the thought of Lynda's lasagna. "I am hungry. I'll take the lasagna and figure out where I'm going to sleep later."

"Good idea."

As they walked past the broken front door, Sara paused. "I need to get this fixed. I can't leave the house open all night."

"I'm sure one of my brothers or my dad can repair it or put up some plywood for you. It will be fine for now. It's still a safe neighborhood.

"Okay. I'll deal with it later."

As they left the house, a cool breeze made Sara shiver, but she appreciated the crisp November air. It felt refreshing compared to the smoky heat of the house.

They walked across the grass and down the driveway. No one ever used the front entrance of the Callaway house. The side door was closest to the kitchen, and when they were growing up, getting food was usually the only reason they went inside.

The delicious smell of garlic greeted her as she entered the kitchen, but the peace and quiet Emma had promised was lost in an angry argument between Aiden, his father Jack, and his older brother Burke. The three were standing in the middle of the kitchen, and they all appeared to be talking at once, raising their voices louder and louder as they fought to be heard. Lynda hovered off to one side, offering peacemaking entreaties, but no one was paying her any attention.

"You need to take responsibility for your actions, Aiden," Burke said heatedly.

The two oldest Callaway brothers had gone head-to-head for as long as Sara could remember. Their extremely competitive instincts had made it impossible for either one to accept that the other might be better or stronger.

Burke was the older by two years and taller than Aiden, broader, too. His hair was a dark, dark brown, almost black, and his eyes were a deeper blue than his brother's. Burke had the look of a winner. He was clean-shaven, his hair short and styled, his clothes neat and unwrinkled. Aiden had a leaner build, a more rugged, sexy look, his hair a little too long, his jaw unshaven, his clothes showing every minute of his day. And some of those minutes had been spent carrying her father out of the basement, so she'd forgive the worn jeans and the dusty T-shirt.

"I have taken responsibility," Aiden said shortly.

"No, you've done nothing but stay silent, the way you always do after you screw up," Burke replied.

Aiden's face paled under the attack, and Sara felt compassion for him. Burke had been a tough act for Aiden to follow. Burke had been the star quarterback in high school as well as the senior class president and had done all that while getting straight A's and winning national scholarships.

Aiden had been a good athlete, too, excelling at baseball, but he'd never participated in school government or gotten good grades. He'd been much more interested in having a good time. And while Burke was impressing people right and left, Aiden was usually getting into trouble.

"Burke is right," Jack interjected, his eyes on his younger son.

"That I'm a screwup?" Aiden asked, sarcasm in his voice. "Tell me something I don't know, Dad."

Jack's jaw tightened. He wasn't as tall as either of his sons, but he still had a big presence and a huge personality. His hair had gone white since Sara had last seen him, and his normally ruddy complexion was very red now, anger burning in his eyes.

"You need to tell us what happened on that mountain," Jack continued. "You owe Kyle that much."

Aiden's jaw tightened. "Don't talk to me about what I owe Kyle. Neither one of you knew him the way I did."

"If you don't clear your name, no one will ever trust you again," Burke said harshly. "If you want to keep working as a firefighter, you sure as hell better come up with a good reason for losing one of your men."

"Go to hell," Aiden said, turning away from his brother. His gaze collided with Sara's.

She swallowed hard, not just seeing anger in his eyes, but also the pain. She had no idea what was going on, but it was clear that he was hurting.

Aiden brushed past her and Emma without a word, the side door slamming behind him.

"You both pushed too hard," Lynda scolded her husband and son. "You need to give Aiden a chance to defend himself. He's only been back a few hours."

"It doesn't sound like he has anything to defend," Burke said.

"You didn't give him a chance. You're always so impatient, Burke."

"He's had three weeks," Jack said, cutting off his wife. "Three weeks to come up with the plain, simple truth. That's all we're asking. You've always been too easy on Aiden."

"And you've always been too hard," she retorted. "The truth is never plain and rarely simple, and you, of all people, should know that, Jack."

Jack frowned at her pointed look. "I'm just trying to help my son."

"I didn't hear either of you offering help, just condemnation."

"I've got to go," Burke said. "I don't have time for this." As he finished speaking, he glanced toward Sara and Emma, his gaze widening as he appeared to realize for the first time that they had an audience. "Sara Davidson, right?"

She nodded, not sure what to say in the midst of so much tension. She'd always felt a little out of step in the Callaway house. They loved and fought with a tremendous amount of passion, which had been hugely different from the quiet stillness of her home where conflict was fought in cold, angry silence.

"Nice to see you," Burke said politely, but it was clear his thoughts were elsewhere.

"You, too," she said.

"I'll walk you out," Jack told his son. "We need to talk."

When the men had left, Emma said, "What was with the full frontal attack on Aiden, Mom?"

"They're worried," Lynda replied. "And sometimes there's a little too much testosterone in this house."

"Sometimes?" Emma echoed.

"Sara, your food is in the oven," Lynda said. "I'm sorry for all the yelling, but I'm really glad you came over. How is your father?"

"He's resting. He'll have some healing to do, but he should make a full recovery."

"I'm so happy to hear that." She paused. "If you'll excuse me, I need to speak to Jack. There's pasta in the oven and salad in the fridge. Emma will take care of you."

"Thanks," Sara said.

"Well, that was a crazy scene," Emma commented. "Never a dull moment in the Callaway house." She grabbed a hot pad and pulled a plate out of the oven. "I hope you're hungry. Mom is always very generous in her portions."

As Emma pulled off the foil, Sara could see that she wasn't kidding. There was enough lasagna on the plate for three people.

"Are you going to eat, too?"

"Already did. You're on your own, but don't worry about finishing it all. Have a seat. I'll get the salad."

She sat down as Emma pulled out a bowl of greens and a bottle of dressing.

Picking up her fork, she took a bite of pasta and was immediately reminded of how hungry she was. Setting politeness aside, she dug into her meal and had finished half the plate before Emma set a glass of red wine in front of her and joined her at the table.

"I guess you were hungry after all," Emma said.

"I'd forgotten what a good cook your mom is. It's been a while since I had a home- cooked meal."

Emma sipped her wine. "That's true. One of the benefits of moving back to the old homestead. Although that benefit is often outweighed by a lack of privacy."

"So give me the rundown on your brothers and sisters," Sara said, as she took another bite. "Who's doing what?"

"Well, Burke was just promoted to chief, one of the youngest in the city, and he works out of a firehouse in the Russian Hill neighborhood. Aiden has been smokejumping for the forest service the past three years. He's based up in Redding, about four hours north of here. Nicole is a teacher at a private high school, but she only works part-time since her son Brandon was diagnosed with autism two years ago."

"Her son?" Sara asked in surprise.

"Yes, Brandon is five years old now. Around age three he started withdrawing, not making eye contact, losing his verbal skills. Nicole has become a warrior mom through it all. She works nonstop with Brandon and has investigated every therapy known to man. Unfortunately, Brandon still hasn't shown much improvement."

"I'm so sorry," Sara said. "That must be incredibly difficult."

"It is. And it's so unfair, because if anyone was meant to be a mother, it was Nicole. That's all she ever really wanted to be."

"How is Ryan handling the situation?"

"I'm not sure. I haven't seen either of them much lately."

"So what's going on with Drew?" she asked, moving down the Callaway lineup.

"Drew flies helicopters for the Coast Guard."

"Ah, another hero type," she said with a laugh.

"It's the Callaway way," Emma replied, grinning back at her. "Until you get to Sean. He's a musician, plays in a band, and waits tables on the side. My father continues to be horrified by his choices. Sean lets everything roll right off of him. He has a studio apartment off the Great Highway, and when he's not working he's usually on a surfboard."

"Sounds like a nice life. And the twins?" Sara asked. "I think they were about thirteen when I last saw them." The twins were the biological children of both Jack and Lynda Callaway, making their family truly yours, mine and ours.

"They're twenty-three now. Shayla turned out to be a genius. She finished high school at sixteen and started college when she was seventeen. She's now in her third year of medical school. She wants to do Emergency Medicine. Colton is a paramedic and just got hired as a firefighter. Colton is more like Aiden than Burke, basically a smart ass. I'm not sure how well he's going to do with all the rules. Frankly, I'm not even sure if firefighting is what Colton really wants to do, but with Drew going into the Coast Guard and Sean playing guitar and drums, Colton got some pressure to go into the family business."

Sara knew about family pressure. Actually, it wasn't so much pressure as it was expectation. Her dad had never told her to be a lawyer, but even without the words, she'd felt compelled to follow in his footsteps.

"How long are you going to be in town?" Emma asked. "Please say you're coming back for good."

"Sorry. I came for the weekend, hoping to celebrate my dad's sixty-fifth birthday. So far my trip is going really badly. I had planned on leaving Sunday, but now I think I should probably stay for a few days and get the cleanup started. My father will be off his feet for several weeks." She sighed. "I really messed things up."

"You? How is this your fault?" Emma asked, arching one eyebrow in confusion. "Wasn't your dad cooking?"

"Yes, but he didn't know I was going to surprise him for his birthday, and he was distracted as well as angry."

"Why?"

"Because he doesn't want me here."

"That's crazy. He's your dad. Although I have to admit that your father always scared the crap out of me, and I don't find that many people intimidating. Even now when I see him on the lawn, I scurry inside like a timid rabbit."

Sara smiled. "I cannot see that happening, but I know exactly how you feel. He's always scared me, too. It's stupid. I shouldn't be afraid to talk to my own father." She set down her fork. "Enough about me. What's up with you? Any men in your life?"

Emma sat back in her chair. "Not for the last three months. I lived with a guy for two years. I thought he was the one, but it turned out he wasn't. We had a bad breakup, and that's why I'm here in the family home again. I needed a place to stay and some of my mom's home cooking and tender loving care." Emma drank some wine, then added, "Coming home has been good for me in a lot of ways. I love my career, but sometimes it's difficult to fight not only fires and arsonists but also prejudice against females. I always have to be on my game, and any mistake I make gets magnified out of proportion. It's stressful."

"I'd think with all the Callaways working in the fire department, you'd be shown more respect. Doesn't your father have a big job in the department?"

"Yes, he's the battalion chief. But my family name actually makes it tougher for me. I have to prove that I'm really good and that I didn't get this job because I'm a Callaway."

Seeing the determination in Emma's eyes, Sara was certain that her friend would prove all the doubters wrong.

"What about you?" Emma asked, an inquisitive light in her eyes. "I don't see a ring on your finger."

"Too busy working. Like you, I've been trying to prove myself, and right now I'm on the partner track."

"Does that track keep you warm at night?" Emma teased.

"No, but it keeps me too busy to think about anything else."

"You were always good at staying focused, Sara. Me, I was easily distracted, especially by hot guys," she added with a laugh.

Emma's words made Sara think about Aiden. She'd certainly been distracted by him a lot as a teenager. "Can you tell me anything about the accident Aiden was in?"

"Not much." Emma set down her wine glass. "Aiden was jumping a wildfire a few weeks ago in the Shasta-Trinity forest, and apparently the winds changed quickly. Their exit routes were cut off, and the crew was separated. In the end, everyone got to safety except Kyle Dunne. There are a lot of rumors about what happened. A couple of the smokejumpers seem to feel that Aiden made some bad decisions that day. We were hoping he would come back and tell everyone what happened, but as you heard, he doesn't seem inclined to defend himself."

"He's probably still reeling from Kyle's death."

"I'm willing to cut him all the slack in the world, but Burke and my father..." She shrugged. "They're impatient, and they want answers."

"Someone hit Aiden today—after he saved my dad's life," she said. "We were standing in front of the house and one of the firefighters walked up and punched Aiden in the face. I think his name was Hawkins."

Emma's lips tightened. "Ray Hawkins. His cousin was on

the fire with Aiden and Kyle, and I don't think he was ever a fan of Aiden's. I suspect he's responsible for a lot of the negative rumors. Not that I know for sure Aiden didn't do something wrong. He can push the envelope."

"Yes, he can," she muttered.

Emma gave her a curious look. "Okay. I've been wondering for more than a decade. It's time to talk. What happened between you two?"

"Nothing," she said quickly.

"You said that before, but I didn't believe you then, and I don't believe you now. You had a huge crush on him when we were in high school, and right before we graduated—"

"I had a crush on a lot of people," she said, cutting Emma off.

"Not like that one. Maybe I should just ask Aiden what went down."

"He'll tell you the same thing," she replied, hoping that was true.

"We'll see." Emma got to her feet.

"Wait. You're not going to ask him now, are you?" she asked worriedly.

Emma laughed. "I should because your face is all red, and that's a sure sign that you're lying. But actually, I was just going to ask him to fix your front door."

"I don't want to bother Aiden," she protested. "Maybe I can do it myself."

"You?" Emma asked doubtfully.

"Okay, maybe not me," she agreed. Her handyman skills were nonexistent. "But I'm sure I can call someone."

"Yeah, we can call Aiden."

Sara followed Emma out the side door. As they turned toward the garage, they heard the sound of hammering. Aiden was already at work on the front door. She was surprised. After the scene she'd witnessed between him and his brother, she couldn't believe her front door was on his mind.

"I was just going to ask you to take care of this," Emma said as they reached Aiden.

"Figured Sara wouldn't want this open all night," he said briskly.

"Thanks," she said.

An awkward silence followed her words and then Emma's phone buzzed.

She pulled it out and checked the screen. "Oh, no. There's a fire at St. Andrew's School. I've got to run. I'll come by tomorrow, Sara, and try to help you with the mess."

"If you have time," she said.

"I'll make time."

"I hope the fire isn't too bad." Sara sniffed, realizing that the smell of smoke in the air was no longer coming just from her house, and that the sirens were getting louder and longer. St. Andrew's School was less than a mile away. "That doesn't sound good," she said to Aiden.

"No," he replied, his attention on the door.

With Emma gone, the silence between them grew uncomfortable. She couldn't go inside while Aiden was fiddling with the door, so she had to wait.

"You're going to need a new door, but this should hold for tonight," he said finally, stepping back to review his work.

"Thanks." As he turned his face into the light, she saw the dark purple bruise on his cheekbone. "How's your face?" she asked.

"It's fine. Nothing for you to worry about."

"You don't need to snap at me. I'm not the one who hit you. I don't even know what you did or what everyone thinks you did."

Aiden ran a hand through his hair. "You're right. Sorry."

"Aiden…" she began, not really sure where she wanted to go with her words, but she felt compelled to say something.

"What?" he asked, his tone not at all encouraging.

"You saved my dad's life earlier, and I'm thankful."

A shadow flashed through his eyes. "You made the mistake of thinking I was a hero once before, Sara. Don't do it again."

Her jaw dropped, but before she could say anything, he was halfway across the lawn.

Maybe it was better that way, because he'd only said aloud what she'd been telling herself all night. This time they were on the same page.

Five

Emma felt a familiar rush of adrenaline as she pulled up in front of St. Andrew's Elementary School. She'd been responding to fires for seven years, but she still felt a sense of amazement every time she saw the flames, felt the heat, smelled the smoke. Not that she'd ever share that information with anyone. She'd fought too hard and too long to earn the respect of her fellow firefighters to act like a "girl."

She couldn't afford any show of emotion when she was on a job, and for the most part she managed to contain herself, but some scenes, like this one, felt personal. She'd spent nine years at St. Andrew's from kindergarten to eighth grade. This school had been a second home, and it saddened her to see that the fire had already engulfed at least two classrooms.

The scene was similar to the fire last month at the local high school, another one of her old stomping grounds. Was it the beginning of a pattern? The high school fire had been smaller, and based on the sloppy ignition point of a gas can and some rags, they'd attributed the arson to vandals, most likely teenagers. The same person or persons could have set this fire, but it was too soon to make that conclusion. She needed to get inside, examine the point of origin, but she would have to wait until the incident commander deemed it safe enough to enter.

She put on her gear and walked across the schoolyard. The commander on the scene was in fact her Uncle Tim.

"What have we got?" she asked.

"Still trying to figure that out. Two points of origin and a hell of a lot of accelerant," he said. "The building was empty except for the night janitor who was working in the other wing. He called it in. He's over there." Tim pointed to a middle-aged man standing by one of the trucks. "He doesn't speak much English."

As she followed his gaze, her heart sank. The janitor was not alone. He was talking to Max Harrison, a homicide inspector with the police department. Max had transferred from Los Angeles three months earlier, and they'd butted heads while working together on a case that had included murder and arson. What was he doing here? From what her uncle had said, there was no one inside the building.

Looking away from Harrison, she turned back to her uncle. "Can I go in?"

"Not yet," Tim said sharply. "You wait for my order, Emma. I'm not in the mood for a rescue."

"Would you say that to one of my brothers?" she challenged.

"Hell, yes," he said. "But the only one who would probably listen would be Burke."

Tim moved away from her as he radioed orders to the firefighters inside the building. She could tell from the intensity of the flames and the color of the smoke that she wouldn't be getting inside for a while, so she headed across the yard to talk to the witness.

Max's gaze met hers as she crossed the playground, and she felt her stomach clench. Every time she was around him, she felt unsettled, and she didn't like it. Since her last romantic breakup, she'd sworn off men for at least a year. She didn't need the complication of love or lust in her life, and she reluctantly had to admit that Max inspired a fair amount of lust. He was in his mid-thirties with blondish-brown hair and sharp green eyes. There was a confidence to him that reminded her of her brothers and probably at least half the men she worked with, which was why she should not let him rattle her. She was used to cocky, arrogant know-it-alls who didn't trust her skills. She'd prove him wrong the way she'd proved the rest of them wrong. And she was not going to sleep with him, she reminded herself.

"Callaway," he said as she joined them.

"Harrison," she returned on a cool note. "What are you doing here? I don't see any bodies."

"Not yet anyway."

"My uncle said the building is clear."

"Your uncle?" he echoed, then shook his head. "How many Callaways are there in the fire department?"

"Enough to make it run extremely well," she retorted.

He gave her a half smile. "That's not what I've heard."

She wanted to ask him what he'd heard, but she knew when she was being baited, and she decided to take the high road. She turned to the witness. "What is your name, sir?"

"Freddie Juarez," the man said.

"You reported the fire?"

"Yes," he replied. "The fire—it is very big."

As he gazed at the fire, he seemed to be almost in a trance, struck dumb by the intensity of the heat.

She wondered if he was more than just a witness. It wouldn't be the first time someone had torched their place of employment and stuck around to watch their handiwork.

"Can you tell me when you first realized there was a fire?" she asked, drawing his attention back to her.

"Smoke. I started coughing. Then I looked out the window and saw the flames. I ran outside and called for help."

"Did you see anyone or hear anything?"

He shook his head. "I was working and listening to music," he said, holding up his earphones.

Before she could ask him another question, a woman and a young girl ran up to them, throwing their arms around Freddie.

She stepped back as the three began speaking to each other in very excited Spanish and turned to Max. "Did he tell you anything else?"

"No."

"Do you have his contact information?"

"I do."

She sighed. "Great. Anything else you care to share? Like why you're here?"

"One of the teachers was reported missing last night by her roommate. There was a trace amount of blood found in the garage of their apartment building. We didn't have enough to launch an investigation, but when I heard the call come in about the fire, I wondered if there was a connection."

"Who's the teacher?"

"Margaret Flannery."

"Sister Margaret?" she asked in surprise. "She's missing?"

"Sounds like you know her."

"I went to school here. Sister Margaret was my fourth-grade teacher, and she has taught at St. Andrew's for forty years. I can't believe someone would try to hurt her. She's a sweet, wonderful person. What else can you tell me about her disappearance?"

"Nothing. It's an ongoing investigation."

"Come on, Harrison. We're working together, aren't we?"

He gave her a short smile. "Are we? I'll remind you of that when I ask you for information on the fire scene."

"I might be able to help you," she said, ignoring his comment. They could both be territorial when it came to information.

"All right. What else can you tell me about Sister Margaret?"

"Well, she's a popular teacher. She runs all the carnivals. She's a huge part of the school and church community."

"What can you tell me about her roommate, Ruth Harbough?"

"She's the school secretary," Emma replied. "The two women have been friends for years."

"Just friends?" he queried.

She frowned. "I don't know. I never thought about it. Does it matter?"

"Just asking questions."

She glanced around the schoolyard. Half the neighborhood was hovering on the street watching the flames. Arsonists loved to watch their handiwork. Was the perpetrator somewhere in the group?

Harrison followed her gaze. "Quite a crowd," he muttered.

"Yeah." She turned her head as her uncle called her name. "Time to get inside before all the evidence is destroyed."

"The fire is still strong," Max said with a frown.

"It's under control," she said, walking across the playground.

He followed. "You're not short on guts, are you?"

"It's part of the job. Fear only gets in the way."

"Sometimes fear can save your life."

"Or kill you," she returned. "Focus and fear don't go well together. I learned that a very long time ago."

"What happened?" he asked.

"Nothing important."

"I doubt that."

She shrugged. "Maybe someday I'll tell you."

He smiled. "I'm going to hold you to that."

His lazy grin made her skin tingle. She forced herself to look away. Max Harrison might be hot, but as far as she was concerned, he was off limits. They had to work together, and she did not mix business with personal relationships.

As she headed toward the burning building, she tried to clear her mind of all distractions. Even though the fire was under control, she would never make the mistake of underestimating its power to leap back to life.

The monster grew larger and larger, taking up every inch of the sky, a raging creature of heat devouring everything in its path. Tall trees crackled with flames, then crashed to the ground one after the other, the smoke so thick it was impossible to see two feet ahead.

A terrible fear ran through Aiden as the firestorm enveloped him. It was too big, too fast, too much. He'd waited too long to retreat.

"Kyle," he shouted, seeing the hazy figure in front of him. "Come back!"

The fury of the fire threw his words back in his face.

What the hell was Kyle thinking? Why was he going up instead of down? Why wasn't he retreating? Had Kyle become disoriented by the smoke? It had to be the explanation. If he could just get to him, he could turn him around.

But the ravaging fire had other plans. He jumped back as a flaming branch landed just inches from his body.

Within seconds the forest around him was blazing with a new line of fire. In the light he could see Kyle twenty yards ahead. Kyle had stopped, pulled off his helmet, his head turned toward the sky as the fire grabbed hold of the sleeves of his coat.

"Kyle," he screamed again.

He ran toward his friend, jumping over rocks, dodging flames, moving so fast he was almost flying, and then he was completely airborne.

He didn't know how long he flew before he hit the ground and then tumbled down the mountain.

His last thought was that he was going to die. Mother Nature had finally beaten him.

But when he woke up in the hospital hours later, he was alive, and Kyle was dead.

Aiden's eyes flew open. He sat up in bed, his heart pounding, his body dripping with sweat, the nightmare in his head so real he could smell the smoke and feel the heat. Drawing in gulps of air, he tried to calm his racing heart. It was just another one of the bad dreams that would haunt him for the rest of his life.

In this dream Kyle hadn't looked at him with accusation, hadn't asked him why the hell he hadn't called for retreat when the winds changed. Not that Kyle had said that to him on that terrible day. At least, Aiden didn't think so, but his memory had been fragmented by the concussion he'd suffered during his fall. The fall had actually saved his life, literally throwing him out of the path of the fire.

Afterwards, he'd tried to put together the events of that day from others' accounts, but there were still gaps and questions that continued to elude him. Had Kyle really taken off his helmet? It seemed unthinkable. Kyle was a trained firefighter, one of the best in the business. He knew what to do and what not to do.

Maybe his dreams were distorted. His memories didn't jive with the accounts given by the rest of the team, some of whom said they'd seen him and Kyle together and didn't understand how they'd gotten separated. Hawkins' cousin had told the investigators that Aiden was too cocky, too reckless, too determined not to let the fire win that he'd lost his ability to reason.

He'd heard those criticisms before. He did push his team and sometimes the limits, but his gut told him that something else had happened that day. He just didn't know what. But he did know that Kyle had been distracted days before the accident, but he hadn't shared what was on his mind, and Aiden hadn't pushed. He should have pushed. But since Kyle had gotten married and become a father, they weren't as close as they used to be.

If only the fire had waited another day, Kyle would have been in San Francisco with his wife and baby son. They'd recently bought a condo in the city after several years of living near the base in Redding. With the new baby, Vicky had wanted to be closer to her family. Kyle hadn't appeared to be as happy with the decision, but he'd gone along with it, saying that marriage was about compromise, and it was something he had to do.

Aiden sighed and rolled over on his side, wondering if he was just rationalizing what had happened. Was his subconscious trying to find a way to shift the blame off his shoulders to someone else – maybe even to Kyle? Hell of a friend that made him, trying to blame the victim instead of himself. He'd been in charge of the crew. It was his responsibility to bring everyone home. He'd failed.

Knowing he wouldn't sleep anymore, he slid out of bed and got to his feet. A glance at the clock told him it was two o'clock in the morning. He had a long time to go before dawn. He moved to the window. His room over the garage looked into the Davidsons' backyard. The familiar sight brought back more memories, but these were much sweeter.

He'd stood at this window many times in his teen years, often watching Sara trying to turn her backyard into a wonderland of flowers and waterfalls. Her mother used to help her in the garden, and the sounds of their laughter had often drifted through his open window.

Sara had been happy in her garden, far happier than in the house where her father ruled with an iron fist. He was a little surprised that she'd come home to visit her father. They'd never had much of a relationship, and as far as he knew she hadn't been home to visit in at least eight or nine years. It had been easier for him when she moved away. She was a distraction he didn't need.

A light suddenly came on in the yard. It appeared to be coming from the back patio. Why would Sara be wandering around outside at two o'clock in the morning?

Without thinking, he threw on a shirt, jeans and shoes and walked down the stairs. There was a gate right next to the driveway.

When he entered the backyard, he saw her sitting in a chair at the patio table, a bottle of wine by her elbow. Sara wore black leggings and a T-shirt with a big, thick sweater. Obviously, she couldn't sleep either. But that didn't mean he needed to talk to her.

He was going to retreat, but he was too late.

She jumped to her feet.

"Who's there?" she demanded, grabbing the nearest thing for a weapon, which happened to be a pillow from the wicker chair.

"What are you going to do with that?" he drawled. "Tickle me to death?" He moved into the light.

"Aiden?" she asked sharply. "What are you doing out here?"

"I saw someone in the yard. Thought I'd check it out."

As he said the words, he realized how familiar they

sounded. He'd shared more than a few late night conversations in this garden with Sara. They'd both been night owls for different reasons. Sara had usually stressed herself out with worry over school or grades or her father. And he'd usually been coming back from some party and not ready to call it a night.

"Couldn't you sleep?" he asked.

Sara lowered the pillow and sat back down. "The house is stuffy. I needed some fresh air."

"You should have gone to a hotel." He took the chair across from her.

"I didn't want to leave the house empty."

"Then you should have armed yourself with more than a pillow if you were going to stand watch."

"Funny. You can go now, Aiden."

"I could," he agreed, but he made no move to leave. He was too restless to sleep and pacing around his small room seemed far less interesting than talking to Sara. "Did you talk to your dad again?"

"I called the hospital before I went to bed, but he was sleeping. I guess that's good—if anything about this can be called good. The house is a disaster."

"I'm sure your father has insurance. If you need a construction bid, you should talk to my Uncle Kevin. He's a contractor. He won't take advantage of you, and I'm sure he can give you a good price."

"I will. Thanks."

Silence fell between them. He wasn't in a hurry to fill it. It had been ten years since he'd seen Sara, and he couldn't help but appreciate the beauty he'd always known was there. As a teenager, she'd hid her body in big clothes and worn her hair in a tight ponytail, not a bit of makeup on her face. She'd been awkward and clumsy, and he'd enjoyed teasing her just to see the light come on in her eyes and the red blush of embarrassment flood across her cheeks.

He'd always known that there was a spark inside of her. He'd seen glimpses of it on a few occasions, but while he'd been intrigued by the idea of bringing her out of her shell, some self-protective instinct had usually kicked in, reminding him that Sara wasn't a girl to play around with. She was his sister's friend, the girl next door, and her parents were friends with his parents. There was no way he could get involved with her. He didn't do serious, and Sara was as serious as they came.

But as much as he'd tried to look at her as an honorary big brother, he'd never really seen her like a sister, or even like a friend. She was more like a challenge, a girl he knew he wouldn't be able to impress with his usual lines. And one night, he'd let things go a little too far.

"You're staring at me, Aiden," she said tersely.

Her face was stiff, her body tense, her obvious dislike of him palpable, which for some reason made him want to linger. He had enough people who hated his guts these days; he didn't really need any more. But this was Sara, and he'd wondered many times over the years if they'd ever meet again. He hadn't expected her to still be so pissed off at him. Obviously she hadn't forgotten their last encounter.

"You've grown up," he said after a moment. "I like the long hair." He liked a lot of other things, too, like the way her breasts moved against her T-shirt, and the way her eyes sparkled. Was she pissed off or turned on? He decided not to ask. Instead, he said, "What's up with you?"

"What do you mean?" she said quickly.

"What's happening in your life?"

"Why do you care?"

"We used to be friends."

"Were we?" she asked. "I thought I was just the irritating friend of your sister."

"That, too," he conceded. "But we had some good times."

"And some bad," she said, crossing her arms in front of her chest.

He knew exactly what she was referring to. "That was a long time ago."

"Tonight, it doesn't seem that long."

"You still blame me for sending you home after the concert, don't you?"

She gave him an incredulous look. "Is that how you remember it? You sent me home after a concert? There was a lot more to that night than that."

"We had fun. And we ended things before they got complicated. That's what I remember."

Her look of amazement deepened. "Seriously?"

He knew he shouldn't ask, but he couldn't stop himself. "How do you remember it?"

She hesitated. "It doesn't matter."

"Apparently, it does."

Anger flickered in her eyes. "You humiliated me, Aiden."

"No," he said quickly. "I protected you. I stopped you from making a bad decision, one you would have regretted."

"I didn't need your protection."

"Yes, you did. You were innocent and naïve. And you'd been drinking. You should be grateful I called a halt."

"And should I be grateful that you told everyone I wanted to have sex with you, but you said no—you, the guy who would sleep with anyone? How do you think that played out for me?"

He tipped his head, acknowledging her point. He'd forgotten the rumors. "That wasn't me. Jim saw us together. He's the one who told people."

"You didn't try to stop him."

"I didn't think it was that big of a deal."

"Well, I did."

He gazed at her for a long moment, wanting her to look at him, but she was picking a piece of imaginary lint off her sweater. "I'm sorry, Sara. Sorry that I let it go as far as it did. I shouldn't have kissed you in the first place. You were three years younger than me, and you were my sister's friend. I get that you were embarrassed, but things would have been a lot worse if we'd kept on going. I did the right thing." He was truly surprised she didn't see it that way now. "There have been a lot of moments in my life where I did the wrong thing, but not that night, not with you. That's the one time I got it right."

"Oh, just shut up," she said. "I don't want to talk about it anymore."

"I hate to think that you've been pissed off at me for the last decade."

"Don't flatter yourself. I haven't thought about you at all." She cleared her throat and shot him a pointed look. "I'm not carrying some torch for you, if that's what you think. That flame died a long time ago. There have been lots of other men in my life."

"I'm sure. We've both grown up, changed."

She gave him a doubtful look. "I'm not sure you've changed. So far today I've seen one man punch you in the face and watched your brother and father come close to doing the same. Care to explain what's going on with you?"

"No. Let's talk about you instead. What brought you back home after all these years?"

"I told you—my father's sixty-fifth birthday. I bought him that bottle of wine," she said, pointing to the unopened bottle on the table. "It cost over four hundred dollars."

He raised an eyebrow. "That's quite a present. Are you rich now?"

She uttered a short, little laugh. "Hardly. But I wanted to

do something special, something to show my dad that our relationship has value, that it's worth saving. My grandmother died a few years ago and it's just my dad and me now. We need to find a way to connect."

"That's a lot of expectations to put on a bottle of wine."

"Too many," she admitted. "I thought at the very least it would open up some communication. When I gave it to him, my dad said it was *nice*, and set it on the table without even looking at the label. Then he told me I shouldn't have come home without being invited."

Aiden shook his head in disgust. He'd never liked Stephen Davidson. The man was as cold as the inside of a freezer. "Your father was always an ass."

"But he's my father. I have to try to love him."

"Why?"

"You wouldn't understand, Aiden. Your family is different from mine. There is an endless amount of unconditional love."

"I wouldn't say it's unconditional," he replied, thinking about the anger in both Burke and his father's eyes when they'd confronted him about Kyle.

"You're wrong. They will love you no matter what you do," she said with conviction. "Trust me, I spent years watching your family and wishing I could have even a tenth of that Callaway love."

"You were close to your mom," he pointed out.

"Yes, but there was always a line," she said. "My mom could never go against my dad, not even in the smallest matter. Her allegiance was always to him. It was strange the hold he had over her. I guess it was love, but it didn't always look like it. Not that I know what love looks like," she said with a sigh. "I keep trying to find a way to prove myself to my father, but it doesn't seem to matter what I do. I went to his alma mater and graduated with honors. I passed the bar, and I'm on track to be partner at one of the biggest law firms in New York. But I can't get my father to look at me with anything but annoyance and resignation."

"Did you do all that for him?" he challenged.

She frowned. "No, of course not. That came out wrong."

He didn't think it had come out wrong at all. "Do you like being an attorney, Sara?"

"Of course I do. Well, most of the time."

"What kind of law do you do?"

"Corporate."

"Sounds …" He couldn't quite find the right word. "Intelligent."

She smiled and for a moment she was the girl he remembered, the girl whose smile had always made him want to impress her. "Nice try," she said. "I know it sounds dull. Look, I don't want you to think that I'm just stupidly and blindly following in my father's footsteps. I made my career choices based on a lot of reasons."

"Hey, I'm not one to judge someone else's choices. As long as you're happy, that's all that matters."

She stared at him. "Are you happy, Aiden?"

"I've been happier," he admitted.

"Emma told me you're a smokejumper now. Fighting a fire isn't daring enough? You have to jump out of a plane first?"

He grinned. "It is an adrenaline rush like no other."

"You and your family…" She shook her head in bewilderment. "I never understood the Callaway attraction to danger."

"And I never understood the Davidson desire to live in the shadows and always play it safe."

"I didn't always play it safe," she reminded him.

And just like that they were back to that night.

She cleared her throat. "Anyway…"

"Anyway," he echoed. "What's the last daring thing you did, Sara?"

"I have no idea," she said finally. "I've been working sixty-hour weeks the last five years."

"It doesn't sound like you've had much time for fun."

"I squeeze it in here and there," she said.

"We could have a little fun tonight," he suggested.

A light flashed in her eyes.

"That's not what I meant," he said quickly. "I'm talking about the wine. We should open it."

"I couldn't possibly do that," she said, but there was a thoughtful expression in her eyes.

"Oh, I think you could. In fact, I suspect you've already considered it. Otherwise, that bottle wouldn't be out here."

Her gaze met his. "My father was so mean to me at the hospital, Aiden. When I came home and saw the bottle sitting on the hall table where he'd so easily put it aside, I had a moment of weakness. But I'm over it."

"Why was he in the basement anyway?"

"I have no idea. He said he had to get something."

"Must have been something important."

"I can't imagine what. I don't remember there being much in the basement besides gardening tools. I would think all the important papers would be in his study." She paused. "I'm very grateful that you came in when you did. I couldn't lift my dad, and the fire was moving so fast."

"Grateful enough to share that bottle of wine with me?"

"Why are you so determined to see me open it?"

"Maybe because I think you need to make a statement. Maybe because I'm thirsty. Maybe because I've had a lousy day, and you have, too."

Her gaze softened. She was yearning to be defiant, to break the rules, and in that moment she reminded him of the very innocent and daring-to-be-reckless girl who he'd let get way too close to him. There was no danger of that now. She hated him. And that was probably for the best.

"It's my father's present," she said.

"One he didn't seem to appreciate," he reminded her.

"The glasses are covered with ash and smoke," she said halfheartedly.

"So we'll share the bottle." He grabbed it along with the wine opener. "Shall I do the honors?"

"You're a very bad influence, Aiden."

"Agreed."

"Fine, but I hope you don't regret this."

He raised an eyebrow. "Why would I? It's your bottle of wine."

"Yes, but the last time we drank together—it didn't end well."

Six

The wine tasted amazing, and she felt warm all over, although the heat might have had more to do with Aiden than with the wine. Sara took another sip, not wanting to acknowledge that she still felt anything for the man with whom she'd shared the most embarrassing moment of her life. But it was still easy to see why her teenage self had fallen for him.

Aiden was a beautifully made man, rugged, strong, masculine, with blue eyes that commanded attention and a sexy smile that made her tingle every time he turned it in her direction.

Damn! She felt suddenly seventeen again. It wasn't like she hadn't been around attractive men, but lawyers in expensive suits were a completely different breed than the rough and tough men who ran into fire. Maybe that's why she'd had trouble falling for anyone else. No one ever seemed to measure up to Aiden.

Not that he was perfect. Aiden was way too cocky, far too reckless and played fast and loose with the rules. In fact, he was pretty much her exact opposite.

She blew out a breath, feeling a little too warm, and handed Aiden the bottle of wine. Alcohol and Aiden had never been a good combination. Not that she'd ever go down that road again. She'd learned her lesson.

As Aiden lifted the wine bottle to his lips, she couldn't help wondering what his relationship status was. She'd thought about him often over the years, usually whenever she saw a fire truck racing down the street.

Aiden handed her back the bottle. She took a drink, and then impulsively asked. "So, is there a woman in your life, Aiden?"

"No," he said, motioning for her to hand back the bottle.

As she did so, she said, "Does no mean not now or never?"

"I wouldn't say never," he said, taking a drink.

"Why are you being so cryptic?"

"Why are you being so curious?" he countered, meeting her gaze.

"Because I'm always curious. It's who I am. It's what I do. I ask questions and investigate. I solve problems."

"That's very impressive. I don't have any problems."

"Really? A fellow firefighter punched you in the face and a few hours later you're in a heated argument with your father and brother. Sounds like a few problems to me."

His lips tightened. "Well, those problems have nothing to do with a woman. I'm single and that's the way I like it. What about you?"

She reached for the bottle, stalling for a second. She wished she had a better answer, because it would have been so much more gratifying to tell Aiden she was madly in love with someone and he'd missed his chance with her. Not that he had a chance now even though she was single.

"Sara?" he prodded.

"I'm single at the moment. I've been busy working, building my career. There hasn't been much time for romance. Practically speaking I'm probably just too analytical for love."

He gave her a thoughtful look. "Love isn't practical, and most relationships don't hold up well to analysis."

"Yeah, I've noticed that."

"You don't still make up those pro/con lists, do you?"

She frowned. "I can't believe you remember that."

"How could I forget? You were always weighing your options. You were afraid to take a step without a ten-point plan."

"You make me sound dull and cowardly."

"More like smart and quirky," he said with a grin.

"Great. Just the way every woman wants to be described," she said dryly.

"Interesting is a better word. How's that?"

"Not much better. Everyone knows interesting is just a nice way of saying someone is a little odd."

He smiled. "I can't win, can I?"

"Probably not." She paused. "I had to be careful when I was growing up, Aiden. I couldn't afford mistakes. My father demanded perfection. Anything less was unacceptable. I'd get grounded for bringing home a B. My father took away my license for six months after I missed curfew."

He raised an eyebrow. "When did you miss curfew?"

"You know when," she said pointedly.

"Ah, another mark against me."

"Not against you. It was my mistake."

"Look, Sara, no one is perfect. You have to accept that."

"It's easier when I'm not faced with my father's disappointment. I shouldn't have come home."

"You had to because you're an optimist."

"I don't think I am," she said slowly.

"Of course you are. You still have hope that you and your dad will become a loving family after reviewing all evidence to the contrary. What's that if not optimism?"

"Stupidity," she suggested, then took another swig of the

wine.

"Hey, don't drink it all," Aiden protested.

She handed over the bottle, wiping her mouth with the edge of her sleeve. "What do you think of the wine?"

"It's very good."

"I think so, too. I wonder if my dad will notice that it's gone."

"It might be good if he did. Maybe it would wake him up to the fact that things and people you ignore eventually disappear."

"He'd love for me to disappear. Until this weekend, I'd pretty much done just that. I hadn't seen my dad in five years, not since my grandmother's funeral. I should have left things the way they were."

"Your father will recover. The house will be redone. It will work out, Sara."

She smiled. "Maybe you're the optimist, not me."

He grinned. "I just know you. When you set your mind to something, you succeed."

"Do you really think you know me after all the years we've been apart?"

"People don't change that much."

She pointed to the bottle. "Now who's the hog?"

He passed it to her. "Sorry."

"This is weird, isn't it?" she asked. "The two of us in my backyard after so many years. I feel young and old at the same time."

"I know what you mean. Being in my old room feels strange and yet oddly reassuring."

"My old room just feels strange. There's no trace of me left in the house, and very little left of my mom. It's as if we were never here." She took a moment and then added. "I never understood what my mom saw in my dad, how they ever came to fall in love, and why they stayed together. I rarely saw any love between them."

"Did you ever ask?"

"Yes, but my mom always told me that there were things about my father I didn't understand. She used to tell me that his love ran deep. Too deep for me to find, apparently," she added with a sigh.

"When I looked out my window earlier tonight, I remembered you and your mom working in this garden."

"Digging in the dirt," she said with a nod. "We couldn't touch the house. My dad hated any kind of clutter or sentimental nonsense as he referred to knickknacks, but he left the garden to us, mainly because he never came out here." She paused, thinking about what Aiden had said. "You used to watch us from your window?"

"Well, not like a stalker," he said with a wry smile. "Occasionally, I'd glance out."

"I used to watch you and your brothers and sisters, too. Your backyard had so much action, especially after you and your dad built that fort. I thought that was the coolest thing ever."

"It was," he agreed. "One of my best accomplishments."

"I saw that it's still there."

"Yes, waiting for the next generation of Callaways, although not too many of us seem in a hurry to marry or reproduce. Nicole is the only one who made it down the aisle."

"Emma told me that Nicole's son Brandon is autistic," she said, handing back the wine.

"Yeah, it's sad. When Brandon was a baby, he was totally normal. He'd laugh and make eye contact, and I used to carry him around on my shoulders. Now Brandon acts like he never met me. To be fair, I haven't been around much the past year. It's no wonder he's forgotten who I am."

"Emma said you live up in Redding."

"Yes, I've been there the last three years."

"But you don't fight fires all year long, do you?"

"No, we take care of the forests in other ways during the off-season. I also do carpentry for a local cabinetmaker."

She wasn't surprised that his off-season job had to do with building. Aiden had always liked working with his hands. She shivered, unable to believe she could still remember his hands running down her arms, his fingers grazing her breasts. God! How crazy was that. She'd had other men touch her since then, so why did she still remember him?

She took another sip of wine. "So when are you going back?" she asked.

"Not sure yet."

"But you are going back, aren't you?"

Doubt filled his eyes. "I don't know. My plans are up in the air."

"What would you do if you weren't a smokejumper?"

"Too many questions, Sara," he said, taking the wine bottle from her hands.

"You always wanted to be a firefighter," she said, watching him take a drink. "Following in the family tradition."

"Not really. Smokejumpers don't protect people, just trees, property, land. It's a step down, according to the men in my family."

"I'm sure they don't believe that."

He shrugged. "It doesn't matter."

She suspected it did matter, but he'd never admit it.

"Anyway, I can't jump fires forever," he said. "I'm getting old."

"Thirty-two isn't old. Is your uncertainty because of what happened to Kyle?"

"Partly." He set down the empty bottle. "We took care of

that."

"We certainly did," she said, feeling warm and a little dizzy. "Maybe we'll both be able to sleep now."

"I haven't slept in three weeks. Sometimes I wonder if I'll ever sleep again. Every time I close my eyes, I'm back in the fire."

"What happened, Aiden?"

"I can't say."

"You mean, you won't say," she corrected.

He shook his head. "No, I can't remember. I fell down a mountain. When I woke up I'd lost several hours of time."

"Does your family know that?"

He shrugged. "I'm not sure if I mentioned it."

"Well, maybe you should. I think they'd have more compassion if they understood that it's not that you don't want to talk; you don't actually remember what happened."

"It doesn't matter."

"It does matter, and now I know why you can't sleep. Your brain is trying to recreate the memories."

"Possibly. I have a lot of recurring nightmares."

"Isn't there anyone else who can help you fill in the blanks? You weren't alone on that mountain, were you?"

"I talked to some of the guys, but Kyle and I were separated from everyone else. After a certain point, it was just the two of us. Anyway, we don't need to talk about that."

"Are you sure? I can be a good listener. And I'm great at puzzles."

He frowned. "We've shared enough for one night, Sara."

"Have we? You don't want to talk about you, so let's go back about twelve years. I have a question that's caused me a few sleepless nights."

"I'm sure I don't want to hear it."

She ignored him. The wine had loosened her inhibitions and broken down her guard, and the question was bubbling past her lips. "Why did you stop kissing me, Aiden? Why did you pull away? Why did you say *I can't do this*?"

"You said you didn't want to talk about that night," he reminded her.

"That was before we started drinking. I told you that you might regret opening that bottle of wine."

"I should have listened."

"Did you ever wish we hadn't stopped?" she asked.

His mouth tightened. "You should go inside, Sara. It's late and we're both a little drunk."

"Why won't you answer the question?"

"Because it was a long time ago."

"That's not the reason. You always want to call the shots, Aiden. I'm an adult now. You don't need to protect me."

He got to his feet and gave her a short smile. "This time I'm protecting myself."

He disappeared into the shadows, leaving her to wonder at his meaning. It would be stupid to think he'd run off because he was feeling something for her. She'd made the mistake before; she wouldn't do it again. It was good that Aiden had left. This was not the time to start something ... or to finish what they'd started before.

Sara woke up Saturday morning with a headache, a reminder that breaking the rules was never a good idea. Flopping onto her back, she stared up at the ceiling. Despite the pain in her temple, she couldn't regret opening the wine and sharing it with Aiden. It had been nice to talk to someone who'd known her since she was young. None of her New York friends knew anything about her childhood or her family. She never talked about her father to them. But Aiden already knew, and he understood. He saw her side, and she'd appreciated that. But she couldn't let herself think of him as anything more than a friend. Despite the mental admonition, she found herself remembering the night they'd moved past friendship.

She'd been seventeen years old, a senior in high school, and Aiden and his friends were going to a concert in Golden Gate Park. Emma was supposed to go, but she'd gotten distracted by her current crush, and so Sara had gone alone. She'd been so terrified of not fitting in or doing something stupid that she'd drunk a lot of vodka. At some point in the night, she and Aiden had separated from the others and, under the shadows of the trees, they'd started making out.

She'd wanted to kiss him for at least three years, so pushing him away had been the furthest thing from her mind. She was ecstatic that he'd finally noticed her, that he wanted her the way she wanted him. He'd told her she was beautiful, and he'd put his tongue in her mouth and his hands on her breasts and she'd wanted more. She'd wanted to have sex with him right there in the park. It didn't matter that they were outside, that people could see them, that she was a virgin. She wanted to be with him. And the desire in the eyes of the guy she'd always wanted had taken her past the point of sanity.

She blew out a breath, shaken by the memories. Putting her hand to her mouth, she realized that while she hadn't consciously thought about that night in a very long time, she'd been comparing that kiss to every other one since then, which was ridiculous. She didn't even know if it was the kiss that had been so good or the alcohol combined with years of a teenage crush. Probably both of those factors had come into play.

In the end, Aiden's hot kiss had turned to cold rejection. He'd pushed her away, saying he was sorry, but he just couldn't do it.

She'd been stunned. Aiden didn't say no to anyone. He'd

probably had half the girls in school, and he prided himself on being a rule-breaker, a risk-taker, a rebel. Obviously, she'd been too dull or too something...

He'd left her feeling humiliated. She'd been willing to hand herself over on a silver platter, and he'd turned her down.

Now he was surprised she wasn't grateful to him for saving her from herself?

Anger ran through her as she recalled his earlier words, but deep down she was as annoyed with herself as she was with Aiden.

Maybe she *should* be grateful that she hadn't had sex with him. He hadn't cared about her. In fact, they hadn't spoken after that night, at least not more than a mumbled hello or goodbye when their paths crossed, which hadn't been often. She'd made sure of that. She'd left for college a few months later. Then her mom died, and there was no reason to go home.

Which brought her to the present...

She was twenty-nine, not seventeen, and she had no intention of falling for Aiden's charm again.

Getting up, she grabbed some clothes out of her suitcase and headed into the bathroom. A quick shower made her feel a lot more like herself. After dressing in jeans and a soft sweater, she headed down the stairs.

The kitchen looked even worse in the daylight. So did the dining room and the hallway where sheets of wallpaper were peeling off the walls.

Her dad would be devastated. He had always been a very neat, organized person. She had to fix it. She'd start with Aiden's uncle.

She left the house and walked next door. Her knock went unanswered. That was odd. It was nine o'clock in the morning. Where was everyone? She glanced down the driveway at the room over the garage. She really didn't want to talk to Aiden again. But what option did she have? She climbed the stairs and knocked.

Aiden opened the door and gave her a sleepy stare.

Her heart skipped a beat at the sight of his bare chest, tousled hair, rough beard and bruised cheek. Thankfully, he still had on his sweats.

"What's up?" he drawled.

It took her a minute to remember why she was there. "I wanted to get your Uncle Kevin's phone number. I tried the house, but no one answered."

"I don't have his number on me, but I'm sure my mom has it. I can get it for you," he said.

"Are you sure? It looks like I woke you up."

"You did."

"Well, at least you slept."

"A few hours anyway." He stepped back into the room, grabbed a shirt and pulled it over his head. Then he walked out to the landing, pulling the door shut behind him. "How did you sleep?"

"Not bad." She followed him down the stairs and into the house.

"First, coffee," he said, grabbing two mugs out of the cupboard.

"That would be awesome," she said.

He poured two mugs and handed her one.

She took a sip. At some point in law school, she'd become addicted to coffee. All those late nights studying for the bar had made caffeine a necessary part of her diet.

"Did you talk to your dad this morning?" Aiden asked.

"Not yet. I want to have some information to share when I tell him he's going to need a new kitchen. Do you think you could get me that phone number?"

"I could, but I'm hungry. Why don't we eat first? I'll

cook."

Before she could answer, he had set down his coffee and was on his way to the refrigerator. He pulled out a carton of eggs. "Scrambled okay?"

"You don't have to make me breakfast," she said, although the idea was making her stomach rumble.

"It's no big deal. I can make you a scramble you won't forget—tomatoes, onions, avocado, cheese."

"You're even cocky about your eggs," she said dryly.

He grinned. "I know my strengths, that's all. What do you say? Have breakfast with me?"

She really needed to say no. This was Aiden, the man who had rejected her a decade earlier and left her heartbroken and feeling completely unsure of herself. It had taken her a long time to recover. Did she really want to spend even a few more minutes with him?

The tingle running down her spine said yes. That same tingle had sent her into his arms a very long time ago. She should listen to her brain instead of her body, but when she opened her mouth to answer him, the tingle won out.

"Yes," she said, hoping she wasn't about to make another big mistake.

Seven

Sara sipped her coffee, watching Aiden's quick and efficient movements in the kitchen. "I can't remember the last time a man cooked breakfast for me," she muttered, then mentally kicked herself for sharing that revealing fact.

"Do you usually cook for them?"

"Sometimes," she said vaguely. It had been a long time since she'd even had breakfast with a man, much less cooked for one. Not that she had much skill in the kitchen anyway. Her mom had tried to teach her, but her father liked his meals just so, and she'd always felt too much pressure to cook, so she'd usually sat on a stool, chatting while her mom made dinner.

A wave of sadness ran through her.

"What's wrong?" Aiden asked, his sharp gaze raking her face as he glanced over at her from the stove.

She started, straightening. "Nothing."

"You'd be a lousy poker player. You have way too many tells."

"And a 'tell' is?"

"A sign of what kind of cards you're holding."

"I was thinking about my mom. She was the cook in our family."

"I'm sorry I missed the funeral, but I was out of the

country."

"Were you?" she asked in surprise. "I just thought you were busy."

"I wouldn't have missed your mother's funeral. I was in Ireland with my cousin Tommy."

She vaguely remembered hearing about his trip back to the "old country," as the Callaways liked to refer to the homeland of their ancestors.

"Did you like it there?" she asked.

"I did. It's a beautiful country."

"I'd like to go sometime."

"You should," he said, as he turned his gaze back to the eggs he was scrambling.

"I'll put that on the *To Do* list."

He smiled. "Still have one of those, too, do you?"

"Doesn't everyone?"

"Not me."

"So you have nothing to do today?"

"Aside from making breakfast and getting you that phone number, my day is wide open."

"Maybe you should try to find out what happened to Kyle."

His mouth drew into a grim line. "I knew I was going to regret sharing that with you."

"You have to find a way to fill in the blanks so that you can defend yourself."

"How do you know I have a defense? Everyone else thinks I'm to blame. Maybe I am."

"Then you should know that, too," she said. "You may not remember anything right around the time you fell, but what about before that?"

Silence followed her words. Aiden tossed the eggs in the pan, then said, "The fire was bigger than we expected. We'd make some ground, then lose it. But we kept working the way we always did. Then the winds changed abruptly. I debated whether or not to retreat. I was having trouble getting information from the other commanders. The radio kept going in and out. Then the fire blew up on us. Our exit routes were cut off. The team separated. Kyle and I were together, but he was way ahead of me. I don't even know if he realized I was with him, or if he was too disoriented by the fire. He just kept walking, sometimes running, and I could see he was heading straight into the fire. I couldn't get his attention. The fire was all around us." He blew out a breath as he finished. "And that's all I know."

"It sounds like an accident," she ventured.

"Does it?" he challenged. "I waited too long to bail out. Kyle's death is on my head."

"Maybe you need someone to blame, too," she suggested.

"Better me than Kyle," he said.

"What does that mean?"

"Forget it."

"Aiden, did Kyle do something wrong?"

"I don't know. But I'm sure as hell not going to try to pin anything on him. Kyle has a wife and a baby son who are mourning him, along with his parents and his brother and sister. They're heartbroken. I won't add to their pain. If they need to blame me, I'm okay with it."

She met his gaze. "I understand, but you need answers for yourself. You're not okay. You don't sleep. You're thinking about quitting. That's nowhere close to being okay."

"I'll deal with it."

"Maybe I can help. I can be very intuitive and objective."

"I'm not one of your clients, Sara, and I'm finished talking. The eggs are almost done. If you want to help me, why don't you make us some toast?"

She sighed. "You can be so stubborn."

"Look who's talking. When did you get to be so pushy?

You used to be timid and shy."

"I grew up and became a lawyer," she said. "I've also been taking care of myself since I was nineteen years old."

"Well, how about taking care of that toast for now?"

"Fine," she said, knowing she wasn't going to get any further at the moment.

She hated injustice. It was something that drove her crazy as a lawyer. If someone was getting a raw deal, she wanted to take up their cause. She wanted to fix things. It was frustrating when she couldn't, when she was supposed to somehow look the other way. Not that she knew if there was injustice involved in Aiden's situation. Perhaps he was to blame. He could be reckless. He could be a thrill seeker. Was it really that big of a stretch to think that he might have thought he could beat a raging forest fire?

She put some bread into the toaster and got out plates while Aiden finished the eggs. A few minutes later breakfast was ready, and they sat down together to eat.

Aiden's cockiness had been well-founded she realized, as she sampled the eggs. The scramble was delicious. "This is good," she said.

"Did you have any doubts?"

"I thought you might be exaggerating your talents, but this time it turns out you weren't. Did Lynda teach you to cook?"

"She did. There were so many of us she was always looking for help in the kitchen."

"I can't believe you were home that often to help. I remember you always being on the go, coming from some athletic practice of some sort, going out with your friends, or making out with some blonde on the sofa in your parents' living room."

He grinned. "Those were some good days. High school was fun."

"Not for me. I was so worried my grades wouldn't be good enough to get me into the right college. When I wasn't studying, I was usually doing something awkward or embarrassing."

"Like what?" he asked, setting down his fork.

"I don't need to relive those experiences with you."

"Come on. I'm curious."

"I got my sleeve caught in my locker, and I couldn't get the combination lock open for about ten minutes. Pamela Danvers and her little gang of cheerleaders stood there and laughed at me. Finally, Emma came to my rescue."

"That sounds like Emma."

"She was great, but she wasn't always around, like when I stayed up all night studying for my AP test and then I fell asleep in the library during study hall. I missed the test, and when I woke someone had drawn pictures on my face."

He laughed. "That is a good one."

"It may be funny. It was not funny back then. High school for me was not the same as it was for you. You were the king of the school."

"No, that was Burke."

"Then you were the rebel prince. Everyone liked your confidence and your daring."

"Both got me into some trouble."

"You always landed on your feet. No matter the odds, somehow you came out on top."

The light in his gaze dimmed. "Maybe I used up my good luck back then."

He was thinking about Kyle again. "Aiden—"

"Don't," he said, with a definitive shake of his head. "I know you mean well, Sara, but this is my problem. And you have enough problems of your own to deal with."

As he finished speaking, the side door opened, and Emma walked into the room.

Surprise flashed through her eyes as she saw them. "Well, this looks…cozy."

"Aiden made breakfast," Sara said quickly, not liking the gleam in Emma's eyes. "I was going to go out, but—"

"But I insisted," Aiden said. "Sorry, there's none left, Em."

"No worries. I ate hours ago." Emma sat down at the table.

"You look tired," Sara said, seeing the shadows under her friend's eyes. "Were you working all night?"

"For a good part of it."

"What's the damage at St. Andrew's?" Aiden asked.

"Two classrooms gone, a couple of others in bad shape. Fire started in the kindergarten classroom with a can of gasoline and some rags. There was no forced entry, so someone had access to the school. The fact that this is the second fire at a school in less than a month is concerning."

"Do you think they're connected?" Sara asked.

"There are some similarities. But what's even more disturbing is that Sister Margaret is missing."

"What?" Sara asked in surprise. She'd transferred to St Andrew's in the fourth grade, and Sister Margaret had been the most popular teacher in the school.

"Is her disappearance connected to the fire?" Aiden asked.

"It hasn't been determined yet if there's a link." She tilted her head, giving them both a thoughtful look. "So what did I miss around here?"

"Nothing," Sara said quickly.

"Nothing," Aiden agreed.

"Yeah, right," Emma said, giving them both a suspicious look. "You know, I always wondered about—"

"I should go," Sara cut in, getting to her feet.

"You still need my uncle's phone number," Aiden told

her as he stood up. "I'll get it."

"Thanks." Alone with Emma, she was acutely aware of the curiosity in her friend's eyes. "Okay, I can see you want to say something, so say it."

Emma's gaze turned somber. "I love my brother, but I don't think you should get involved with him."

"I'm not."

"Sara—"

"I'm not," she repeated. "I came to get your uncle's phone number. Aiden said he might be able to give me a bid on fixing my dad's house. Aiden was making breakfast and offered to share. That's it. I got over Aiden a long time ago."

"Did you?"

"Yes," she said. "I told you that last night."

"I hope that's true, because..." Emma paused, glancing toward the door leading into the hallway. She lowered her voice a notch as she said, "I love Aiden. He's my brother. But he's not good with women. He doesn't have relationships. And now he's in a dark place. I don't want him to hurt you."

"I can take care of myself, Emma."

"You may be a tough lawyer on the outside, but I think on the inside you're still that sweet girl with a big heart who maybe cares a little too much."

She didn't like that Emma's assessment was so accurate, because she'd worked very hard the last few years to toughen up her soft side.

"I'm not that girl anymore. I'm a lot meaner. Some people at work even call me a bitch."

Emma laughed.

"It's not funny."

"Sara, you couldn't be a bitch if your life depended on it."

"I can be. I am," she protested.

"You are what?" Aiden asked as he entered the room.

"Nothing," she muttered quickly.

"Sara says she's a bitch at work," Emma put in with a grin.

"No way," he said with a shake of his head. "Not sweet Sara."

She frowned at his words. He might mean them as a compliment, but they only reinforced the fact that Aiden would always see her as the good girl.

"Here's my uncle's phone number," he added, handing her a piece of paper. "I'm sure he can help you out."

"Thanks," she said. "For this and for breakfast."

"No problem. I had to eat. I'll see you around."

After Aiden left, she turned to Emma. "See—no sparks. Where Aiden is concerned I'm just the girl next door. I always was and I always will be."

"You sound disappointed," Emma commented.

She straightened. "I'm not. I'm only here for a few days anyway."

"I wish you'd stay a while. Now that you're back, I realize how much I missed our friendship. I don't want to lose it again."

"I have to go back to New York," she said. "It's where my life is." As she said the words, that life seemed very far away.

"You could practice law in San Francisco. You could be closer to your father, and to me."

"I have considered moving back, but I'm on a track, and it's not the right time to get off. Speaking of my father, I need to get to the hospital. And then I need to see about getting the house fixed."

"Okay, but why don't we go out tonight for a drink, Sara? My brother Sean and his band are playing at a bar in Haight-Ashbury. It's actually a fundraiser for Kyle's widow and his baby son. There will be some of the old gang there. I'm sure you'd enjoy yourself."

"Is Aiden going?" she couldn't resist asking.

"I don't know. I haven't mentioned it to him." Emma paused, giving her another speculative look. "So, really, no sparks left?"

"No. I'll see you later." She headed out the door before Emma could see the lie in her eyes.

Eight

→⇒⇒⇐⇐←

Aiden paced around his room, feeling more alive than he had in weeks. After Kyle's death, numbness had crept over him. He'd been living in a surreal fog where everything was hazy, including his memories. Since arriving in San Francisco, things had changed.

The fire next door had forced him to act, to be the man he used to be. It had felt good to do something positive. Not that saving Sara's father made up for anything. Hell, Stephen Davidson would have been saved five minutes later by someone else in the fire department. Sara didn't need to be grateful to him, although he'd liked seeing something other than anger in her gaze.

When he'd pushed her away all those years ago, he'd known that he'd hurt her. The pain in her brown eyes had stuck with him for a long time. He'd told himself it was for the best. Sara was his sister's friend, and the girl next door – the *good* girl next door. If she'd been anyone else, he wouldn't have stopped. They'd have had sex right there in the park. But Sara was just too innocent to ruin, and he knew that she liked him way too much, mostly because she didn't really know him. While he was flattered to be the star in her teenage fantasy, he was not the man for her. He'd known that when he was nineteen, and he knew it now.

He just wished she hadn't grown up to be beautiful, smart, and sexy. Not that he should be surprised. All the ingredients had been there when she was younger; she just had to get over her awkward, shy, clumsy stage. She'd certainly done that. She was much more self-assured now, confident, and apparently a ruthless bitch of a lawyer. He found himself smiling at that thought. No way was Sara a bitch. She had an innate sense of kindness and compassion for other people. She might have toughened up on the outside, but inside she was still soft and maybe a little vulnerable.

Her relationship with her dad had messed her up, and last night had shown that she hadn't come to terms with that relationship yet. Stephen Davidson was an idiot—an asshole. He had an incredible daughter and he couldn't even see it. Aiden had half a mind to go to the hospital and tell him that to his face. But he had a feeling that action would only make things worse for Sara, and he didn't want that.

He wanted only good things for her.

Why wasn't she attached to someone? Why wasn't she married? Why didn't she have a house full of kids by now? She was such a loving person. He'd always admired her intelligence and had known she'd do great things, but he'd never seen her as only a career woman. In fact, that was one of the reasons he'd shied away from her before. He'd felt deep down that Sara was a woman who would settle for nothing less than everything from the man she loved. And as a teenager, that "everything" had been terrifying.

It was still scary. Loving someone that much was a huge risk, a risk he'd never been willing to take. He didn't see that changing anytime soon. So he would stick to women who felt the same way he did. Which meant he needed to stay away from Sara, because all morning long he'd found himself wondering what it would be like to kiss her now. Would it be as good as he remembered? Would it be better because they were older, because she wouldn't be so shy, so tentative, and he wouldn't be fast and impatient?

He blew out a breath, desire heating up his blood and tightening his body. He needed a shower – a cold shower.

It was not the time for his libido to spring back into action, especially not with Sara. He probably didn't need to worry. His earlier rejection had obviously stuck with her, and she wouldn't be in a hurry to give him another opportunity to push her away.

Frowning, he wondered if the reason behind Sara's all-consuming career was an unwillingness to put her heart on the line. She'd spent her entire life trying to get her father's approval. In fact, she was still trying. And he could see more clearly now how she must have felt when he'd shoved her away all those years ago. She'd taken it as one more rejection. But he had wanted her; he just hadn't been ready for a girl like her. And he didn't think he was ready now, either.

Damn! He did not like the direction of his thoughts.

Moving into the bathroom, he turned on the shower, stripped off his clothes and let the icy spray cool him down. As his tension decreased, he turned the water to warm and closed his eyes.

He wanted to think about something that wouldn't make him tense. Unfortunately, every part of his life was in turmoil. He'd thought coming home would help clear his mind, but he should have known better. His family wanted answers, and he had none to give. It had been three weeks since he'd woken up and learned that Kyle was dead, and he still didn't know what had happened. Why wouldn't his brain release the memories? There had to be something he wasn't seeing.

It wasn't just that he wanted to be able to defend himself, although it had stung to read some of his coworkers' statements. But they had a right to their opinions. They'd put their lives on the line working under his direction. Now some of them had lost faith in him. How could he blame them? How could he go back to Redding next year and lead?

Even the few people who supported his decisions, who were at least somewhat convinced that Kyle's death was an accident due to unforeseen fire activity, had suggested that he might want to rethink his career options. His boss had tried to spin the idea by saying it would be tough for him to come back after such a terrible loss, that he might not want to put himself in the same situation, that it wouldn't be a failure to make a change in his life.

Hell, yes, it would be a failure. He'd lost a man on his watch, and that would never change. And not just a man, but also his best friend.

He drew in a long, ragged breath, wondering if the pain would ever lessen. It seemed unimaginable.

It had to be even worse for Vicky. His thoughts turned to Kyle's wife. Kyle had met Vicky in a bar in San Francisco in the off-season. It had been a whirlwind love affair. A month later, Vicky had dropped everything and moved to Redding with Kyle. They'd gotten an apartment in his building, so he'd seen a lot of them. At first, it had been annoying to always have Vicky along, but Kyle was over-the-moon happy, so what could Aiden say? His friend was happier than he'd ever been.

Aiden had been the best man at their wedding. He'd been the first one they'd told when they were going to have a baby, and he'd been in the hospital when Robbie had been born. Three months later, they'd asked him to be the godfather. He'd promised Kyle that he would always look out for his son, but for the past several weeks he hadn't kept that promise. He needed to do that now. He just hoped Vicky would let him in the door.

—⇒▷◁⇐—

Sara entered her father's hospital room with a wary smile, unsure of her reception. Her father was in a private room, and his broken leg was propped up in a very uncomfortable-looking contraption. His hair was mussed, and he was unshaven, and didn't look at all like the man she'd grown up with. He'd never left his bedroom, much less the house, without every hair in place. But the one thing that was familiar was the frown on his face.

"I thought you'd have gone back to New York by now," he said.

"I wouldn't leave without saying goodbye." She moved to the side of his bed. "How are you feeling?"

"Not good."

"Do you need anything? Should I get the nurse to give you something for the pain?"

"I'm handling it," he said.

"Okay. I called Kevin Callaway. He's a contractor. He said he could come over this afternoon and give us a bid for fixing the damage."

"You don't need to be involved in that."

"You can't take care of it right now, and you can't come back to the house in the condition that it's in. You have to let me help you. I won't make any decisions without consulting you first, but at least let me lay some of the groundwork."

"I guess I have no choice."

Thank you would have been a better answer, but since he was in a lot of pain, she would cut him some slack. "Did the doctor say when you will be released?"

"Because I live alone, he wants me to go to a rehab facility for a few weeks."

She nervously licked her lips, not sure what to say. She couldn't take weeks off work, but the thought of her dad in a rehab facility was not appealing, either. "Maybe I could stay in the house with you for a few days, and then we could hire a nurse to come in after I'm gone," she suggested.

"No," he said, shaking his head. "You need to go home. I will deal with my situation."

She wanted to think that he was making that choice because he was worried about her losing her job, but she couldn't convince herself that was the reason.

"Why won't you let me help you? I'm your daughter."

"You've done more than enough."

There it was—the blame. He hadn't come right out and said she was responsible for the fire, but the accusation was in his eyes. "I wasn't the one who left a pot on the stove or who set a pile of newspapers way too close to the flame," she said, refusing to let him pin this disaster completely on her.

"You're right," he said, surprising her. "It was my fault. You can go home, Sara. There's nothing for you to feel guilty about."

Was his acquiescence just a faster way of getting her out of his life?

"I'm going to talk to the contractor first, get a bid," she said decisively. "You can decide what you want to do with it, but at least you'll have something to look at."

"I don't want you messing around my house, going through my things."

"Well, that's too bad, because someone is going to have to help you, and I don't see anyone else here."

He sighed. "I'm tired, Sara."

"I'm tired, too, tired of banging my head against a wall. Why is it so difficult for you to talk to me, to accept me?"

"I'm not trying to hurt you, Sara. I just don't have anything to give. I'm sorry, but that's the way it is."

"Why? Why is that the way it is?" she challenged. "Mom used to tell me that you were capable of a tremendous amount of love. I guess she saw it, but I didn't, and I never understood why."

His jaw tightened. "I'm in pain. I can't have this conversation with you now. Go home. Live your life. Forget about me. Forget about the house. I will take care of everything when I get out of here. Just leave it all alone." He let out a weary sigh and closed his eyes.

Sara stood by his bed for another moment, staring down at his face, at the lines of age around his eyes and mouth—a mouth that rarely smiled. Why was he so determined to have her leave when he was obviously going to need help? He'd rather go to a rehab facility or have a stranger give him assistance than have his own daughter take care of him? It didn't make sense.

She left the room and walked out to her car, thinking she had to be missing something. His behavior was just not normal, and his desperation to get rid of her so fast made her wonder if he was hiding something.

Did her father have secrets? She'd never thought he was interesting enough to have secrets, but something was off. Aiden had asked her the night before why her father had found it necessary to go down to the basement when his house was on fire.

Maybe the answers she was looking for were in that basement.

Aiden stared at the names on the mailbox: Kyle and Vicky Dunne. He drew in a tight breath knowing that Kyle would never live in the first and only home he had ever purchased. The condo had been a huge financial stress. They'd had to borrow money from Vicky's grandparents to make the down payment, and Kyle had been worried about keeping up with the mortgage. But Vicky had fallen in love with the Russian Hill neighborhood, the shops just around the corner, the children's park nearby, and Kyle had wanted to give her a home she loved.

It would probably be easier for Vicky to live in this condo. There were not as many physical reminders. Kyle had only spent one weekend there. He was supposed to have officially moved in the day after he was killed.

Aiden's stomach turned over and he felt physically sick, but he'd come too far to turn around and leave. He'd respected Vicky's wishes and stayed away from the funeral, but he needed to speak to her. He needed to make sure that she and Robbie were okay. He pressed the intercom.

Vicky's voice came over the speaker. "Yes?"

"It's Aiden. I'd like to talk to you for a minute."

Silence followed his request, then she said, "There's nothing left to say, Aiden."

"There's a lot to say, Vicky. I made a promise to Kyle. I intend to keep it. You're going to have to leave the condo eventually. I'll wait here until you do." He hoped he wouldn't have to make good on the threat or that Vicky wouldn't call the cops on him and report him for harassment.

A moment later, the buzzer rang. He opened the door and walked up to the second floor. Vicky stood in the doorway. She looked exhausted, emotionally spent. She wore faded jeans and a big sweatshirt that had baby spit-up on the shoulder. Her brown hair was pulled back in a ponytail, and there were dark shadows under her puffy eyes. She'd aged ten years since he'd last seen her.

"What do you want, Aiden? Absolution?" she asked, her tone harsh and unforgiving. She folded her arms in front of her chest, making it clear she had no intention of inviting him inside.

"How's Robbie?"

"He's asleep. He has no idea that his life has been ripped apart, that his father is never coming home." Her voice broke.

"I don't want to talk to you, Aiden. There's nothing you can say that will make any of this better."

"I know that, Vicky. I miss him, too. I loved Kyle. He was closer to me than some of my brothers."

"Then why did you let him die?"

Her question stole the breath out of his chest.

"Kyle would have followed you anywhere," she added. "He had so much respect for you. He never questioned your decisions. But some of the other men did, and they're still alive because they didn't follow you the way Kyle did." Her shoulders began to shake, and she put a hand to her trembling mouth. "You're still alive, Aiden. How can I look at you and not see him? You were always together. You were superheroes. You were invincible. That's what Kyle used to say."

Her words let loose an agonizing pain in his chest. He bit down on his bottom lip, feeling like she was ripping his heart into very small pieces. But he had to let her get out whatever she needed to say.

Tears fell out of her eyes, and she ruthlessly wiped them away. "You promised me that you would keep Kyle safe, and that didn't happen. So I don't care about any other promises you made."

"I'm sorry, Vicky." He wanted to give her a hug, but her body was as stiff as a board, and it was clear that she wanted nothing from him.

"Is that it? Are we done?"

"I want to help you and Robbie."

"To lessen your guilt?" she asked scornfully. "You think that will make it better?"

"I think it's what Kyle would want me to do. I didn't let him die, Vicky. I tried to get to him. He wasn't following me. I was following him."

"You should have gotten off that ridge a lot earlier.

That's what Dave Hawkins told me. But you were convinced you could beat the fire."

He had wanted to win that day, but a lot of factors had played into his decisions. "The fire blew up around us, Vicky. We had seconds to find a way out. And for whatever reason, Kyle went in another direction than everyone else."

"Why would he do that?"

"I don't know. Maybe he was blinded by smoke."

"How do you not know?"

"I fell down a hill into a ravine. I was knocked out, and when I woke up I couldn't remember everything that had gone down. There were pieces from my memory missing, and they still haven't come back."

"Well, isn't that convenient? You don't remember, so you can't be blamed."

He didn't know this cold, angry woman. She was a far cry from the fun-loving wife and mother he'd spent time with the past two years.

"It's not at all convenient," he countered. "When did you last talk to Kyle?"

"The day before he died."

"Was he worried about anything?"

Her gaze narrowed. "Like what?"

"I'm not sure. He seemed distracted days before that last jump. He wasn't talking to anyone, and that wasn't like him. He wasn't normally quiet."

"He didn't seem any different to me, and if you're trying to find some reason to blame him, then that's despicable."

"I'm not trying to blame Kyle," he said forcefully. "I'm just trying to figure out what happened."

"If Kyle was distracted, it was because he wanted to be done with smokejumping. He wanted to be with Robbie and me. But he was feeling bad about leaving you behind, Aiden. He said you needed him to stay grounded."

He frowned. "That's what he said?"

"Yes. He told me you were reckless, that you took too many chances, just what everyone else has been saying about you. But he had to be there to support you because that's what he'd been doing his whole life." She paused. "You didn't like that he got married, that he had a wife and a child. I broke up the dynamic duo, didn't I?"

"I was happy for him," he said. "And for you."

"Well, now neither one of us has him." She shook her head. "Kyle wanted to leave early. He wanted to get down here to start a new chapter in his life, but he told me that you wouldn't let him go. You needed him to stay to the last day. He didn't know it would be the last day of his life."

"He never asked me that," Aiden said, beginning to wonder if what Vicky was telling him had any credence at all. "I swear to you—he never asked me."

"Just go, Aiden. And please, don't come back."

She shut the door in his face. He stared at it for a long moment and then slowly walked back to his truck. He felt like he'd gone ten rounds in the boxing ring, and every punch Vicky had thrown had landed hard.

But some of what she had said did not ring true. And if she wasn't lying to him, then Kyle must have been lying to her. Why?

He now had even more questions than he had before. He needed facts, cold, hard facts.

Who better to help him than someone analytical and objective, and allegedly a really good investigator?

Nine

—➤➤❰❰﹤—

Sara walked down the stairs to the basement of her father's house feeling more than a little wary. The smell of smoke still lingered in the air, and in her mind she could see her father's broken body lying on the cement floor. He was lucky he hadn't cracked his head open.

When she reached the last stair, she glanced around the dark, shadowy room. Nothing unusual jumped out at her. There were the gardening tools she'd expected to find, along with some paint cans and a couple of folding chairs. Moving further into the room, she noted the water heater and just behind it a filing cabinet. On top of the cabinet was a cardboard box.

Frowning, she wondered if her father had rushed downstairs to retrieve some paperwork, but to her knowledge, he'd always kept anything of importance in his study. But he had come into the basement for a reason, a reason worth risking his life for, and she needed to figure out what that was.

Pushing herself forward, she picked up the cardboard box. It was taped shut, not particularly heavy, but it felt like there was something inside. She set it down on the ground and pulled open the top drawer of the two-drawer filing cabinet. It was empty. The second drawer held tax returns.

She flipped through the folders, noting that the dates went back ten to fifteen years. There was nothing more current in the drawer.

Her tension started to ease. She could see her father wanting to retrieve tax returns. He was a stickler when it came to receipts. But then again, they were very old. She placed the box back on top of the cabinet and looked around for some scissors. There were gardening shears in a nearby bucket. Good enough. She slit the tape, opened the top, and stared at her own face.

The box was filled with photos, the very first one the portrait shot she'd taken as a senior in high school. It was not her favorite shot. She'd felt uncomfortable with the purple drape falling off her shoulders, and she had a huge zit on her forehead.

Okay, there was no way her father had risked his life to retrieve this photo. She dug a little deeper and found more school pictures. These must have been the extra shots that hadn't fit into the photo albums her mom kept.

She let out a sigh of relief. There was nothing sinister in the basement.

"Sara?"

She jerked at the sound of her name. Aiden stood at the top of the stairs.

"How did you get in?" she asked, surprised by his sudden appearance.

"You left the front door open," he said, as he jogged down the steps.

"Right. I was going to move some of the trash outside and then I got distracted."

"What are you doing down here?"

"Trying to figure out what my father was after, but all I found were old tax returns and school pictures, nothing mysterious. I don't know why I thought for a moment there would be something strange down here. My father is not a man of mystery. He goes to work every day at eight and comes home just before six. He has one martini, sometimes two, and after dinner he works in his study until bedtime, which is usually around ten."

Aiden tilted his head and gave her a curious look. "Is that all you know about your dad?"

"Unfortunately, yes. And I think he's happy that's all I know about him. I can't remember an occasion where we had a conversation about anything personal. If he spoke to me at all, it was usually about grades or school or planning for the future. He had absolutely no interest in who my friends were, what books I liked..." She paused, thinking how odd it was that he hadn't sent the box of photographs to her with the rest of her belongings. He must have forgotten.

"Sara," Aiden asked.

"What?"

"You drifted away in the middle of a sentence."

"Am I missing something?"

"Uh, I don't know." He glanced around the basement. "Nothing looks out of the ordinary."

"Exactly. So why did my dad come down here?"

"You could just ask him."

"Like he'd tell me."

"Well, does your dad have a safe?"

"Not that I know of."

Aiden walked around the room, peering into some of the dark, shadowy corners. "I don't see any dead bodies."

"Not funny," she said, feeling an odd chill run through her body. It was just Aiden's comment and the spooky room that were making her feel on edge. "Let's go upstairs. I'm not a big fan of closed rooms. I get claustrophobic." She grabbed the box. "I think I'll take this with me."

Aiden grabbed it out of her hands. "I've got it."

She didn't bother to argue. She felt an intense need to get some fresh air. Unfortunately, the kitchen was just as suffocating as the basement. "Would you carry that up to my room for me?"

"Wherever you want it," he replied.

When they reached her room, he dumped the box on the bed and glanced around. "Well, this is homey."

"I told you my dad had cleared out all traces of my existence."

"Why are you staying here? Why not just go to a hotel? It would be a lot less depressing."

"I want to keep an eye on things, and this room is fine. I won't be here that long."

"Did you talk to my uncle?" Aiden asked.

"Yes." She glanced down at her watch. "He's coming over in about fifteen minutes to look around the damage."

"Good. I take it your dad's mood didn't improve between last night and today."

"No. But I'm going to do what I think is right. And he can take it or leave it." She paused. So why are you here?"

His expression grew somber. "I need your help."

She felt a little tingle of pleasure at the thought of Aiden coming to her for help. Their relationship had always been so one-sided growing up. She'd been the adoring one, and he'd been the adored. It was nice to turn the tables. Not that he was here to adore her… "What do you need?"

"Someone objective, analytic, and smart. Since you were bragging earlier about your strengths—"

"Bragging? That's your department."

"Whatever. You said you were a good investigator. And I think I need one."

She saw the new certainty in his eyes. "You want to find out what happened to Kyle."

"Yes. I need to know if there was anything going on in

his life that contributed to his death."

"Weren't the two of you close? Wouldn't you know what was going on in Kyle's life?"

The last few years we weren't as tight. After Kyle got married, he got busy with family life. When they decided to buy a condo in the city, they were gone almost every weekend. Once Vicky moved back, Kyle seemed down, distant. I figured he was missing his wife and kid. I tried to get him to go out with the rest of the team for drinks or dinner, but he usually said no. Those last few days he was packing up, getting ready for the move. I offered to help, but he turned me down." He let out a frustrated breath. "I think now that I gave him too much space."

She gave him a thoughtful look. "You said you *figured*— using the past tense."

"So?"

"So, reading between the lines, it sounds like you think there might have been more going on with Kyle than just being depressed about his wife and kid being in another city."

"Very sharp on the details, aren't you?"

"I told you I'm a good listener, and that's not an answer."

He sat down on the edge of the bed. "I might be trying too hard to come up with something."

"Just say it, whatever it is. Let's get it on the table." She sat down on the chair by her desk.

"You're a lot more direct than you used to be."

"No point in wasting time. Tell me what you're worried about."

"This doesn't go outside this room?"

She met his gaze head on. "No, it doesn't."

"Okay. I saw Kyle in town one day, and he was having a heated conversation with a woman I didn't know. They were standing on the sidewalk in front of a hotel. She put a hand on his arm, and the gesture seemed intimate. A few minutes later, they walked into the hotel."

"Did you ask Kyle about it?"

"No. I was waiting for him to tell me. I couldn't ask him if he was cheating on his wife."

"Couldn't you? I didn't think you and Kyle worried about boundaries."

He tipped his head. "In the old days, maybe not. But like I said, Kyle had become more distant. I don't want to believe he was having an affair. Kyle loved Vicky."

"Vicky was gone, and he was lonely."

"That's not a reason for having an affair."

"Men have had affairs for absolutely no reason at all," she pointed out, unable to keep the sharp tone out of her voice.

He raised an eyebrow. "Are you speaking from personal experience, Sara?"

She hesitated, but Aiden's demanding gaze compelled her to add, "I haven't been married, but I have been cheated on. And my boyfriend had no explanation except to say it didn't mean anything, and I shouldn't worry about it."

"Ouch. Did you kick him to the curb?"

"Oh, yeah."

"You know, it probably didn't mean anything, Sara. Sex and love are not the same thing."

"Well, you would say that," she said.

"What does that mean?"

"Come on, Aiden, you've always been a player. You had a million girls around when we were growing up. Since you're still single and still... Anyway, I'm sure you don't spend too many nights alone."

"Still what?" he asked. "You've developed a bad habit of drifting off in the middle of a sentence."

That was because she was talking way too much. "You know what you look like, Aiden. I don't need to make your head any bigger."

"So you think I'm attractive." The teasing light in his eyes reminded her of the boy she'd fallen so hard for.

She really needed to leave town before her old crush came completely back to life. "Let's get back to Kyle. If there was another woman, maybe we can find her."

"I might be completely off base," he said.

"You have good instincts. What other theories do you have?"

He stared back at her for a long moment. "I wasn't sure how Kyle could afford the condo. Smokejumpers don't make a lot of money. A while back, when we were a lot younger, Kyle got caught up in gambling. He said he'd learned his lesson—that the house always wins – but I wonder if he got himself into some financial trouble."

"That doesn't seem like something he would keep from you."

"He might. I got pissed off at him the first time around. He lost some of my money along with his."

"So gambling, women… anything else?"

Aiden's mouth turned down into a frown at her words. "I feel like an asshole. Kyle was a good man. He probably wasn't doing anything wrong. I shouldn't be doing this."

"You haven't done anything except talk to me. You don't have to feel guilty for wanting to find the truth, Aiden. What you do with it is up to you." She paused. "Have you spoken to Vicky? She might be able to answer some of your questions."

"I tried a little while ago. She had a lot of things to say, none of them good. She said that Kyle had asked to leave the season early and that I had said no. That wasn't true. I don't know if she was lying to me or Kyle was lying to her." His lips tightened. "She is so angry. I feel terrible for what she's going through, but she won't let me help her. She blamed me for Kyle's death."

"That may change with time," she said gently, wishing she could ease some of the pain in his eyes. "Vicky needs someone to blame. But you need to figure out if she's blaming the right person."

Shadows darkened his blue eyes. "It's possible the decisions I made that day were wrong, that I wasn't seeing the situation clearly. What I do remember suggests something else was happening. It's not really about who is to blame. I just need to know."

She could see the anguish in his eyes and wondered if his mind was protecting him in some way. Maybe he wasn't remembering because he just couldn't go to that terrible place in his head. Was she doing him a favor by helping him? Or was she going to end up hurting him?

"I don't want to get anyone from the Redding crew involved in whatever we're going to do. I've already talked to the people I trust the most. And the others I've read what they had to say. If something was going on with Kyle, he took great pains to hide it, and I want to make sure I don't inadvertently smear his name on my way to the truth."

She nodded, thinking about the best way to proceed with such little information. "I've worked with a private investigator, Jeanne Randolph, on cases for my firm. She's an ex-cop with a lot of really good connections. I can call her and see if she can help."

"I'll pay whatever she charges."

"Okay." Wanting to lighten the mood, she added, "You'll like her. She's blonde."

The shadows lifted from his eyes. "That's not actually a requirement," he said dryly.

"Could have fooled me. I never saw you with anyone who didn't have golden hair."

"Maybe when I was in high school," he conceded. He paused. "There's one other thing, Sara. I don't want my family to know what I'm doing, and that includes Emma. So if you don't think you can keep her out of it, we should stop right now."

She had a choice to make. Emma wouldn't like her keeping a secret that involved her brother. Then again, she was trying to help Aiden. He didn't want to involve his family or his fire crew, which didn't leave him with many options. All that aside, it was Aiden, and he wanted her help, and there was no way she was going to say no. "I won't tell Emma," she said, meeting his waiting gaze. "This is your business, and I'll respect that."

"And you'll respect that whatever we find out will be mine to decide what to do with? Because I may do nothing."

"Not even if the truth will clear your name?"

"That depends on whether that truth will hurt Kyle."

She admired his loyalty to his friend, and she hoped he wouldn't have to make that choice. "Let's not get ahead of ourselves."

"So how do we start?"

"I'll call Jeanne. I'd like to get some of Kyle's information first: name, birthdate, any other information you have like a social security number or a driver's license."

"I don't know that I have any of that," Aiden said.

"Jeanne is good at working with very little. Let's get some paper. I'm sure my father must have some in his study."

They went downstairs and entered the room that had always been her father's private sanctuary. Stepping through the doorway, Sara felt very much like an intruder. "I can't remember the last time I was in here," she muttered, glancing around the room. Her father's den was very male with a big mahogany desk by the window, shelves and shelves of books, mostly law books, although there were a few other nonfiction and biographies in the mix. Her father was all about facts. No fiction for him.

A brown leather couch and a coffee table were on the adjacent wall. Like the other rooms in the house, this one was neat and organized. The only sign of life was a stack of recent mail that her father had placed in his in-box. She smiled cynically. Her father had always been most comfortable when he was working, so he'd created an actual office in his home, his place of retreat.

Aiden nudged her shoulder. "Are you okay?"

"Just thinking about how this room was probably the only room in the house where my father felt at home."

"It's a man-cave," he agreed. "A little on the boring side, but it suits your dad." He paused. "Not your mom, though. She was warm, friendly. I remember all the times your mom and Lynda would sit at our kitchen table with their tea and cookies. They'd talk for hours."

"My mother was hungry for conversation and company. I think when I got older and was out of the house more, she felt the loneliness more deeply."

"Why do you think your parents stayed together?"

"Probably out of a sense of duty and responsibility. That's the kind of people they were. Once they made a promise, they kept it." She thought about all the times she'd wished her mother would run away with her. They'd go someplace warm where the sun beat down on their heads and people played music and laughed, and there wasn't icy quiet all the time.

"Sara," Aiden prodded. "Where are you?"

She smiled at him. "On a beautiful beach, watching my mom enjoy her life instead of suffering through it. She could have had so much more if she'd left my father. It's just so unfair. She loved life, and he barely tolerates it. But she's gone, and he's still here. And it's not that I don't want him to be here," she said hastily. "That sounded bad."

"I get it, Sara. You don't have to explain."

"I feel disloyal, not just when I say the words out loud, but when I think them in my head."

He smiled at her. "That's because you went to Catholic school and learned about guilt."

"True."

"Love and hate are complicated emotions," Aiden said. "Sometimes they're the same."

"I don't want the kind of love my mom had. I want more for myself."

"You should have more, Sara, a lot more. Don't settle for someone who isn't willing to lay down his life for you."

"I'm sure that guy won't be difficult to find," she said dryly. "Most men aren't willing to put down their phones for me."

He grinned. "You haven't met the right guy."

She had met the right guy—a very long time ago. He just didn't feel the same way about her. She moved to the desk and opened the top right-hand drawer and pulled out a notepad. "Write down whatever you think might help Jeanne do some research into Kyle's life," she said, pushing the pad and a pen across the desk. "Go back in time, high school, college, fire academy, friends, addresses. If you know where he did his banking, put that down. Any gambling connections would be helpful." She paused, as he made no move to pick up the pen and start writing. "If you've changed your mind, Aiden, it's all good."

He looked into her eyes. "I just have a bad feeling about this."

"Afraid of what you will find, or what you won't find?"

"Both." A moment later, he picked up the pen.

Ten

Emma felt sick to her stomach. Her job as an arson investigator required objectivity, but staring at the burned out classroom where she'd gone to kindergarten felt very personal. She had so many memories in this school, and in this particular room. She could remember sitting on the bright, colorful carpet listening to the teacher read stories about incredible places and kids having extraordinary adventures. She'd drawn pictures at one of the three communal tables, painted watercolors on the easels that stood at the back of the room, and built castles out of blocks.

The kindergarten room had been a place of magic, a trip into imagination, a child's first entrance into the world of school and learning. Now the magic was gone, and there was nothing but blackened remnants of furniture and piles of ashes. She drew in a deep breath. She loved her job, but sometimes she hated it, too. But she would find joy in bringing whoever had done this to justice.

"Callaway."

His voice made her jump, spin around, and she was annoyed with herself for feeling so unsettled by Max Harrison's sudden appearance. She should have expected him to show up. He always seemed to be in her way these days.

"Harrison," she said crisply.

"Any clue as to who set this?"

"Unfortunately, no. The arsonist covered his tracks."

"Or hers," he said.

"Ninety percent of arsonists are male. Your gender seems to enjoy fire more than mine. Do you have any information on Sister Margaret?"

"Unfortunately, no," he said, echoing her words. "It's still possible she left of her own volition."

"But you said there was some blood found in her parking garage."

"A trace amount. She could have cut her finger."

Despite his logical words, she sensed that he did not believe Sister Margaret had cut her finger. "Your instincts tell you something happened to her, don't they?"

"From the interviews I've conducted with her friends and with her employer, it seems that her disappearance is out of character. The fact that there was a suspicious fire at her placement of employment is also concerning." He paused, tilting his head, as he gazed into her eyes. "Have you considered the possibility that Sister Margaret set fire to the school?"

She was genuinely shocked by the suggestion. "No, of course not. Why on earth would she do that?"

"I've had enough training in fire investigation to know that arsonists, especially female arsonists, often target their homes or their places of employment."

"That's true, but Sister Margaret is not an arsonist. She's a sixty-something-year-old nun. She teaches fourth grade and runs the choir. She organizes fundraisers for the school and the church. She's a wonderful, amazing person."

"You don't sound very objective, Callaway."

"I know her. She would never set fire to the school. She loves this place. It's her second home."

"Which classroom was hers?" he asked.

Her lips tightened. "You already know the answer to that question—the one next door, but this is the room where the fire started."

"Her classroom was destroyed, too."

"I thought you were trying to find her, but you sound like you're more interested in arresting her."

"I'm just doing my job."

"So am I," she said. "And there's no evidence pointing in Sister Margaret's direction."

"There's no evidence pointing anywhere. You've got nothing, Callaway. But I have a missing nun, some blood evidence, and a fire at her place of employment. Her roommate also told me that the good sister had been replaced on the choir and was thinking of retiring because she didn't care for the new principal."

"It's not unusual for someone of her age and long tenure at the school to consider retirement," Emma replied. "I understand why you're making the connection, but I don't believe there's a link between Sister Margaret's disappearance and the fire. Last month we had a similar fire at the high school. It's more likely we have a fire bug whose favorite target is a school."

"Did you know that Sister Margaret used to work at the high school?" he asked.

She didn't appreciate the gleam in his eyes or the fact that he had more information than she did. "I wasn't aware of that. It had to be a very long time ago."

"Twenty-three years ago. She worked there for four years before transferring to St. Andrew's."

"You're on the wrong track, Harrison."

"We'll see. So, I heard one of your brothers is playing a gig tonight for the smokejumper who died."

"Yes," she said slowly, hoping he wasn't planning to go. It was bad enough she had to deal with him on the job. She really didn't want to spend her off time with him.

"Are you going?"

"Yes, of course. Kyle, the man who died, was very good friends with my brother Aiden. They worked together for a long time."

"So how many brothers do you have, Callaway?"

"Five brothers and two sisters."

"Big family. How many are in the fire department?"

"Too many to count if you include first and second cousins."

"Family tradition, huh?"

"Yes. Speaking of family... She glanced at her phone, a text message from Nicole flashing across the screen. "I need to make a call."

"Maybe I'll see you tonight," he said.

"Maybe not. I'm sure there will be a big crowd."

His smile broadened. "Not a problem. You're a standout, Callaway."

Her nerves tingled at the look in his eyes. "Look, Harrison, I'm not interested in any kind of a relationship with you that isn't one hundred percent professional."

"Did I ask you for anything else?" he countered.

"I know when a man is interested in me. You need to stop. I am single now, and I intend to stay that way."

With that proclamation, she left the classroom, hoping that she hadn't just made a complete fool of herself by assuming he was interested in her when he really wasn't. But she hadn't imagined the sparks between them. She knew what heat felt like. Max Harrison was one fire she was going to stay away from.

Emma got into her car and punched in Nicole's number on her phone. "What's up?" she asked when her sister came on the line.

"I need a break, Em. I was wondering if you wanted to go out and get a drink or something. Ryan is actually home and I need to get out of here."

"Sure," she said, surprised that Nicole would actually consider leaving the house without Brandon. "I'm going to the Dunne fundraiser later tonight. Sara and I are going to meet for dinner before that. Why don't we make it a threesome?"

"Are you sure Sara won't mind?"

"Of course not. She was asking about you yesterday. It would be fun to have some girl time. I have to stop by work. Can I get you in about an hour?"

"I'll meet you at Mom's. I have to run a couple of errands first. Thanks, Em."

"For what?"

"For saying yes," Nicole said. "I know I haven't been a very good sister lately."

"Don't be crazy. You've had your hands full. I totally get that. I'm thrilled you're actually going to take some time for yourself."

"Is Aiden going to be at the fundraiser tonight?"

"I don't know."

"I hope he goes. He needs to find a way to make peace with what happened."

Emma smiled to herself as she set down her phone. Aiden and Nicole were a lot alike. Neither one of them could accept the unacceptable with resignation. They fought until they couldn't fight anymore.

—➤➤◄◄—

Aiden had just turned down Nicole's street when he saw her car going in the other direction. Maybe that was a good thing. He wanted to talk to Ryan alone.

Ryan greeted him with a tired smile. Tall and lean with light brown hair and dark brown eyes, Ryan wore navy blue slacks and a white button-down shirt, part of his pilot's uniform. Ryan had been flying since he was fourteen years old. It was his greatest passion—after Nicole.

"Can't say I expected to find you on my porch," Ryan said. "I heard the family had search parties out for you."

He gave him a dry smile. "I'm sure they did."

"Come on in. If you're looking for Nicole, she just left."

"That's fine. I want to talk to you."

As Aiden entered the house, he saw Brandon playing with Legos on the floor of the living room. "Hey, Brandon," he said loudly. The kid didn't even turn his head.

"Don't waste your breath," Ryan said. "Brandon wouldn't acknowledge you if you were standing on your head in a clown's costume. Believe me, I've tried. Do you want something to drink?"

"Sure."

Aiden followed Ryan into the kitchen, taking a seat at the counter while Ryan opened the refrigerator door. "Vegetable juice, orange juice, milk, water."

"I'll take some orange juice," he said.

"Coming up." As Ryan poured the juice, he said, "So what did you want to talk about?"

"Just wanted to check in and see how things are going."

"Not well." Ryan set the juice in front of Aiden. "But Nicole will give you a different spin."

"How so?"

"She'll tell you that Brandon is improving, that she can see a light in his eyes, that he's coming out of his dark world."

"And you don't believe that's true?"

"I haven't seen it. I think she just wants it so badly to be true that she's starting to believe her own spin."

"Positive thinking can be good," he said.

"But not delusional thinking. At some point, she may have to face reality. Brandon may never get better. We may never get our son back." He shook his head as if he couldn't believe he'd just said the words out loud. Then he let out a long sigh. "It sucks."

"Yeah, it does," he agreed, taking a sip of his juice. "But you and Nicole will get through it. You're both strong, and you love each other."

Ryan's gaze shifted slightly. "I'm not sure Nicole even knows I exist anymore, except when it comes time to pay for more therapy. That's where I seem to be the most valuable."

"That's not true."

"Hey, you haven't been around. So don't tell me what's true."

Aiden could see that Ryan was getting wound up. "Take it easy. I'm not judging you. I'm just worried. Is there anything I can do to help?"

"Short of finding us a miracle cure, I can't think of anything," Ryan said tersely.

"Maybe you'll still get that miracle," he said, wishing Ryan had more of Nicole's positive attitude. Then again, maybe Ryan was being more realistic and Nicole was just unwilling to accept the truth.

"I hope so. I should get back to Brandon, not that he'll care, but I told Nicole I'd try to engage him in activity."

"Where was Nicole headed?" Aiden asked.

"She said she was going out with Emma, which shocked the hell out of me. She has really isolated herself from anyone who isn't connected to Brandon's treatment program. I'm glad she's going to step into the outside world for a few hours. Maybe it will give her some perspective," Ryan replied as they headed to the living room.

"You should take a break together. What about a long weekend away? I'm sure Lynda would babysit."

"She's offered, but Brandon does best with Nicole. He doesn't interact with her either, but she's still some sort of a safety net for him." Ryan paused as they entered the living room. Brandon was engrossed in his building blocks. "He likes to match stuff up," Ryan said. "When he finds a pair of the same shape and color, he actually looks happy for a split second. Some kind of minor victory, I guess."

Ryan moved around the couch and knelt on the ground next to Brandon, careful not to get too close to his son. "How about I help you build something, Brandon," he suggested.

Brandon didn't respond.

Ryan picked up some pieces and started putting them together. "We could make a truck or a dinosaur," he said. "Maybe you could help me, Brandon. Can you find me a piece like this?"

Brandon's gaze remained focused on the pieces he was rearranging.

Ryan held the piece closer to Brandon, so that it was practically under his nose. "Can you find one that looks like this, Brandon?"

Brandon's fingers stilled on the block he was playing with, and his gaze lifted ever so slightly. Then he went back to work on what he was doing.

"It's okay. I'll look for it," Ryan said.

Aiden had to admit he was impressed that Ryan's voice held no trace of the frustration and anger he'd shown when they were talking in the kitchen. He might be going crazy on the inside, but he wasn't showing that to his son.

"Do you want to help me build something?" Ryan asked, directing the question toward Aiden.

He smiled. "You know, that might be the best offer I've had today." He joined them in front of the fireplace. "But I'm building the dinosaur. You stick with the truck."

"Forget the truck; I'm going to build a plane," Ryan said

with a trace of a smile.

"Well, we'll see whose is better," Aiden said.

"Always the competitor."

"That comes from having seven siblings," he said, digging into the box of Legos.

"Your family has been very supportive," Ryan said. "I don't know what we'd do without them. Jack and Lynda, Emma and Shayla all babysit, and Burke watches out for Nicole when I'm out of town."

"Good old Burke," he drawled.

Ryan gave him a speculative look. "You two fighting already? You haven't been home that long."

"Long enough."

"Are you going to tell me what happened to Kyle?"

"I can tell you what everyone thinks happened."

"How about what you think?"

"My memories are blurry."

"Well, I'm sorry about Kyle. He was a great guy. Are you blaming yourself for that?"

"It's hard not to."

"You have good instincts and you know how to fight fires, Aiden. I'm sure you did everything you could to get your men out safely."

He really wanted to believe that, but he needed some facts to back up the theory. While grabbing a handful of blocks, he glanced over at Brandon. While they'd been talking, Brandon had lined up blocks two by two, but he didn't appear to be interested in building anything with them.

Ryan followed his gaze. "Brandon is obsessed with pairs. I guess his brain is working something out. I can't imagine what. I wish I could help him."

The pain in Ryan's eyes was intense. No matter what Nicole thought, Ryan had not given up on his son. Whether or not he'd given up on Nicole was another matter.

Eleven

⟶⟫⟪⟵

"This is great," Emma declared, glancing around the table. "My big sister is out on her own in probably two years, and I'm with my best friend, who I haven't seen in a decade. I'm so glad we're all together."

"It is nice," Sara said, exchanging a smile with Emma.

After meeting with Kevin Callaway and discussing bids for a kitchen remodel, she'd spent the afternoon looking at kitchen cabinets, sinks and appliances. She was going to gather the information and leave it with her dad. If he wanted to dump it in the trash, that was up to him, but she would have done her part. Now she could relax and just enjoy herself.

"I can't believe we let so much time go by," Emma said.

"I feel bad too," she said, "but we were busy growing up."

"That's true," Emma said, sipping her mineral water. She'd already proclaimed herself the designated driver.

Sara glanced over at Nicole, thinking she was being awfully quiet. Nicole was one of the nicest people she'd ever met. She didn't have Emma's sharp edges, or Aiden's reckless spirit, or Burke's commanding presence, but Nicole had a deep well of generosity and kindness that just drew people to her. She'd always thought of Nicole as a big sister, someone she could ask for advice when she was confused or floundering. Right now, it seemed like Nicole was the one who was floundering.

"Are you okay, Nicole?" she asked.

Nicole gave her a weak smile. "I'm sorry I'm not great company. I seem to be distracted a lot these days. Please don't take it personally."

"Of course not. I wish I could help."

"I have a lot of people who are trying to help," Nicole said. She sat up straighter in her chair. "It's just going to take time, that's all, but I'm going to get my son back, and everything will be good again."

She nodded. Nicole had as much Callaway spirit as the rest of her siblings, but she seemed to be facing some pretty big obstacles.

"I wonder if I should call Ryan," Nicole added, glancing down at her watch.

"Ryan is fine," Emma said. "He can take care of his son for a few hours. You need to relax. You should have some more wine."

"I've had enough wine. I'm not a single girl like the two of you." She gave a slightly wistful sigh. "I can barely remember those days."

"That's because you weren't single very long," Emma said. "You fell for Ryan hard and fast. One look, and he was the one."

"He was the one," Nicole echoed.

Sara wondered if there wasn't just a little too much emphasis on the word *was*.

Emma suddenly stiffened, her mouth turning down in a frown as her gaze fixed on someone at the other side of the room.

Sara shifted in her chair so she could see who Emma was looking at. The focus of her attention was a good-looking man wearing dark jeans and a gray sweater. "Who's that?" she asked.

"Max Harrison," Emma replied, her lips tightening. "He's a cop, a very annoying cop. He's working on the investigation involving Sister Margaret."

"How is he annoying?" Sara asked.

"He thinks he knows everything when he knows nothing."

"Sounds like every guy I know," Sara said with a smile.

"True, but he gets under my skin. I ran into him earlier today at St. Andrew's. He had the nerve to suggest that Sister Margaret might have been responsible for setting the fire, that she might have had some beef with the administration."

"Wait, what are you talking about?" Nicole interrupted. "I didn't hear about this."

"There was a fire at St. Andrew's last night," Emma replied. "And Sister Margaret is apparently missing. But I know she did not set that fire."

"That would be crazy," Sara agreed. "She loved that school."

"Exactly what I told him, but he didn't seem inclined to take me at my word."

"I'm sure he's just doing his job," Nicole said. "He might be more objective than you."

Emma frowned at her sister's criticism. "I have found no evidence to support his theory. If I had, I would keep an open mind."

"Yes, but that school meant a lot to you, too," Nicole said.

"I know what I'm doing, Nic."

"Okay, fine," Nicole said.

"I just really dislike him," Emma muttered, her gaze moving back to her object of dislike.

"Or..." Sara said, noting the gleam in Emma's eyes. "You

actually like him, and that's why he irritates you."

"Oh, please," she said with disdain. "That is ridiculous."

"She's right. You have that look, Em." Nicole exchanged a nod with Sara. "Good call. I'm getting slow. I didn't pick up on that right away."

"I do not have that look," Emma said, her annoyance now centered on them. "You two are way off base. I am off men for at least a year."

"You haven't told me about your last relationship," Sara said, realizing they'd skated around that topic. "You mentioned something about a breakup…"

"It's a long story."

"Now seems like a good time to tell it. We have a half hour."

"We'd need a week and maybe a shrink to help us analyze things. It was complicated, messy, awful, wonderful and then awful again. It was too much drama, and too much emotion, and I had to get out. I was becoming this weepy girl, and I didn't like it."

Sara smiled. Emma had always taken pride in her tough edges. But she'd never been as tough as she thought.

"Let's talk about something else," Emma added. "Oh, there's Burke." She waved to her oldest brother.

Burke gave a nod and then headed toward them.

Wearing black slacks and a charcoal gray coat over a black shirt, Burke drew more than his fair share of looks on his way to the table. With his almost black hair and his blue-gray eyes, Burke was an attractive man with a serious, intense edge. He had a commanding presence, but he could also put people off. Sara had never felt comfortable around him. He'd been five years older than her, a gap that had seemed like a million years when they were kids. He was a good man, but she couldn't help wondering if he ever had any fun. Although most people probably wondered the same thing about her.

"Em, Nic," he said shortly, then gave her a polite smile. "Sara. Sorry about last night. I don't think I was very welcoming."

"I understand there's a lot going on."

"Yes," he agreed, turning to Nicole. "It's good to see you out of the house."

"Actually, I'm leaving," Nicole said, getting to her feet, despite Emma's protest. "I'm sorry, Em, but I have to go. Thank you. I haven't had this much fun in a long time. You are a great sister. And Sara, it was wonderful to see you, too. I hope we don't have to wait another ten years for you to come for a visit."

"I hope not, too."

"How are you getting home?" Burke asked Nicole.

"I'll get a cab out front."

"I'll help you with that," he said, walking Nicole through the crowded restaurant.

"Your brother is always a gentleman," Sara commented.

"He does have good manners." Emma paused, her gaze moving toward the front door. "It looks like there's going to be a good crowd tonight."

Sara nodded, seeing a swarm of people moving toward the stage in the adjacent bar area.

"Sean will be thrilled by the turnout," Emma added. "I just wish it wasn't for such a sad reason. Hopefully, we can raise some money to help out Kyle's widow and his baby son. I just wish Aiden would come. I know he's taking some heat for the decisions he made, but he wouldn't have done anything to hurt Kyle, not on purpose. I get angry every time I hear someone express doubts about that. It pissed me off that Vicky asked him not to go to Kyle's funeral, but it was better that he wasn't there because I heard a lot of nasty comments about Aiden that day."

"I didn't realize you'd gone to the funeral," Sara said.

"Most of the family went. Kyle spent so much time at our house, my parents felt like he was one of their kids."

"I suspect your parents feel that way about a lot of kids."

"Well, they feel that way about you," Emma said with a warm smile. "Our moms were as close as we were. My mother was so sad when your mom died. We all wanted to take care of you, but you went back to school. I always wondered how you handled it. Your emails were pretty short and we always seemed to miss each other's phone calls."

"I buried myself in my classwork and let the days go by," she said.

"You're a strong person, Sara."

She'd had to be strong; she didn't have anyone to lean on.

She sipped her water as the waitress set down their check, her gaze moving idly around the room. She saw Burke again, this time talking to an attractive brunette. "Who is your brother talking to?"

Emma glanced over her shoulder. "That's Hannah Abrams. She works in dispatch."

"Are they a couple?"

Emma immediately shook her head. "No, she got married last year. It was too bad. She would have made a nice sister-in-law, but I think she and Burke only went out a few times." She paused. "Burke hasn't been with anyone seriously in a while. He was engaged about five years ago, but his fiancé was killed by a drunk driver." Emma's gaze filled with sadness. "Burke was working that day. His truck responded to the scene."

"Oh, my God," Sara said, horrified by the thought.

"It was beyond awful. Ever since then, Burke's serious side has gotten darker. He's overprotective when it comes to family. That's why he walked Nicole outside. He checks in on everyone all the time. I think that's why he's so angry with Aiden. He wants to help him, but Aiden won't let him, and as usual they're butting heads."

"They always seemed competitive growing up."

"That hasn't changed. In some ways it's good. They push each other to be better. But sometimes that competitive drive stops them from just being brothers." Emma slid some cash under the bill and said, "Let's check out the bar. I think the band is going to start soon."

They made their way through the crowd. There were a few tables in the bar, but most people were standing on the dance floor. Sean and his band were setting up. Sara recognized Emma's little brother right away, although he wasn't so little now. He wore faded jeans and a light green T-shirt. His hair was much longer than his brothers', curling down past his neck. He definitely had a rock star vibe about him.

"Sean is super talented," Emma said as they paused in the middle of the room.

"I can still remember him walking around your house with a guitar."

"Drove me nuts," Emma said with a nod. "He wasn't playing songs back then, just hitting chord after chord."

Sara laughed. "I remember. I guess all that practice is paying off."

"It is. I'm going to get you a drink and me some more sparkling water. Save me a spot."

Before she could tell Emma she didn't need another drink, her friend had disappeared into the crowd.

Sara glanced around the room, wondering if she'd see any other familiar faces from her past. Almost immediately her gaze came to light on Aiden, and her heart skipped a beat. She really hadn't thought he would show up. Then again, Aiden had never been short on guts.

There were dozens of people between them, but when his gaze locked with hers, everyone else faded away. Her breath got stuck in her chest, and a wave of heat ran through her. It was crazy to be attracted to someone who'd already rejected her once. Hadn't she already learned that painful lesson? So, why the same crazy, world-tilting reaction whenever she saw Aiden? He wasn't a superhero. In fact, right now he was probably one of the most hated men in the room.

He moved towards her, and she silently willed for someone to get in the way. She needed to get herself together, to remind herself that she was not a teenager anymore, and he was not her high school fantasy.

But he looked really good in jeans and a black knit top under a black leather jacket.

They were not in high school anymore, but he was definitely still fantasy material.

When he stopped in front of her, she forced a casual expression on her face. "I didn't think you were coming."

"Changed my mind a half dozen times. Let me know if you see any knives headed towards my back."

"So far, all the daggers are just looks," she said, aware that people were watching them, and she didn't think she was the one drawing attention.

"Great."

"Did you get my message about the investigator?" she asked. "She's going to call you tomorrow morning."

"I got it, and I appreciate the help."

The crowd around them shifted, moving her closer to Aiden, so close she could smell the musky scent of his aftershave. Her breasts teased the front of his chest, sending another tingling surge down her spine. She drew in a shaky breath. "It's warm in here."

He gave her a knowing smile. "It always seems to be that way when we're together."

"I think it's all the people in the room, Aiden."

"No, you don't."

His gaze caught hers, and something passed between them, something real and honest and very hot.

She was in trouble. She was having a hard time fighting her own desire. No way she could fight him, too. Then again, she'd misread his intentions once before. She couldn't do that again.

The microphone crackled, and she was relieved by the interruption. She dragged her gaze away from Aiden's to look at the stage.

Sean stepped up to the microphone. "Thanks, everyone, for coming," he said. "This is a special night. We're playing for a man who was a really good friend to a lot of us in this room, and for me he was like a big brother. In fact, Kyle is the first one who encouraged me to stay true to my dreams, and those dreams always included this guitar. He's gone, but he won't be forgotten. Tonight is for Kyle. Enjoy."

Sean played the first chord, leading the band into action.

As she listened to the music and watched the band play, Sara was very aware of Aiden standing just behind her. She could feel his breath moving the hair on the back of her neck. Occasionally, she thought she could feel his hand resting on her waist, but she was afraid to look back.

Where was Emma? She could really use a drink right about now. Actually, drinking was probably a bad idea. Too many vodka cranberry drinks had sent her into Aiden's arms the last time.

Fortunately, she didn't have to talk, didn't have to do anything but listen to the music. Sean was even better than she'd expected, not just as a musician, but also as a singer. His tone was silky smooth, husky and romantic on the ballads, and sharp-edged on the faster numbers.

After another trio of songs, the band took a short break, and she had no choice but to turn around. Fortunately, Emma was heading her way.

"Sorry, I got sidetracked," she said, handing her a glass of wine. "I kept running into people. I'm glad you came, Aiden."

"I couldn't seem to stay away." He took a breath. "Maybe I should have."

Burke pushed through the crowd. "I need to talk to you," he said to Aiden. "Let's go outside."

"No."

Burke's gaze turned to steel, but Aiden didn't waver.

Sara could feel the tension emanating from the two men. They were brothers, but right now they seemed like enemies.

"You two need to talk," Emma said.

"Stay out of it," both men said in unison.

Emma gave them both a scathing look. "Fine, I'm out of it. I'm going to see how long the line is for the restroom. Sara, do you want to come?"

"Absolutely," she said, eager to get away. As they moved through the crowd, she saw Aiden and Burke finally move toward the front door. It looked like Burke was going to get the conversation he wanted.

"Talk to me," Burke ordered as they hit the sidewalk outside the restaurant.

Aiden sighed. Having shared a room with his older brother for fifteen years, he knew all of Burke's moods, and this one was the worst. Burke was a fixer. If something was broken, he had to be the one to fix it. Maybe it came from being the oldest of eight kids, or maybe it was just inherent in Burke's personality, but he couldn't stop trying to solve every problem in the world, even those that didn't concern him.

"I've told you that I don't know what happened to Kyle," he said. "I had a concussion. I lost some of my memory. You can check with the doctors if you don't believe me."

Burke stared back at him, weighing his words. "Why didn't you tell us that a long time ago?"

"Because I didn't feel like talking."

"So you don't remember anything?"

"Bits and pieces. A lot of it is blurry. I know we were having trouble with the radios. Information was sketchy. The winds were changing. The fire was growing faster than anyone had anticipated. And then we were caught. Our exit routes were blocked by fire. Obviously, some of the team believe I waited too long before giving the order to retreat, that I pushed the men too hard, that they were too tired when it came time to run for their lives. You read the reports, I'm sure. I'm betting you even talked to a few people," he added.

"A few," Burke admitted. "Some of your better friends support the fact that it was an accident. Others are not so generous. Hawkins has been running his mouth all over town. Everyone loved Kyle, so it's difficult for some to see the situation clearly."

Burke was being more generous in his assessment than Aiden had anticipated.

"So what are you going to do, Aiden? Are you going back to Redding next year?"

"I don't know. The Chief suggested I consider other options during the off-season."

"You're going to let him run you off when it's not clear you did anything wrong?" Burke asked, anger edging his voice.

"If my crew has lost confidence in me, how can I go back?"

Burke met his gaze, and for the first time he saw understanding in his brother's eyes. Firefighters had to work together. They entrusted each other with their lives. Once that trust was broken, it was almost impossible to reclaim.

"I want you to defend yourself, Aiden. If you don't remember what happened, then tell people that. Don't just shrug and walk away and let them say whatever they want. It's arrogant and frustrating and it just pisses people off."

"They're going to say whatever they want anyway. My crew is spread out all over the country right now. I won't see most of them for another six months. Who exactly do you want me to defend myself to?"

"Dad would be a start. He's angry that you've shut him out. He has connections. He can get the truth out."

"I don't know what the truth is," he said forcefully. "Maybe I did screw up. Maybe I did push the crew too hard. I'm not defending myself, because I don't have a defense."

"Someone has to know something. There were dozens of men working that fire."

"But no one was with Kyle and me. We got separated from the others."

Burke put his hands on his hips and blew out a frustrated breath. "So, what are you going to do?"

He wished his brother would stop asking him that. He didn't want to mention the investigator Sara had set up for him, because he didn't want Burke getting involved in that, not until he knew if any of his theories about Kyle might be true. "I told you, I don't know."

"You might be able to work here in the city," Burke said slowly. "If you want to come back."

"You sound really excited about that possibility," he said dryly. Burke was making the offer out of a sense of family loyalty, but it was clear from his tone he didn't really want him on his crew.

"You have excellent skills, Aiden. You're smart, quick, and courageous. But sometimes you do push the envelope, take too many chances, and that can make you dangerous."

"It can also make me good. Thanks for the offer. I'll think

about it. Right now, I'm going back to the bar."

Aiden was about to move when his gaze caught on a woman getting out of a cab. There was something familiar about her. As she turned, her face caught the light. "Becky Saunders," he muttered. "What's she doing here?"

"Becky Saunders?" Burke echoed. "Isn't that Kyle's old girlfriend?"

"From high school." Something tugged at his memory. Kyle had said something about Becky several weeks earlier. "She called Kyle recently. Damn, what did he say about her?"

"Does it matter?"

"Probably not, but something was up with Kyle the last few months."

"You never said that before, either," Burke said, his gaze narrowing. "Why do I get the feeling there's a lot more you aren't telling me?"

"I'm going to talk to Becky."

"I'm right behind you," Burke said. "Believe it or not, I do have your back."

"Appreciate it, but I want to talk to her alone. You intimidate people so much they can't speak."

"I don't do that," Burke protested.

"Are you kidding? You scare the crap out of just about everyone."

"Except you."

"Well, I know you better than most people—or at least I used to," Aiden added, knowing that like so many of his relationships, the one with his older brother had been strained for a long time. "If you really want to help, try to get Dad off my case. I need some time to figure things out on my own. I don't need the pressure of clearing the Callaway name right now. If I can do that in the future, I will. If I can't, then you're all free to disown me."

Twelve

After leaving Burke on the sidewalk, Aiden entered the bar in search of Becky Saunders. Unfortunately, the first person he ran into was Ray Hawkins.

"You have a lot of nerve coming here, Callaway," Hawkins said.

Aiden sighed. He wasn't itching for a fight, but this time he wasn't going to just take a punch. "You've already had your one free swing. Get out of my way."

The other man stared back at him. "Never thought you'd let down a fellow firefighter."

The accusation burned through him. Out of the corner of his eye, he saw a few other firefighters closing ranks behind Ray, and he couldn't count a friend among them.

"What's going on?" Burke asked, appearing by his side. "Is there a problem, Hawkins?"

Hawkins stuttered, "Uh, no, Chief. No problem."

"Good, because this is a fundraiser for Kyle's family. That's why we're all here, right? I'm sure we don't want to do anything to ruin it."

Hawkins and his buddies muttered words of agreement, then backed away.

Aiden had to admire Burke's power. A few simple words, and he had his way. "I told you that you scared the crap out of everyone," he said to Burke. "This time it came in handy. Thanks."

"Like I said, I've got your back, Aiden. You'd know that if you looked behind you once in a while, but you're always in a hurry to get somewhere else."

"Speaking of which—I see Becky. I'll see you around."

He moved toward the back of the bar area where Becky was standing alone. He was happy to find her on her own and far enough away from the speakers that he might actually be able to talk to her.

When he reached her side, she gave him a startled look.

"Aiden. I didn't expect to see you here." Her gaze darted around the room as if she was worried that other people were watching them.

"I didn't expect to see you here, either."

"Kyle and I were in love once."

"About fourteen years ago," he said, giving her a thoughtful look. "I wasn't aware you'd stayed in touch."

"We reconnected a few months ago. I couldn't believe it when I heard Kyle had died. I had just spoken to him three days earlier."

"I didn't know that. I'm surprised Kyle didn't mention that he was talking to you again."

"Well, you never liked me. You tried to get Kyle to break up with me in high school."

"Because you were cheating on him, Becky," he reminded her. Becky had been a wild girl in high school, and Aiden had warned Kyle that she wasn't to be trusted. But Kyle hadn't been able to see past her blonde hair or big breasts. Becky was still attractive, but she was skinnier, and her eyes had the look of someone who'd seen a little too much action.

"That was a one-time mistake," she said defensively. "I had too much to drink. You didn't have to tell Kyle. It wasn't going to happen again."

"He was my best friend. Of course I had to tell him. And who's to say it wouldn't have happened again. We both know you were giving it out pretty freely back then."

She gave him a scornful look. "You were so quick to judge me, but you were just as bad, Aiden. You slept with half the girls in our grade."

"Half is a bit generous," he said dryly. "And I didn't have a girlfriend, so it wasn't cheating."

"Whatever," she said with a wave of her hand. "It was a long time ago."

They watched the band for a moment, and then he asked, "So what did you and Kyle talk about recently?"

"Life, stuff," she said vaguely.

"Did he tell you about his marriage?"

"Yes, he talked about his wife and baby. He was proud to be a father, but he was stressed out moving to San Francisco."

"He told you that."

"Of course. He was worried that his wife had high expectations that he wouldn't be able to meet. He wasn't sure how they could afford the condo they'd bought, but his wife loved it, so he was going to find a way to make the payments and pay her family back for the loan. It's funny that Kyle would hook up with someone with expensive taste. He was never into money."

"He told you all that?" Aiden couldn't keep the surprise out of his voice. "After all these years, he just told you his life story?"

"Why is that so strange?" she asked. "Kyle needed someone to talk to, someone outside his work friends and his family, and I fit the bill."

"How did you find each other again? Did you look him up?"

"No, he looked me up," she retorted.

"When was that?"

"A couple of months ago. Why are you asking me so many questions?"

"He didn't mention to me that he'd talked to you."

"Well, obviously, he didn't tell you everything."

"Were you having an affair with him?" The question burst out before he could stop it.

Becky stiffened. "No. I don't break up marriages, even when there are problems."

"What problems?"

"If he didn't tell you, then I can't say. Our conversations were private." She paused. "I just wish I hadn't missed his last call. It would have given me one more chance to..." She cut herself off. "It doesn't matter now. It's so sad. I need to leave. I shouldn't have come, but I couldn't stop myself."

"Wait, Becky," he said, putting a hand on her arm. "What were you going to say? You wish you'd had one more chance to..."

Indecision wavered in her eyes. "I forget," she said. "It wasn't important. It won't bring Kyle back." She pulled her arm away. "Leave it alone, Aiden. Let Kyle rest in peace."

His stomach turned over as he watched her leave, their conversation making him more than a little uneasy. Becky knew something, but what?

Of course Aiden would be chatting up a blonde. Some people never changed, Sara thought, although this blonde didn't look very happy. In fact, she seemed to be angry, throwing Aiden's hand off her arm before storming out of the bar.

Aiden turned his head and caught her watching him. She felt a rush of heat run through her body. Damn him. One look and she melted into a puddle.

Aiden walked quickly in her direction. "I have another name to give to your investigator."

"Does the name belong to that blonde you were talking to?"

"Yes, that was Becky Saunders. She went to school with me."

"Right, I remember her now," she said, putting the face to the name. "She went out with Kyle, didn't she?"

"Yeah. I had no idea they had renewed their friendship a couple of months ago. She was very cagey about it, too."

"Do you think they were having an affair?" she asked, lowering her voice so they couldn't be heard. Not that it was possible to overhear much in the crowded, noisy bar.

"She said no. Not sure if I believe her."

Before she could ask him another question, Emma interrupted their conversation. "Sara, I just got a text from Shayla. Her car broke down, and she needs a ride. I have to pick her up. She rescued me from a flat tire a few months ago, and I owe her."

"No problem. I can leave now."

"Or I could give you a ride home," Aiden suggested.

She hesitated, knowing that Aiden probably wanted to talk to her about Becky, maybe run a few more theories by her, and while she wanted to help him, she'd had some wine, it was late, and he was looking really hot. Her old crush was coming back to life, and she knew it was once again all one-sided. He wanted to talk business. She wanted to strip off his clothes and see the body she'd been imagining all these years.

Emma gave her a questioning look. "It's up to you, Sara."

"I'll catch a ride with Aiden," she said, trying to sound nonchalant.

"All right, but don't forget what I told you," Emma reminded her as she grabbed her keys from her bag and headed to the door.

"What did she tell you?" Aiden asked curiously.

"To stay away from you," she said, drinking the last bit of her wine before setting it down on a nearby table.

"That might be good advice," he said slowly. "I don't want to drag you down into my mess. Anytime you want to bail…"

"Then I'll bail," she finished, meeting his gaze head on. "Let's go."

***

After saying goodbye to some old neighbors and friends she'd chatted with earlier, Sara and Aiden made their way out of the bar.

"My truck is over there," he said, pointing down the block.

"Wow, good parking karma."

"At least something is working for me."

"How was your conversation with Burke? I don't see any new bruises."

He gave her a dry smile. "No fists flew, so I guess it was good enough."

"You two have had a combative relationship since you were young. You were always competing, arguing over what games to play and who was in charge and what the rules were."

"Burke usually won those battles."

"Well, he might have won the leadership spot, but you used to drive him crazy because you never followed his rules."

Aiden tipped his head. "Guilty. Sometimes I broke the rules just to piss him off. That was fun."

"Probably not for him," she said with a wry smile.

"Being an only child, I never really understood the sibling dynamic. You and Burke would pummel each other one minute and then the next you were laughing."

"We were done fighting," Aiden said with a shrug. "Unfortunately, it's not quite that easy any more. Our problems are bigger and the fights last longer."

"I think Burke wants to help you, Aiden."

"I know," he admitted. "But Burke doesn't help; he takes over, and this is my problem, not his."

They paused at the corner, waiting for the light to change. Sara drew her sweater more closely around her, wishing she'd opted for a bigger coat, but she hadn't thought much about wardrobe when she'd packed for her quick trip home. She hadn't expected to be out in the city or seeing anyone but her father. The fire had certainly changed both their lives.

She might not have even seen Aiden if he hadn't come to her rescue, and she might not have seen Emma either, which would have been a shame. She'd forgotten what it was like to have a friend who'd known her since she was nine years old. Tonight had been the most fun she'd had in a long time, and it had reminded her of the good times in her childhood. She'd lost some of those memories when her mother died.

"It's funny," she said aloud.

"What's that?"

"How long we've known each other. I was nine when we moved in next door to you, which would have made you twelve."

"I don't remember you much at nine. Were you friends with Emma right from the beginning?"

"We knew each other from school, but I was shy, and there were so many of you, I'm sure I faded into the woodwork. I used to sit on my porch in the afternoons, pretending to be reading, but really I was watching you and your brothers run the street games with the Moretti twins and Kyle, of course. You'd occasionally let Emma or Nicole play, but only if you absolutely had to. It was mostly boys only."

"It was a rough game," he said. "I didn't want my sisters to get hurt."

"Nice try," she said.

He grinned. "The girls had their own games, and they didn't let us play."

"Like you wanted to play restaurant."

"Actually, that was a good game, especially when Nicole made cookies to sell in the restaurant."

She smiled, thinking about those long, endless summers of fun. "You had a good childhood."

"I did. I was lucky."

They crossed the street and walked to Aiden's truck. He opened the door for her, and she got in, buckling her seat belt. As he slid behind the wheel, she said, "So, where are we going?"

"Let's just drive and see where we end up."

"That's not my usual style, but okay," she said with a small smile.

He smiled back at her. "The most interesting destinations are not always on the map."

"True, but I never get lost, and I'm betting you do."

Shadows filled his eyes. "All the time."

He pulled into traffic, and for several minutes they just drove. When he made no move to break the silence, she said, "Do you want to tell me more about your conversation with Becky?"

"She said that Kyle sought her out a few months ago. It's just so strange to me that he didn't mention talking to her. He would tell me the most boring moments of his day in great detail, but he leaves that out? It doesn't make sense. And then she started to say something and cut herself off. Something about missing his last call a few days before he died, wishing she could have had one more chance to do something, but she wouldn't say what. I pushed her, and she took off. She's hiding something, Sara. I know it."

"Then she's a good place to start. When you talk to Jeanne tomorrow, be sure to tell her everything you just told me."

"I could be reading into things." He glanced over at her, a question in his eyes.

"You could be," she said.

He frowned. "I was not looking for that answer."

"Just being honest, Aiden. You're very close to the situation, and you're still grieving for your friend. You want there to be a reason for what happened, a reason that doesn't make you accountable. You're not so different from Vicky in that regard. You both want something or someone else to blame. It might have just been a tragic accident. Your job is inherently dangerous. Every time you jump a fire, you're putting your life on the line."

"I just want to make sure I didn't put Kyle's life on the line. But you're very smart, Sara. You have the ability to look at an entire situation instead of just a few pieces. You must be a good lawyer."

"I am good," she said without hesitation.

He laughed. "Now, who's the cocky one?"

"I'm just stating a fact. I'm really good with academic-type problems, and that's what the law is. There are precedents for anything, and research and investigation are some of my stronger skills. I just wish sometimes that I'd chosen a different area of law, something a little more exciting, more meaningful."

"Is it too late to change?"

"It would take me way off track, and I've worked so hard to get to where I am. You have no idea how many hours I've put in. I don't do anything else but work. Just taking this weekend off was a huge accomplishment. I had to work extra hours all last week."

"It sounds like a grueling grind."

"It is, and I've been running for a long time. After my mom died my sophomore year in college, I had to focus on something that would take my mind off the pain. That was school. My classes were my life. My grades were an obsession. Law school was more of the same. I thought I could take a break when I finally got a job, but that was a crazy thought. There were more goals in front of me, and if someone gives me a test, I have to pass. It's ingrained in me." She paused. "I am talking way too much."

"Don't stop. It sounds like those thoughts have been trying to get out of your head for a while."

"They have been, but I keep pushing them back in. I have a great job, and I make good money. I can afford to live by myself in Manhattan, which is a phenomenal accomplishment, but..."

"But it's not enough. There's a little something called life that you seem to be missing out on."

"I keep telling myself I'm going to have that life when I make partner."

"After that there will be another goal, another mountain to climb. And for what? Is it really for you, Sara? Or are you still hoping to impress your dad?"

"I'll admit I'd like to see some respect in his eyes just once in my life, but that isn't solely what drives me. I want to succeed for myself."

"You already have succeeded. You just told me that," Aiden said. "You've got a great job, money, a place to live. If you want to make a change, then you should do it."

"That's easier said than done. People don't walk away from my firm. It's one of the best in the country. I couldn't do better. And my resume would take a hit if I left."

"All practical considerations," he conceded. "But while every job has its dull days, you should love some of what you do. Otherwise, why do it?"

"Do you love your job?" she asked.

He didn't answer right away, then said, "I used to."

His profile was hard, his gaze turned toward the road, but she suspected his mind was somewhere else. "Did that change because of Kyle's death?"

"Partly. But like you, I've had to consider the toll the job is taking on my life. The fire season demands total commitment. There's no time for anything or anyone else. It's also physically demanding. We jump into areas that no one else can get to. We have to live off whatever we can carry in our packs, sometimes for days at a time, battling hot and monstrous fires that are beyond your imagination."

Despite the negativity of his words, she could hear the passion in his voice. "But you like the magnificence of the challenge."

"I do," he admitted. "I like the adrenaline rush, pushing myself to the limit, and the sense of satisfaction that comes when we beat down a fire. But even the wins come with losses, not just people but also land. The fire dies, but the devastation can last for years."

"Still, you make a difference, so why would you quit?"

"I'm not sure they want me back."

"They can't fire you for no reason, and you said that the incident reports were vague, that people thought things could have been done differently, but nobody was sure you made a definitive mistake."

He cast her a quick smile. "That's a lawyer talking. The real issue is whether anyone could ever trust me again. You can't work a fire with people who can't trust you with their lives."

"Is it really about their trust, or about whether or not you can trust yourself?" she challenged.

"That, too," he admitted.

"Well, I hope we can get you the answers you need. I'm sure your family would help, too, if you asked them."

"I don't want anyone in the family, especially those members who work in the fire department, to be put in the position of defending me. I won't take down the family."

She admired his loyalty. It was actually one of the traits she'd first noticed about him. "Do you know when you first changed from being Emma's annoying big brother to being kind of cool?" she asked.

He shook his head, giving her a quick smile. "I have no idea what I ever did to impress you."

"I was a freshman in high school at the time, and you were a senior. One day at lunch, a bunch of bullies tackled Joey Randall and tried to stuff him in the garbage can. You stopped them. You stood up for him while everyone else was just watching."

"I couldn't stand those assholes."

"But no one else acted, only you. You're loyal and courageous, Aiden. I don't believe you were responsible for Kyle's death. There's no way on earth that you would have let him die if you could have saved him." She said the words with conviction, realizing how true they were. "What amazes me is that anyone who knows you could believe otherwise."

"I appreciate the vote of confidence, Sara, but you haven't been around me in a long time. You don't know what kind of man I am anymore."

"People don't change the core of who they are."

"I don't know about that. I have a feeling Kyle changed right in front of my eyes, and I didn't even see it."

"You don't know that yet, Aiden."

He shrugged. "We'll see."

She glanced out the window, noticing that they were going in the opposite direction of their neighborhood. "So how long do we just pick random streets to drive down?"

"Don't worry. I've come up with a destination, Sara."

"Care to enlighten me?"

"Sometimes surprise is good, Sara."

"I said that to my dad, right before the house caught fire."

He laughed. "This surprise will be better."

"It probably couldn't be worse."

She settled back in her seat, watching the city go by. In San Francisco the neighborhoods had distinct personalities and changed every few blocks. Haight-Ashbury was still considered hip after being the mecca for the hippie and flower child peace movement in the sixties. The Sunset was more for families and young couples. Russian Hill was filled with singles looking for action at the local bars. Then there was Chinatown, the south of Market area that was coming alive with restaurants and clubs since the building of the new baseball park, and downtown where the skyscrapers housed the hustle and bustle of the business world.

Ten minutes later, Aiden turned toward the water, weaving his way down Union Street and into the Marina, the upscale neighborhood where houses and apartment buildings looked out onto the Bay. They left the main road and drove along the outskirts of the Presidio, an old army base. The property had a spectacular view of the Golden Gate Bridge.

A few minutes later, Aiden pulled into a deserted parking lot. Nearby was a paved path that ran along the beach and was popular in the daytime for walkers and joggers. Tonight the area was quiet and dark, most of the illumination coming from the lights on the bridge and a few passing ships making their way from the Pacific Ocean into the bay.

"Feel like taking a walk?" Aiden asked, as he shut off the engine.

"It's kind of cold."

"You can wear my jacket."

"Then you'll be cold."

"I have a sweatshirt somewhere," he said, reaching into the back of the cab. "Here it is."

"I'll just wear that," she said.

"Are you sure? It's not stylish."

"I don't care about that. It looks warm." She stepped out of the truck and slipped the big sweatshirt over her head. It was warm and smelled like musk and Aiden. She chased that thought out of her head, firmly reminding herself they were just two old friends, and that nothing else would ever happen between them.

She couldn't let Aiden back into her heart. It had taken far too long to get him out. They were ships passing in the night, in the same place at the same time for now, but not forever. Their other lives would soon call them back home.

They walked down the path together, not talking, just enjoying the beauty of the night, the water, and the bridge, which served as a majestic gateway to the west. Out here, her real life seemed even farther away. And being alone with Aiden on a moonlit night with such a beautiful vista in front of them was making her regret her recent resolve not to turn this into something romantic. Because really, this moment, this night, reminded her of all the dreams she'd ever had about Aiden.

Aiden paused by a low sea wall, the waters of the bay just a few feet away. "You're quiet," he commented.

"Just enjoying the walk," she said.

"And thinking," he said. "I have the feeling that at any given time, there are a million thoughts running through your head."

"I do tend to have a busy brain," she admitted.

"So what are you thinking about now?"

She hesitated. "I shouldn't tell you."

"Now you have to tell me. You can't leave it like that," he said with a teasing smile.

She couldn't help smiling back. "Fine, but it will make you uncomfortable."

"I'll take my chances."

"I feel like I'm living out my teenage fantasy. We ran into each other at a party. You asked to give me a ride home, then you wanted to take me for a drive. Now I'm wearing your sweatshirt and walking on the beach with you."

"You fantasized about doing all that?"

"Yes, and don't try to act surprised. You knew I had a crush on you."

"It was hard to miss. You kept dropping things and running into furniture when we crossed paths."

"Don't remind me," she said, embarrassed by the truth.

"You were cute," he said.

"Great, just what I wanted you to think—that I was clumsy and cute."

"And smart. Do you know when I first saw you as someone besides one of my sister's annoying friends?" he asked, repeating her earlier question.

"I didn't think you ever stopped seeing me that way."

"It was on the night of your junior prom. You and Emma got dressed at the house and were taking pictures in the yard. I was in college by then, and I was shocked at the way you looked in that purple dress."

She was stunned that he remembered what she was wearing. "Seriously?"

He nodded. "Oh, yeah. It was the first time I realized you had really nice breasts."

His words brought a wave of heat to her cheeks, and she instinctively crossed her arms in front of her chest. "You didn't even talk to me that night."

"You left me speechless."

"Why are you telling me this now?"

"Because you thought the attraction you felt was all one-sided."

"It was," she said. "I got proof of that a year later when you rejected me."

"Protected you," he corrected.

"You're just trying to be nice, Aiden."

"I'm not." He moved a little closer, and she found herself backing up against the wall.

"What are you doing?" she asked, a breathless note in her voice.

"I'm wondering if your fantasy ended with a simple walk on the beach. Or, if maybe something else happened?"

A tingle ran down her spine at the predatory look in his eyes. "That's exactly where it ended," she lied.

"I don't believe you, Sara."

"Well, back then, I might have wanted you to kiss me, but that was then and this is now."

"And now you don't want me?" he queried.

She wanted to say no, she didn't want him, but all she could think about was how sexy he looked in the moonlight, how much she wanted that full mouth on hers, how good it might feel to be in his arms again. She drew in a shaky breath. Things were getting way out of hand. She was getting lost in the past, in the dark isolation of this romantic night. This wasn't real. In an hour or even five minutes from now, they'd go back to being who they were, and those people were never going to end up together.

Not that Aiden was thinking about the future. He'd always been a man to live in the moment, to take an impulsive leap, and she'd always been someone to weigh the pros and cons before she acted.

There was desire in his eyes, and she was old enough to

know when a man wanted to kiss her. She wasn't imagining it this time—was she?

"You're thinking really hard, Sara," he drawled, his hands coming to rest on her waist.

She caught her breath at his touch, her mind suddenly spinning. All sense of reason and logic was being crowded out by the sheer desire.

"Sara?" he said.

"Just kiss me already."

She'd barely gotten the words out when his mouth covered hers. His lips were warm, firm, and while the kiss started out soft and tender, it quickly changed to hard and passionate. He pulled her up against his chest, and she went into his embrace willingly. She opened her mouth under his, taking his tongue inside, loving his taste, his touch, the softening of her body against his hard angles.

The kiss was better than her fantasies, better than her memories, and she didn't want it to end, didn't want to have to talk about it, explain it, or rationalize it. She just wanted to feel his heat, to be a part of him the way he'd always been a part of her.

Somewhere in her brain, she knew she needed to be the one to pull away, to say no, to end the kiss. She couldn't let Aiden be the one—not again.

But it was so difficult to find the right moment to end it.

Then voices penetrated the thick fog of passion. Loud voices.

She pulled away as two teenage couples came down the path. They had their arms around each other and were passing a bottle of alcohol back and forth between them. They barely glanced at them as they passed.

Sara let out a breath. She should have been grateful for the interruption, but she wasn't.

"Sara," Aiden began.

She immediately shook her head. "Don't say anything, please."

"I didn't mean—"

"Aiden, stop. Let it be. It was just a kiss. Don't make it into anything else. We should go back to the car."

"Are you sure you don't want to talk—"

"I don't. I really, really don't." She moved out of his embrace and started walking down the path.

Thankfully, Aiden followed. The drive home was made in silence. But when Aiden parked in front of her dad's house and turned off the engine, he stopped her from getting out of the car. "Wait, Sara."

She waited, but now that he had her attention, he didn't seem to know what to say.

"It's not a big deal," she said, breaking the silence. "We got caught up in the moment. And now the moment is over. It was just a kiss," she repeated, silently willing that to be true. "I don't have a crush on you anymore, if that's what you're worried about."

"I don't want to hurt you."

She stared back at him. "I don't intend to let you." And with that, she got out of the car and walked into her father's house, resisting the urge to look back.

Thirteen

After a sleepless night, Sara got up Sunday morning just after seven, threw on sweats, grabbed her keys and phone and went for a run. About a half mile into her jog, she remembered that she really didn't like to run, but she needed to find a way to burn off the restless energy that had been building since she'd kissed Aiden. She should have followed Emma's advice and stayed away from him. Instead, she'd gotten caught up in his sexy charm and let her inner teenager take over.

Today, she would get back to business. She needed to make some decisions. It wasn't like her to be so indecisive, but things had changed a lot since she'd first made her weekend getaway plans. She still had a flight booked for six o'clock in the evening. She could get on it and go back to New York and the life she'd built the last seven years. Or, she could stay in San Francisco and…

What?

Help her father when he clearly didn't want her assistance?

Get further involved with Aiden, who would no doubt disappear as soon as he came out of the fog of grief he was living in?

The only reason he'd turned to her was because he didn't

want to get his family involved in his problems. He had not suddenly discovered that she was irresistible.

Although it was fun to imagine that Aiden now thought she was beautiful, sexy and desirable. Wasn't that just the ultimate revenge? The nerdy girl turns into a swan and the sexy bad boy finally sees her for who she really is?

Unfortunately, her revenge would have worked better if she hadn't kissed him again, if she'd been as untouchable and unattainable as he'd once been for her. She really needed to stay away from him.

Too bad he lived just next door.

Right now, he was probably in bed, maybe wearing nothing...

She'd seen him with his shirt off, and his muscled arms and rippling abs were a thing of beauty, not to mention the fine dark hair that ran along his chest and down toward the waistband of his jeans.

She cleared her throat, not wanting to think of Aiden naked, but she couldn't help herself. His teenage body had been impressive, but years of physically demanding work had turned him into a rugged, sexy male, and she was more than a little attracted to him. Last night, she'd gotten so caught up in kissing him, if he'd thrown her down in the sand, she would have had sex with him on the beach and not even considered where they were or how cold it was. When she was with him, she was always hot.

But he wasn't always as hot for her, she reminded herself again.

Damn! This run wasn't working at all. She might be sweating, but she still had way too much time to think. Turning toward home, she picked up the pace, sprinting when she reached her street. As she neared her house, she saw Emma on the sidewalk. She was talking to a guy who appeared to be in his mid-thirties. He had blonde hair and was dressed in khaki slacks and a dark brown sport coat. Judging by Emma's stiff posture, the conversation didn't appear to be friendly. And as she drew closer, their raised voices were impossible to ignore.

"I told you I don't want to see you anymore, Jon," Emma said. "It's done. We're over. Accept it and move on."

"You have to give me another chance. This wasn't all my fault."

She shook her head. "You've had all the chances I can give you. Just go, please."

"Em, baby."

"Stop! I'm not your baby. I'm not your anything. We were not good together. You're just feeling lonely. You miss having a girlfriend, but it's not me you miss."

"That's not true."

"It is true, and we both know it."

Emma turned to go, but the guy grabbed her arm.

Sara ran over to them. They looked at her in surprise. "Everything okay?" she asked.

"It's fine," Emma said, pulling her arm free. "Jon was just leaving."

"We're not done talking," he protested. "I know I hurt you, but you hurt me, too."

"I'm not doing this with you. I've said all I had to say. Go home."

Jon gave her an angry glare. "You can be such a bitch." He strode to his car, got in and pulled away, the tires squealing.

Sara looked back at Emma and saw her mouth tremble just a little before she quickly forced back the emotion. "Who was that?" she asked.

"My ex," she said. "Jon Wickmore the third."

"Did he hurt you?"

"Not today," she said with a humorless laugh.

"But before…"

"He didn't hit me," Emma said. "He just cheated on me. We'd been living together for almost a year, and I had no idea that when I was at work, he was sleeping with other women. Of course he's sorry now, but I'm not going back to him because the cheating wasn't the whole issue. He didn't like my job. He thought I put it before him, and to be fair, I did sometimes. Anyway, it's over."

"It sounds like it's for the best."

"I think so." Emma gave her a painful smile. "I just thought I was in love with him; that's before I saw him for who he really was. I was too caught up in lust and passion to see what was right in front of me. I won't make that mistake. That's why I've sworn off men for at least a year." She paused, her gaze narrowing as she noted Sara's sweatpants. "So, you're a runner now? Aren't you the girl who would use any excuse to get out of P.E.?"

"I don't like to run, but I try to get in a little exercise because I spend so much time sitting. And I'm coordinated enough to put one foot in front of the other. All those other sports that involve balls and rackets and clubs are not for me."

"You should have called me. I would have gone with you."

"It was a spur-of-the-moment decision."

"What happened with Aiden last night?"

"Nothing," she said quickly.

"Really?" Emma gave her a suspicious look. "Then why are you blushing?"

"I'm just red from my run."

"I know you two didn't come home right away because Aiden's truck was not here when I got back from rescuing Shayla."

"We took a drive. We talked. That's it. There's nothing

else to say."

"Got it. So what are you doing today?"

"Trying to decide whether or not I should go home."

Emma's brows knit together in a frown. "Let me make that decision for you—don't go. We're just getting reacquainted. I don't want to say goodbye yet."

"I'd love to stay a few days," she said slowly. The idea had been going around in her head for most of the last twenty-four hours. "But then I think, what's the point? My dad doesn't want me here. He wants me gone."

"Screw what he wants. He's going to be in the hospital for a while anyway, so it's not like you'll be tripping over each other."

"That's true."

"He should be happy the house isn't sitting empty."

"I'm not sure happy is an emotion my father feels very often." She paused. "I sometimes wonder if he has any friends. I know he has colleagues at work and he spends most of his time there, but have you ever seen anyone at his house? Does he ever have any parties, barbecues, or people over for dinner?"

"My mom has asked him to come over to our house a few times, and he always declines. I've never seen any party action."

"It's weird to think anyone would be happy being that alone."

"Your father is just different, Sara. I obviously don't know him as well as you do, but he just seems like a shadow of a person."

"That's a good way to put it," she said.

"So think about staying. It would be fun to have you around. We can call Julia and Kristine. They'd love to see you," Emma added, referring to some of their old friends.

"I haven't talked to them since high school."

"They're actually nicer now," Emma said.

"I'll think about it. What are you up to today?"

"The family is heading to church in about an hour. You could come with us. And then join us for the traditional Callaway Sunday lunch."

"Your family still does that?" she asked in surprise. The Callaways had always invited family and friends to come for lunch after the noon service at St. Andrew's. It was a long-honored tradition.

"It's not as big of a crowd as it used to be, but there's always good food. If you don't want to join us for church, just come for lunch. Aiden might be there," she added with a twinkle in her eye.

"That's not necessarily a plus," she said dryly.

"Oh, I'm betting it is," Emma said with a laugh. "I never totally understood your crush on my brother, but last night, for the first time, I saw Aiden look at you the way you always looked at him. Maybe think about that while you're deciding whether or not to make that flight tonight."

Sara couldn't help but think about Emma's words. They ran around and around in her head. She'd seen that same look in Aiden's eyes, but it was nice to have it confirmed by a third party. But she didn't know what to do about it. Should she stay in San Francisco for a few more days? See where things went with Aiden? Spend time with Emma? Maybe try to have another conversation with her dad?

Or should she go back to the life she knew, the one she excelled in, the one that was a little bit lonely? If it was lonely, she only had herself to blame. She couldn't make friends in the outside world if she never left her cubicle. She didn't need to move back to San Francisco to make some changes.

Frowning at the chaotic confusion in her head, she distracted herself with more immediate work. She grabbed a half dozen garbage bags and headed into the kitchen to start the cleanup. When they were full, she realized she'd barely made a dent. But it was a start.

When the lingering stench of smoke got to be too much, she went upstairs and jumped in the shower. She'd always done some good thinking in the shower, but she was still dithering when she stepped out, toweled off and dried her hair. She put on some clean clothes and then stared at her open suitcase. She could pack, or she could unpack.

Maybe she should toss a coin. It was not a bad option. She certainly wasn't going to ask her father again. He'd made his viewpoint clear yesterday. So if she didn't stay for him, then who was she staying for? Aiden?

That was crazy. She could not turn her life upside down for him.

She just wished the taste of his mouth didn't still linger on her lips.

Shaking her head, she told herself to stop it and looked for another distraction. She found it in the box of photographs she'd discovered in the basement. Maybe she should go through those, find a couple that she really wanted and take them back to New York with her.

Happy to have some sort of a plan, even if it was a short-term activity, she grabbed the box, plopped it in the middle of the bed and sat down.

The first few pictures she found were from her elementary school years. She'd been such an awkward child, braces on her teeth, hair that never parted evenly, pale skin from all the time she'd spent indoors, her nose buried in a book.

She caught her bottom lip between her teeth as she pulled

out a photo of her and her mom when she was about five years old. She had her hand in her mother's, and it was clear she was holding on tight. She looked like she was about to cry, and her mother was trying to reassure her. She wondered who had taken that photo, and if it was her father who'd made her cry.

Sighing, she put the picture aside and turned the box upside down, shaking the photos out so she could see all of them at once.

A very old photo caught her attention. Her parents held a baby in a white baptismal gown. But the baby didn't look like her. In fact, she didn't remember seeing this photo before, and when she was a kid, she'd helped her mother compile many a family photo album.

Very weird. An uneasy feeling tightened her muscles. She picked up another photograph. This one was more shocking than the last. Her father was at the park. He was pushing a toddler in a swing, and he was smiling at the camera. It was the biggest grin she'd ever seen on his face. It almost didn't even look like him.

Maybe he had loved her when she was a baby.

But as her gaze settled on the child, she didn't feel any sense of recognition. The toddler had on blue shorts and a T-shirt with a big dinosaur on it. She'd never worn those clothes. That kid wasn't her. In fact, she was pretty sure it was a boy.

Her uneasiness deepened. Who was the child? Why was her father with some strange kid at a park? He'd never taken her to the park, pushed her on a swing, or helped her down a slide. She didn't have any cousins. The little boy had to belong to one of her dad's friends.

She shuffled through more photographs, more pictures of her mom and dad and a baby, then a toddler, that she didn't recognize. But the three of them were always together. They looked like a family—a happy family.

Where the hell was she?

Her stomach turned over. She wanted to take the photos, shove them back into the box, and put it back where she'd found it—in the basement.

Had her father risked his life to get these pictures?

With trembling fingers, she rearranged a series of photos, trying to put together a timeline. There was a house she didn't remember, a car that she hadn't seen before. Her parents seemed really young and very happy. These were not the people she'd grown up with. It was as if she had entered an alternate world, one where they existed, and she didn't.

She turned one of the pictures over. There was a date. The shot had been taken four years before she was born. No wonder she didn't recognize any of the details.

But who was the child? Her parents had never talked about watching anyone else's son.

She rifled through more of the pictures, looking for clues. Finally, another date, and this time a name—*Stephen, Jr.*

Her heart pounded against her chest. *Stephen, Jr.? A child named after her father?*

It didn't make sense. She was the firstborn, the only child. No one had ever told her about another baby—not her father or her mother or her grandparents. Had they all conspired to keep a secret? Why?

Something bad must have happened.

She flew through the rest of the photographs. There were no pictures of the child past the age of three or four, no school pictures, no family shots.

A million questions raced through her head.

The analytical part of her brain screamed at her to pay attention to what was right in front of her, to stop trying to pretend that this was some crazy daydream. Her parents had had another child. Maybe it wasn't their birth child. Maybe it was a kid they adopted or cared for while the parent or parents were gone. That thought made her feel marginally better.

But then she remembered the name, *Stephen, Jr.*

Getting up from the bed, she moved over to the desk and opened her computer. She typed in Stephen Davidson, Jr., and ran through the results. Both first and last name were very common, so there were literally hundreds of names. She entered more data, San Francisco, the date on the photograph. Nothing definitive.

She tried a new search for birth records in San Francisco over a couple years.

And there it was.

Stephen Davidson, Jr., father Stephen Davidson, mother Valerie Laura Davidson.

Sara sat back in her chair, stunned beyond belief. The date was six years before she was born. She'd once asked her mother why they'd waited eight years to have a baby. Her mom had mumbled something about not being ready. But they'd been ready. They'd had a kid together, a child they hadn't told her about.

Anger and pain ripped through her along with a terrible sense of betrayal. The rush of emotions made her head spin.

What had happened to the baby? To her *brother?*

Nausea swept through her. She ran to the bathroom and threw up. When she finally rose, she was shaking. She ran cold water over her face and then pressed a dry towel against her forehead and over her eyes. With her eyes closed, she could almost pretend that nothing had changed, but that wasn't true. Everything had changed.

She had an older brother. Where was he?

Setting down the towel, she returned to the bedroom, knowing that there was only one explanation. It wasn't the answer she wanted to find, but there seemed to be no alternative.

She checked death records, obituaries, and there it was.

Stephen Davidson, Jr., age 4, survived by his loving parents, Stephen and Valerie Davidson.

There was no mention of how he'd died, and the date was two years before she was born. She walked back to the bed and stared at the photos, especially the ones of her dad smiling. He'd been a happy father then. He'd obviously loved his son. And she'd just figured out why her father had risked his life to rescue a box of photos, why he hadn't wanted her to go through his things, why he'd been almost desperate in his desire to get her out of his house. He hadn't wanted her to find out about her brother.

She flopped on her back and stared at the ceiling. She didn't want to cry, but she suddenly felt very emotional. Tears began to stream down her face, and she wasn't even sure exactly what she was sad about. She'd never met her brother, so how could she grieve for him. She was angry with her mother for never telling her about her brother. But her mother was gone. There would be no confessions, no truth between them now.

And then there was her father …

He'd loved that child. He'd been able to be a dad to his son, but not to his daughter.

He hadn't loved her. He hadn't wanted her.

She'd known it all along, but now she had proof, hard evidence.

And the tears kept coming…

Fourteen

"We need to have a talk, son," Jack Callaway told Aiden as he joined him at the buffet table.

The Callaway lunch was in full swing. Dozens of relatives were gathered in the house. Aiden had hoped the crowd of extended family and friends would have prevented a conversation with his father, but apparently not.

"Now is not a good time," he said.

"Tonight, after everyone goes home," Jack said, meeting his gaze. "We need to discuss your future."

"My future is my business."

"You've made it everyone's business," Jack retorted. "You're not just dragging yourself down in the mud, you're taking the family name with you. Now Burke tells me you don't remember what happened. That's some information that needs to be shared with other people." He paused as Lynda interrupted them.

"Whatever you two are talking about can wait," she said firmly. "We've got a house full of people, and I need your help in the kitchen, Jack."

"Tonight, Aiden," his father said. "Don't make me come looking for you."

He didn't bother to reply. He'd get some lunch and then decide whether or not he wanted to have that conversation with his father. Except for possibly Burke, Jack didn't seem able to accept that his children were adults and could live their own lives. Not that he'd been doing a great job with his life lately, but that was still his business.

He picked up a plate, grabbed two sandwiches, and a generous helping of potato salad and moved into the living room. Two of his aunts were on the sofa and his grandmother sat across from them in an armchair. She didn't seem to be all that interested in their conversation, nor did she pay him any attention either. Her somewhat vacant smile reminded him a little of Brandon. He wondered what was going on with her. He was going to sit down next to her, but his cousin Anne nabbed the seat before him, so he headed across the room and sat down on the bench in front of the piano.

A few moments later, Emma joined him. "What are you doing all by yourself?" she asked.

"Hardly by myself," he said dryly. "Half the neighborhood is in this house."

"It is a big turnout today. Tons of great food, too."

He nodded, his gaze catching on a group of people walking up to the front door. For a moment he thought he saw Sara, but it wasn't her. He wondered where she was. He'd thought she'd come by for lunch, if not to see him, then to see Emma. Or she could be avoiding him. Once again, he'd let himself get carried away with her. Only this time, he hadn't had any intention of calling a halt. If they hadn't been interrupted, who knows how far they would have gone.

"Earth to Aiden," Emma said dryly.

"What?"

"You're somewhere else today. Are you looking for Sara?"

"Is she coming?"

"I invited her earlier. She was noncommittal. She told me nothing happened last night, that you just gave her a ride home. Care to confirm that story?"

"You should mind your own business."

"Sara *is* my business. She's my friend."

"And a grown woman," he pointed out.

"I just don't want either one of you to get hurt."

"We can take care of ourselves. If you want to worry about someone, maybe you should worry about Grandma. She's been staring into space for five minutes. And now she appears to be talking to herself.

"I am worried about Grandma. Mom said that Grandpa is taking her in for some tests this week. She's been confused and forgetful. It's kind of scary, Aiden."

He nodded, worried even more now that his suspicions had been confirmed. His father's mother, Eleanor, had always been a sweet and loving grandmother to all of them, and he couldn't imagine his grandfather without her. The two of them had been married for almost sixty years.

"I'm going to talk to her." He set down his plate on the bench and then crossed the room, pausing by her chair. "Grandma, can I get you anything?"

She looked at him in confusion. "Drew?" she said.

"I'm Aiden," he reminded her. "Drew isn't here today."

"Aiden doesn't live here anymore," she said.

"I'm visiting," he told her. "I got home a couple of days ago."

Her gaze met his, and the clouds lifted just slightly. Her smile seemed almost dreamy. "You look just like your grandfather. Like Patrick."

"You do look like Grandpa," Emma agreed, joining them. "Same blue eyes."

His grandmother suddenly grabbed his arm. "We can't keep it a secret anymore, Patrick. It's going to come out. I'm so worried."

He stared at her in confusion. "Grandma, what are you

talking about?" he asked.

"I know I promised, but it's so hard."

An uneasy feeling settled in his stomach. He glanced over at Emma. Her sharp gaze had narrowed. She answered his unspoken question with a shrug.

"Grandma," he started, then was interrupted by his grandfather.

"Ellie, there you are," his grandfather said. "Let's get you some food."

"Patrick?" she asked, as she held out her hand.

"Yes, sweetheart, it's me," he said.

She smiled. "I thought so."

His grandfather helped his grandmother to her feet, then gave Aiden a quick look. "We're going to talk later, Aiden. You, me and your father."

"Great," he muttered.

"Looks like you're going to be on the hot seat," Emma said, as their grandparents left.

"What was Grandma talking about?"

"I have no idea. She thought you were Grandpa."

"And they seem to have a secret," he said.

"Well, who knows what she was saying? She could have been referring to her secret spaghetti sauce recipe that she won't share with anyone in the family."

"I suppose," he said, not at all convinced. There had been an urgency in his grandmother's eyes. But then again, she'd thought he was her husband, so how could he take anything she said seriously?

"So, Aiden, what are you going to do now? Are you going back to smokejumping? Have you considered applying for a job here in the city?"

"I don't know yet, and I wish everyone would give me a chance to figure things out. I'm more than capable of making decisions about my life."

"Jeez, relax, I was just asking," she said.

"You and everyone else in the family. Coming home was a big mistake."

"We just care about you, Aiden."

He knew that was true, but the weight of their love felt more oppressive than supportive. "I've got to get out of here," he said.

"Aiden, I'm sorry. You don't have to leave."

"It's fine. I need some air."

"Tell Sara to come by and eat. And make sure she doesn't go back to New York without saying goodbye."

"I'm just going outside."

She gave him a disbelieving look. "Sure you are."

Aiden walked around the block, then added another and another, finally ending up back in his driveway, torn between going to his room and going next door. Emma's comment about Sara going back to New York had stuck with him. He didn't want her to leave without saying goodbye, either. Actually, he didn't want her to leave at all, but her home was on the other side of the country. Their lives were in different states. He should leave her alone.

Five minutes later he rang her doorbell. Her rental car was out front, but she didn't answer. He rang the bell again. Maybe he'd missed her, and she'd gone next door while he was walking off his frustration. He was about to leave when the door opened.

He stared at her in shock. Her brown hair was tangled and messy, her eyes and nose were red and swollen. She looked devastated.

"What the hell happened?" he asked.

She stared back at him, her lips trembling.

"Sara, talk to me." He grabbed hold of her hands. They were ice cold.

"They lied," she said.

"Who lied?"

"My parents. My mother and father lived a big, fat lie."

He was confused. "What are you talking about?"

"I'll show you," she said, pulling her hands away from his. She turned and headed upstairs.

He shut the door and followed her up to her room.

On her bed were at least twenty or thirty photographs. They'd obviously come from the box she'd found in the basement.

She searched through the pictures, found the one she was looking for and held it up. "Look at this. What do you see?"

"Your parents and you."

"No, that's not me, that's another baby. And look at my dad," she added. "Have you ever seen him smile like that?'

"No, but I don't think I'm someone he would smile at."

"Neither am I. Only *this* child was worth a smile."

"Who is this baby? I don't understand what you're talking about."

"I'm sorry. Wasn't I clear? This is my brother, Aiden, my older brother, the child my parents never told me about, the son my father always wanted. He was even named after my dad, Stephen, Jr."

His amazement grew with each word. "That's impossible. You would have known. Someone would have known. Someone would have said something."

"Someone like my mother, who I thought I was really close to? That kind of someone?"

"Sara," he breathed, seeing a tremendous amount of pain in her eyes. "Are you sure?"

"There's a name on one of the pictures," she said wearily, sitting on the edge of the bed. "I did an Internet search and found birth records. I also found an obituary for a four-year-old. He was born six years before me. I don't know how he died. I don't know why his existence was kept from me, kept from everyone." She paused, tilting her head. "Do you think your parents knew?"

"I – I don't know. You didn't move here until you were..."

"Nine," she said. "Of course your parents didn't know. It all happened long before we moved here."

"I don't know what to say." He was stunned by the revelation.

"It's strange. I remember asking my mom about where they used to live before I was born, and she never had much to say. She was always vague about it. I don't recognize the house in any of the photos, so it was probably different than the one where I was born." She paused. "Maybe this is just the tip of the iceberg. What else don't I know about my parents?"

He could see the anger, frustration and fear bubbling up inside of her. "You need to talk to your father."

"I can't imagine what I would say."

"How about – why have you been lying to me my whole life?"

She stared back at him. "I want to ask him that, but I can't do it right now, Aiden. I'm too confused. My head is aching, and my heart is pounding out of my chest, and if I go to see him now, I don't know what I'll say. I need to be better prepared. I need to calm down. I feel so shaken. The earth is moving all around me, and I can't find solid ground to stand on. My flight leaves in two hours, but I can't get on the plane like this. I also don't want to stay here in his house, with his lies staring me in the face. I need to breathe. I need to think. I need time, Aiden."

He knew exactly how she felt. Their circumstances were

different, but their needs were the same.

"Let's get out of here," he said impulsively.

"Where—where would we go?"

"I don't know."

"We can't just take off without a destination."

He smiled. Destroyed and distraught, Sara was still Sara. "Your bag looks like it's mostly packed," he said, tipping his head toward her suitcase. "Let me throw some stuff into the truck, and we'll go for a drive."

"With our bags?" she asked, wariness entering her eyes.

"You said you didn't want to stay here."

"I don't, but…"

"You can trust me, Sara."

She drew in a big breath and then said, "All right. I'll meet you at the truck." As he turned toward the door, she added, "Don't take too long or I might change my mind."

━▶▶◀◀━

It took Aiden five minutes to throw his clothes into a duffel bag. When he jogged down the driveway, he could hear laughter and conversation coming from the open windows in the kitchen. Fortunately, no one seemed to be looking outside. He didn't want to answer questions, didn't want to have to explain what he was doing or where he was going, because he had no answers. Like Sara, he just needed some time to think, and it was obvious his time at home had run out. His father and grandfather were determined to have some sort of discussion, a conversation he was not in the mood to have.

Sara was waiting at the truck when he got there. She didn't say anything to him, just handed him her suitcase and then got into the passenger seat. There was a determined expression in her dark brown eyes now, a decided improvement over the pain and grief he'd witnessed earlier. She was getting herself together. Hopefully, putting some distance between her and those photographs would help.

As he started the engine, he saw Emma come out of the house. Sara saw her, too.

"Just drive," Sara ordered. "Now."

He pulled away from the curb. In his rearview mirror he could see Emma standing on the sidewalk with a thoughtful expression on her face.

"I should have talked to Emma," Sara said a minute later, guilt in her voice. "That was rude."

"You'll talk to her when you're ready. She'll be fine."

"I can't imagine when I'll be ready."

As he turned the corner, Sara rolled down her window, letting the cool air dry the lingering tears on her face. It was a beautiful, sunny day, warm for early November, the temperature in the high seventies, the sky pure blue, not a cloud to be seen.

It was a good day to be going somewhere—he just wasn't sure where.

He weaved through the city streets without much thought, and when he found himself heading over the Bay Bridge toward Berkeley, he kept on going. She wanted miles between her and her father, and he was happy to gain some distance from his family.

Coming off the bridge, he continued north, heading toward the Napa wine country. As they left some of the bigger cities behind, the scenery grew more rural. Driving through the Napa Valley, they passed lush vine-covered fields and historic stone buildings that housed wine cellars and offered tastings on Sunday afternoons. He could feel Sara's tension ease and she finally broke the quiet of the last hour.

"Look, hot air balloons." She pointed to a half dozen bright, colorful balloons soaring over the valley. "I wonder if it's peaceful or scary. I'm sure it wouldn't scare you to be that high."

"Actually, I'd feel more comfortable with a parachute strapped to my back."

She glanced at him, her gaze curious. "What's it like, Aiden? Jumping out of an airplane?"

He thought for a minute, searching for the right words. "It's monumental, exhilarating, mind-blowing. I don't even know if I can explain it. Right after you jump, you go into free fall, your body hurtling towards the earth at an incredible speed. It's amazing. Then the chute opens, and your life is saved. That moment is followed by an incredible quiet, a sense of wonder and amazement. It doesn't last long enough. Soon, you're trying to use the wind to land on the ground and not in a tree."

"You love it," she said with a small smile.

He smiled back at her. "The jumping never gets old. The rest of it—let's just say landing is not always that smooth and clean."

"Have you ever landed in a tree?"

"More times than I'd like to admit. I've also dumped myself into a lake, some really sharp rocks and even a patch of poison oak."

"But none of that stops you from doing your job once you're on the ground," she said.

"Sometimes it slows me down, but unless I've broken something, I don't stop. I'm there for a purpose." He felt a rush of pride at the admiration in her eyes. He'd seen so much condemnation and criticism in recent weeks that he'd forgotten what it was like to be someone who was good at his job.

"You were always a daredevil. I remember when you and your brothers set up your own version of a skateboard park in front of the house. It started with a ramp going down the driveway, over a pile of boards and around some garbage cans. It was wild. I sat on the porch thinking any minute one of you was going to kill yourself. I even had the phone handy in case I had to call 911."

He grinned, remembering how much fun they'd had that day. "That was a great course. Unfortunately, it only lasted until my father came home."

"Actually, I think it ended when Sean broke his wrist," she said dryly.

"I forgot about that. Collateral damage," he said lightly.

"I don't think your brother saw it that way."

"Hey, I didn't think he should be on the course at all. Sean always got hurt. He tried to climb the tree out front and fell into the garbage can. He tripped over the stairs during tag and sprained his ankle. He rode his bike into a rosebush and ripped up his legs. I could go on and on. I told him to stay off the skateboard. He didn't listen."

"He was the little brother. He wanted to be like you and Burke and Drew."

"He's gone his own way now with his music."

"He's very good. I was impressed. He has a soulful quality to his singing. It made me wonder what his story is, where he's finding all that emotion."

"I don't know, either," he said, her words reminding him that he'd lost touch with Sean along with so many of his siblings. It had been a long time since they'd had more than a three-minute conversation.

"How does your father handle Sean being a musician, breaking with the family tradition to do something of service for the community? Singing doesn't exactly go with the Callaway code of serve and protect."

"I think he always knew that Sean wasn't going to be a firefighter. Sean had a bad experience with fire when he was a little kid, and for months after that he'd hide under the bed when he heard the sirens. My dad tried to take him to the firehouse, break him of the bad memories, but it didn't work."

"What was the bad experience? I don't remember hearing about that."

"Sean was in the car with my dad. They were just coming home from the store, and they stopped at a light. My dad saw smoke and flames coming out of a house. He called it in, then jumped out of the car and ran into the house. Sean was alone outside when a little girl came running out of the house, her pajamas on fire. My dad ran after her and rolled her in the grass, but she was screaming, and I guess Sean was traumatized. He was like six at the time."

"I can't blame him. That must have been terrifying for a little kid."

"My dad tried to tell him that she was going to be all right, that her burns weren't bad, that he'd gotten her out in time, and that firefighters were the good guys. But Sean never wanted anything to do with the job." Aiden paused. "I thought he might follow Drew into the Coast Guard since he liked to swim, but it was always about music for him. My dad keeps telling him to get a real job, but Sean is a stubborn Callaway like the rest of us." He paused, adding, "My father hates it when he can't control his kids. We're all grown up now, and he still treats us like we're twelve. It drives him nuts when he can't make us do what he wants."

"Then you must have sent him all the way to crazy by now."

"No doubt."

"Your father is lucky he has Lynda to talk him down. She always seems like she's calm and centered."

"She does a lot of yoga."

"Maybe I should try that. I'm far from calm and centered right now. Lynda has the perfect personality to balance your father's volatility; they're a good match."

"Lynda does her best. My father doesn't always listen to her."

Sara turned her gaze on him, a curious look in her eyes. "Why don't you call Lynda *Mom*? You're the only one of your siblings who doesn't. I always wondered why."

He hadn't had to answer that question in a long time. "Habit," he said. "I couldn't think of her as my mother in the beginning. I was five when my mom died and eight when my dad and Linda got together. I knew she wasn't my real mother, and it felt wrong to replace her. Plus, I wasn't sure Lynda was going to stick around. My dad dated a few women in between my mom and her. For a while, it seemed like there was a new woman at the dinner every other week. Lynda was one of the few who wasn't scared off by a man with four boys, one of whom was still in diapers."

"I didn't realize your father had dated anyone else. I suppose that was natural."

He sighed. The death of his mother had left a hole in his heart that he'd never quite filled. He'd moved on as they all had, but he still thought about her sometimes, wondered why no one ever talked about her. "There was nothing natural about any of it," he said a moment later. "My mom was way too young to die. She got cancer when Sean was only a year old. She was in her mid-thirties—a year older than I am right now." He shook his head, filled with regret and anger that his mother hadn't had anywhere close to a full life.

"I'm sorry, Aiden," Sara said softly. "I didn't mean to bring up a touchy topic. We didn't move in next door until you were all one big blended family, so I never really thought about your real mother, or even about Emma's real father. Although I do remember early on when Emma and Nicole would go visit him on the weekends. She hated to do that, and then suddenly the visits just stopped. I guess he got married and moved away somewhere. Emma seemed mostly relieved."

"I didn't know their father. He never came around our place. If Emma and Nicole saw him, they went to his house." He paused. "It's been a long time since I thought about those days. We moved into Lynda's house right after the wedding. Not much of my mother came with us; a few photos, that was about it. I understood that my dad was trying to be respectful to Lynda, but it seemed wrong to just erase my mother, as if she'd never existed, never made a mark on our lives."

"Maybe that's the real reason why you can't call Lynda *Mom*. You're still protecting your real mother's memory. I can understand that."

"I don't mean it to be disrespectful," he said quickly. "Lynda raised me. She's been great. My dad got lucky when he found her."

"What was your real mother like?" she asked.

"She was pretty; blonde hair, blue eyes, great smile. I remember her laugh. It was hearty for such a small person. She wasn't much over five feet tall. She liked to go barefoot all the time. She used to take us down to the beach because she loved the ocean. She actually taught me how to surf." The memory widened his smile. He could still see her in his mind, running into the surf, her hair flowing out behind her.

"She sounds adventurous."

"She was. She liked a good challenge."

"Like you."

"I did feel like she understood me. But she made a point of having alone time with each of us. I don't know how she managed it, although my grandmother was around a lot to help out." As he thought about his grandmother, he remembered the odd exchange they'd had at lunch. "My grandmother isn't doing well," he added. "She was at the house for Sunday lunch, and she started talking to me like I was her husband." He looked over at Sara. "She said something about it was time to tell the secret."

"More family secrets," Sara said, her lips tightening. "That doesn't sound good."

"Grandma wasn't lucid. She could have been talking about anything."

"Or something."

He frowned, directing his attention back to the road. "She didn't know what she was saying. I was shocked at how out of it she was. She's always been healthy, active, sharp; it's disturbing to see that change."

"Well, I hope she's okay. And if there is any big Callaway secret, perhaps it's better if you don't go looking for it. A part of me wishes I could turn back time and not find that box in the basement, not go through those pictures, not learn that my entire life was built on deception."

"In the end it could be good, Sara. You've always felt a distance from your father and you blamed yourself. Perhaps you were pointing the finger in the wrong direction. You need to find out why there was a need to deceive you."

"I can't think of a reason that would make sense. Do you think I'm a coward for not confronting my father right away?"

"No. I think you're regrouping, and that's smart. But then, you're a smart girl."

"Thanks. So where are we going, Aiden?"

"Home," he replied, knowing that subconsciously that's where he'd been heading all along. "And I'm not talking about San Francisco." He turned his head to meet her gaze. "Are you okay with that?" There were a lot of shadows in her still puffy eyes, and he could see the indecision in her expression. "Trust me, Sara," he added.

"Okay," she said finally. "Show me where home is."

Fifteen

As they got farther away from San Francisco, Sara felt her muscles begin to relax. The more miles between herself and her father's house, the better. She needed time to think about everything she'd learned, and Aiden was giving her both time and space. She suspected his offer to take her away was not entirely selfless. The Callaways loved deeply but also demanded a lot from each other. The expectations set by generations of Callaway men could be a heavy load to carry, and Aiden was dragging under the weight.

"Did you talk to Jeanne?" she asked suddenly. "You were going to connect this morning, weren't you?"

"Yes, we had a long conversation. I gave her as much information as I could, and she said she'd get back to me with whatever she could find. She said it would be easier if I would agree to let her speak to members of my team, but I asked her to hold off on that for now."

"You don't want to tie her hands too tightly."

"I want to see if we can get anywhere without involving the other guys."

"That makes sense." She shifted in her seat, crossing her legs as she looked out the window. Her eyes felt red from all the crying she'd done earlier, and she wished now she'd taken some time to put on a little makeup. She felt a little embarrassed that Aiden had seen her in such an emotional state, but she couldn't do anything about that now. She'd chalk it up to one more time that he hadn't seen her at her best.

Now that she wasn't feeling so tense, she could appreciate the fact that she was getting to spend more time with him. They were getting to know each other as adults, and they were getting along really well. She told herself not to read too much into it. They were both going through some rough personal times and, for whatever reason, they were able to help each other out, but it was all so very temporary.

She thought about their earlier conversation, about Aiden's real mother and the loss he'd suffered. She wondered now if his unwillingness to commit to a relationship with a woman had something to do with losing his mom at such a young age. He'd obviously loved his mother deeply, so deeply that even after twenty-something years, he couldn't call his stepmother *Mom*. Maybe it was habit as he'd said, but she thought the reason might be out of respect for his mom's memory.

She knew what it was like to lose a mother. It hurt like hell. She'd been destroyed for months after her mom's passing, and she felt the loss now as keenly as she had ten years earlier. She'd been older than Aiden when it happened, but she'd still felt adrift without her mom, her anchor. It must have been doubly worse for Aiden. Maybe it was the memory of that pain that kept him from love.

Not that he didn't love his family and his friends, but that was a different kind of love. A woman would demand all of him—his heart, his soul, his body, and his mind. If he kept things light and casual, he didn't have to worry about that.

In some ways, she did the same thing. She went on a lot of dates, but she didn't have long-term relationships. No one was ever quite right. Maybe she should be analyzing herself instead of Aiden. Or maybe she should skip the analysis and just live in the moment.

Turning to Aiden, she said, "Tell me about Redding, about your home. What should I expect?"

"Not much," he said dryly. "The city is on the small side, about eighty-thousand people. It sits on the banks of the Sacramento River, and it's nestled between several mountain ranges. Lake Shasta is nearby for boating, and the redwood forests provide great camping opportunities. The city was bigger back when the lumber industry was booming. Now it's become more of an escape for people looking to get out of the high-priced big cities and find more affordable housing. It's a nice community. When I'm on duty during fire season, I sleep in the barracks at the base. The rest of the time I live in a small apartment about five minutes away."

"So you stay in Redding all year long?"

He nodded. "I moved up here full time about three years ago."

"And Kyle did the same?"

"Yeah. The first year we shared a place. The next year he met Vicky. She moved into our place, and I got a smaller apartment upstairs."

"So you saw a lot of each other."

"Yes, we did. After the baby was born, Vicky started pressuring Kyle to quit smokejumping. She wanted to move back to San Francisco, and she wanted him to work there. He eventually agreed. It wasn't his first choice, but he wanted her to be happy, and he knew it wasn't easy for her to be on her own during the fire season. We could be gone for days at a time, and she was stuck in a place where she didn't have friends or family, except a few of the other wives or girlfriends."

"That does make sense."

"Perfect sense," he agreed. "I was just sorry that Kyle

had to give up on his dream. Everyone thinks that Kyle followed me to Redding, that I was the instigator, but the truth was that smokejumping was his passion. I might have gotten him into firefighting, but he's the one who wanted to smokejump. I followed him. At first, I thought he was nuts. We were running ten miles a day, carrying eighty-pound packs in a hundred degree weather; it was crazy."

She heard the passion in his voice. "But you loved it."

"Well, you always said I was crazy," he said, flipping her a smile.

Her heart turned over at his sexy grin, reminding her that being caught up in an emotional whirlwind had not dampened her attraction to Aiden one bit. She was probably the crazy one, agreeing to take off with him, knowing that spending more time in his company was only going to make it more difficult to say goodbye. But it was too late for regrets.

"If you all lived in the same apartment building," she said, "I'm surprised that Vicky would turn on you the way she has. How could she believe that you'd do anything to jeopardize your best friend's life?"

"She thinks I let Kyle down. By the time Vicky came along, I'd been promoted a few times, and she saw me as the leader, someone who'd watch out for Kyle. She used to take me aside every now and then and tell me that she felt better knowing I had Kyle's back. She'd make me promise to bring him back safely. I didn't keep my promise."

She heard the pain in his voice and didn't like that Aiden was taking the blame for what was most likely a tragic accident. "How much farther do we have to go?" she asked, changing the subject.

"About twenty minutes. Around that bend up there you're going to start to see some real nature. Tomorrow, I'll show you some of my favorite spots."

The word *tomorrow* reminded her that they were going to

be spending the night together, and she couldn't help thinking about where she was going to sleep, and whether or not they'd finish the kiss they'd started the night before. Her body tingled at the thought at the same time her mind screamed *caution.*

Aiden suddenly put a hand on her thigh, and she jumped.

"It's going to be okay, Sara," he said, meeting her gaze.

She didn't know exactly what he meant, but looking into his beautiful blue eyes she knew there was no place else she'd rather be right now than with him.

Fifteen minutes later, Aiden pointed to an airfield in the distance. She could see several small planes on the tarmac. "That's the base," he told her. "Not many people around this time of year. It gets busy again in the early spring when we start selecting rookies and preparing for the next season."

"So, you'd normally be working now at what?" she asked.

"I do different things during the off-season: forestry work, teaching fire safety classes, working on equipment. When I'm not doing that, I do some carpentry. A former smokejumper named Bo makes cabinets, and whenever he needs extra hands, he knows who to call. Bo is a real character. He's in his fifties now. He had twenty-two seasons under his belt when he wrecked his knee and had to quit. He has more stories than anyone I've ever met."

"Did you talk to Bo after the accident?"

"Yeah, he was in the hospital when I woke up."

"Had he had a similar experience to yours?"

"He told me a few stories, but I wasn't really in the mood to listen."

"How long were you in the hospital?" she asked, unable

to picture Aiden in that setting. He was such an active man.

"Just overnight. I checked myself out."

"Of course you did," she said dryly.

"I was fine, Sara, and I couldn't stay there. I couldn't lie in a bed with nothing to do but think about Kyle."

"What about all your other friends? You said you had some supporters on your crew. Did you spend time with them?"

"Everyone was leaving. Fire season was over. Their plans were made, plane tickets had been booked."

"I just don't understand why you're so alone, Aiden. I thought firefighters were like brothers."

"We are like brothers," he said tersely. "But when you let one of those brothers die, no one in the family is too happy to see you."

"You and Kyle were separated from the group, so how does anyone besides the two of you know what happened?" she challenged. "It sounds to me like you're starting to believe their stories instead of what your gut tells you."

"If I believed their stories, I wouldn't have hired an investigator."

"Okay," she said, relieved that he wasn't giving up. "Good."

"And I wasn't completely abandoned. Some of the guys made an effort to talk to me. I just wasn't in the mood to see anyone. I needed to deal with Kyle's death on my own."

She was relieved to hear that not everyone blamed Aiden. But she knew Aiden would not feel better until he knew the truth for himself, whatever it was.

A few minutes later, Aiden pulled into a parking spot in front of a modest four-story apartment building. The building was at the end of a street, and on the opposite corner was a beautiful park with lots of trees, a garden, and a play structure in the distance.

"This is a pretty neighborhood," she said.

"The park sold me," he said. "Kyle and I used to play basketball over there on the weekends." He cleared his throat. "Anyway, this is home. Ready to see the inside?"

"Absolutely."

They grabbed their bags and headed up the stairs. "Of course you would live on the top floor," she commented. "And in a building with no elevator."

He grabbed the handle of her suitcase, relieving her of the burden. "It has an elevator. I just never use it. Walking is faster. And I have to keep in shape."

He was definitely in good shape, she thought, as she got a nice view of his ass on the way up the stairs.

Aiden gave her a funny look when they reached his door. "You're all red. The stairs weren't that bad, were they?"

"I'm fine. It's just hotter here than it is in New York." Okay, that was a stupid answer. She cleared her throat. "Are we going in?"

He turned the key and opened the door. "After you. It's not much."

The one-bedroom apartment with a small kitchen off the living area might not be much, but it was Aiden's home, and she could see his personality everywhere she looked. The furniture was very male, big, overstuffed couch with a bunch of loose pillows and a recliner with a perfect view of what appeared to be a sixty-inch television screen. There were newspapers on the coffee table and a couple of novels, which surprised her a little. She'd always thought of Aiden as a man of action and not as a reader.

Speaking of action… The walls were covered with amazing photographs: athletes engaged in extreme sports, skiers going off tops of mountains, surfers taking on huge waves, and rock climbers reaching the summit of a steep peak. Moving closer to the wall by the kitchen, she realized some of the photos were actually of Aiden and Kyle.

There was a rafting shot with Aiden and Kyle in the front of the boat, two other men in the back, making their way through some nasty whitewater. There was nothing but pure joy on their faces.

"When was this taken?" she asked.

"Two years ago. That was on the American River."

"Looks dangerous."

"It's more fun that way."

"Sure." She moved down the wall, happy to see what else Aiden did in his spare time. No boring activities for this man. She saw him reeling in a fish, climbing up a steep rockface, and jumping out of an airplane. "Was this at work?" she asked.

"That was my first rookie jump," he said. "They gave us a souvenir."

"I can't believe you jump out of planes," she said, reminded of how very different they were. "Are all these other guys smokejumpers?"

"Most of 'em. We spend a lot of time together during fire season, and when we're not fighting fire, we're still usually together."

"Do you ever do anything tame—golf, bowling?" she asked.

He grinned. "Some of the guys golf, but it's a little slow for me.

"Is this Vicky?" she asked, pausing in front of a party picture. Kyle had a birthday hat on his head, and a pregnant woman stood behind him with her hand on his shoulder.

"Yeah, that was last year. I should take all these pictures down," he added, his tone turning somber.

"Don't rush it," she said, putting a hand on his arm as he reached toward the photograph.

"I can't leave them up. I can't look at Kyle at his birthday party and think about how he's never going to have another one," Aiden said, his voice rough with pain. "Damn." He pushed past her and ripped the photo off the wall, followed by another and another. He was suddenly obsessed with getting the pictures down.

Sara stepped back, waiting and watching, wishing she could help him, but there was nothing she could say that would help. Aiden had to get through the pain in his own way.

Eventually, there was nothing left on the wall but nails and odd patches of gleaming paint that had been hidden behind the photographs. Aiden stood in the middle of the pile, hands on his hips, his breath coming fast and ragged. Finally, he looked at her.

"God, Sara," he breathed.

His expression tore at her heart. "I know. It hurts," she said softly.

She went to him, wrapping her arms around his waist, pulling him as close as she could. He needed someone to hang on to, to anchor him, and she could do that.

After a slight hesitation, he put his arms around her, hugging her so tight she could feel every tense muscle in his body.

"What can I do?" she asked, gazing up at him. "How can I help?"

He stared down at her, his blue eyes dark and glittering. Then he lowered his head. His mouth sought hers with the same desperate urgency he'd shown a moment earlier. His lips were demanding, hot, and needy. She started out wanting to give him comfort, but that turned quickly to passion, because this was Aiden. And he knew exactly how to set her senses on fire. She matched him kiss for kiss until they ran out of breath.

And then Aiden jerked back, his jaw tightening, his

hands clenching into fists, so that he wouldn't reach for her again. "I've got to get out of here."

"I'll go with you," she said.

"No," he said forcefully. "You. Me. Not a good idea." He grabbed his keys and headed out the door, letting it slam behind him.

Shaken, she blew out a breath and then sat down on the couch. What the hell had just happened?

One minute they were talking and then they were kissing like there was no tomorrow. She'd never experienced so much intensity, so many emotions. She'd been on edge all day, and when Aiden had snapped, she'd gone right along with him, wanting to forget everything and just be in the moment.

But the moment was over, and Aiden was still in a lot of pain.

Her heart went out to him.

But he didn't want her heart, she reminded herself. Like the last time, he'd pushed her away.

After leaving his apartment, Aiden walked through the park, his lips burning with the taste of Sara's mouth, his heart in turmoil, his mind full of condemnation for taking advantage of a woman who was far too generous for her own good. Her beautiful, compassionate brown eyes, her soft lips and tender smile had been his undoing. She'd opened her arms to him, and he'd wanted to lose himself in her. But he couldn't use her to ease his pain.

So he walked and he walked, his emotional pain turning physical as his injured leg protested the exercise. But he didn't slow down. He welcomed the physical ache. It was much easier to handle. He eventually left the city to take a trail into the woods. He'd walked and run this trail many times. It was used often in training runs, and there were memories along every step of the rocky path.

As the memories threatened to breach his control, he started to run. His muscles screamed in protest. He really shouldn't be jogging, but he pushed himself to do it anyway. He needed to burn some energy and maybe, just maybe, he could outrun the past.

It didn't work. With the setting sun in his face, he came to a halt, breathless and exhausted with sweat running down his face, back and shoulders.

Flopping down on the ground, he took in gulps of air, feeling like he'd just finished one of the grueling runs that were required to be a smokejumper. When he'd gone through rookie training with Kyle, he'd been shocked at the amount of physical strength and endurance required to do the job. He'd thought he was in good shape before he got there, but he wasn't even close. He and Kyle had never worked so hard in their lives. The training had tested their stamina, endurance, courage and mostly their will.

They'd never considered quitting. They'd been more worried about not making it. Kyle had been particularly stressed out before their final test.

"Don't let me quit, Aiden," he'd said. "Whatever I say, no matter how tired I am, don't let me give up. I want to do this. I want to be proud of myself. I want to do this more than I've ever wanted to do anything."

"Right back at you," he'd told him. "You run, I run. We don't stop. Ever."

The pact had carried them through that run and through many more runs. In fact, it had carried them through all the challenges they'd faced together—except for the last one.

"Sorry I let you down, buddy," he muttered, staring up at the sky.

The dusky twilight turned to a blazing orange red.

Instead of sky, he saw the forest on fire, the flames splitting the trees, the smoke thick and black, and Kyle walking away from him.

Where the hell was he going?

But now, like before, there was no answer.

Sitting up, he took several more breaths, then stood up. It was getting dark and he was miles from home. Sara was probably worried. He reached into his pocket for his cell phone and realized he'd left it on his coffee table. There was nothing to do but head home. The pain in his leg was bad now that he wasn't so distracted by grief, and he had to go slow. By the time he made it back to the apartment, it was eight o'clock at night. He'd been gone for hours.

He had no idea of the response he'd get when he finally opened his apartment door. He had enough experience with women to suspect he wasn't going to get a great welcome.

Sixteen

Aiden had expected Sara to be pissed off, maybe sulking, maybe even gone. But when he let himself into his apartment, he found her in the kitchen, stirring something in a pot on the stove. The air smelled like garlic and onions, and for the first time in a long time, a bit like home. To say he was shocked was an understatement.

"I hope you're hungry," Sara said, turning her head to give him a warm smile.

That smile held absolutely no hint of resentment or anger, and it rattled him as much as the dinner she appeared to be making.

"I am starving," he said, as he limped across the room.

Her sharp gaze took in his hobbling stride. "You're hurt."

"I just walked too long," he said, pausing by the stove.

"You look like you just finished a marathon," she said, her eyes running down his sweaty face and body. "Do you need some ice? Maybe a shower?"

"I'll get to all that. First I want to apologize."

"It's fine, Aiden."

"I shouldn't have—"

"Stop," she interrupted, holding up a hand. "I said it was fine. You don't have to apologize. I know what grief feels like, and I know why you had to get out of here."

He could see the understanding in her eyes, which only made him feel guilty. "Still, I shouldn't have left you like that. You've had a tough day, too."

"Well, surprisingly, I feel better. I'm far, far away from my problems, and I have you to thank for that. So I decided to make you dinner."

"You're being very nice," he said, surprised by her attitude.

"I'm a very nice person. Haven't you figured that out yet?"

He smiled back at her. "Actually, I've known that all along. You were always a sweetheart, Sara. Far too good for me."

She shook her head, her expression turning rueful. "I never liked being the good girl. It was so boring."

"It's who you were and who you still are," he amended. Sara had definitely come out of her shell since high school. She wasn't afraid to be smart in front of people anymore, and she could stand up for herself. But deep down she still had a core of softness and warmth that was just inherent in who she was.

"Bad girls had and still have more fun," she said. "Anyway, you should check your phone. It rang a few times while you were gone."

"Probably my family trying to track me down. My father and grandfather both wanted to have a discussion with me tonight."

"No wonder you were so willing to hit the road," she said dryly. "And here I thought it was all for me."

"It was for both of us. When you told me you needed time to just think and breathe, I felt exactly the same way. I figured we could do it together." He grabbed his phone and checked his missed calls. There were several from family members along with a couple of text messages from Emma, telling him he better take care of her friend. "Did you hear from Emma?" he asked.

Sara nodded, her eyes filling with guilt. "I didn't pick up the call, but I sent her a message saying I'm okay and not to worry. I feel bad about taking off on her the way I did. She must be wondering what's going on."

"You'll fill her in when it's time. In the meanwhile, she'll live." He moved over to the stove. "That sauce smells amazing. I thought you said you couldn't cook."

"I have three dishes I know how to make, and this is one of them. It's not fancy, but it's pretty tasty."

"I know you didn't find any food in my refrigerator, so…"

"So I walked to the store, which thankfully was only about a mile. You took the keys to your truck with you."

"I realized that later."

"And I bought a few things for dinner and breakfast. I threw out all the expired food in your fridge. It was starting to stink."

"I left in a hurry."

"Where exactly did you go?"

"I just drove. To be honest, I wasn't paying any attention. When I would start to fall asleep, I'd pull over, camp out or find a motel for the occasional shower. I ended up in Wyoming."

"That's crazy, Aiden."

"That's when I realized that no matter how far I went, I wasn't going to be able to get away from myself. So I headed back to San Francisco, thinking maybe being around the family would help me remember who I was. That didn't really work out. Although I did find you there. That was a nice surprise—at least for me. You weren't too happy about it."

"I wasn't expecting to see you, and the fire shook me up. I thought I was just going to surprise my father for his birthday and, wow, look how that's turned out. My whole life, my entire sense of identity, is in question. Talk about not knowing who you are, I have no idea who anyone in my family is."

He nodded. "We can talk about it."

"No, not yet," she said quickly. "Let's just have dinner. It's almost ready. Why don't you sit down and put your leg up."

"Good idea," he said, moving over to the table.

"I met one of your neighbors earlier, a very attractive redhead named Mallory. She asked me to tell you that she was thinking about you and that you should call her."

"Thanks," he said, taking a seat.

"So who is Mallory? An old girlfriend?" she asked, a curious gleam in her eyes.

"I wouldn't call her a girlfriend. We went out a few times." He grimaced as he propped up his leg on a nearby chair.

"Do you need some ice?" Sara asked, not missing a thing.

"It will be fine."

She didn't look like she believed him, but she let it go. "So what happened with Mallory?"

"Nothing. We had some laughs. That was it. There was no big drama."

"She likes you. I recognized that look in her eyes when she asked about you."

"Mallory likes a lot of people," he said with a shrug. "Believe me, I did not break her heart."

"Would you know if you had?" Sara challenged.

"I don't get involved with women who are looking for a serious relationship. I'm up-front about that. I always have been. Except maybe with you. But that night with you was unexpected. I didn't handle it well, obviously." He paused, waiting for her to make a comeback, but her gaze was focused on the stove. "What about you, Sara? You're as single as I am. What's your story?"

"I have no story. I told you I work all the time, and I haven't met anyone I liked well enough to change that." She paused, her expression contemplative. "Love has always been a mystery to me. I saw love when I looked next door, but I didn't see it in my own home. I certainly never wanted to model my parents' relationship. And I've never wanted to be with a man who could make me as sad as my mom used to get. She tried not to show her unhappiness to me, but I could see it. Sometimes I could hear their raised voices late at night. I used to worry sometimes that she'd leave and not take me with her. I did not want to get stuck with my dad." She turned her gaze to Aiden. "But that's exactly what happened. I got stuck with my dad, and he's not any more happy about it than I am. Anyway, I don't want to talk about him—or even about love. My few attempts at the emotion haven't turned out so well."

He had a feeling he'd been one of those attempts, and it bothered him. He'd never meant to hurt her.

"Love can be good," he said slowly.

She raised an eyebrow. "You're going to advocate love now?"

"Well, I've seen it in my grandparents. My father's parents have been married for sixty years, and they're devoted to each other."

"That is unbelievable," she said.

"And my father and Lynda seem to have a strong relationship. Sometimes on the outside it looks one-sided, like she does everything for him, but the old man can be a romantic."

Sara nodded. "He is romantic. I remember on one of Lynda's birthdays your dad hired a plane to fly over your house with *I love you, Lynda* in skywriting."

"That's Jack Callaway—bigger than life. He's always been about the grand gesture."

"Well, I was impressed. So was Emma. We sat on the curb watching that plane and talking about how one day we were going to find guys like that. Turns out they're more difficult to find than we thought," she said with a wry smile.

"Maybe you haven't been looking in the right spot."

"Maybe you haven't either," she retorted.

Their gazes caught and something passed in between, something amazing and a little terrifying.

Then Sara looked away, turning her attention back to the stove. "This is ready."

"I'll get some plates."

"No, just sit, rest," she said. "I can handle putting dinner on the table."

That was the easy part, he thought. After dinner, they had the rest of the evening to handle, and he had a feeling bringing Sara home with him was going to be one of the worst ideas he'd ever had.

Dinner conversation was casual, neutral, and Sara felt herself relaxing after the tense few moments before the meal when Aiden had given her a look that told her he was just as aware as she was that there was something going on between them, even if neither one of them wanted to admit it.

Or… Maybe she'd imagined that look. She had a long history of hoping Aiden would suddenly wake up and see that he was in love with her. She couldn't go down that road again. That fantasy was part of another life.

After they finished eating, Aiden went to take a shower, and Sara busied herself with the dishes. He'd offered to do them later, but she'd brushed off the suggestion. It wasn't that big of a deal, and she needed a distraction from thinking about Aiden's beautifully rugged body under a spray of hot water.

She wondered what he'd do if she joined him in the shower. He'd probably welcome her at first and then push her away when he came to his senses. That seemed to be the pattern with most of their encounters.

Frowning, she started the dishwasher and headed into the living room. She flipped through several channels on the huge television. For a man who liked nature so much, Aiden obviously spent some time on the well-worn recliner in front of the TV.

She paused on a game show. She loved intellectual games. In college, she'd been part of a super bowl academic team that had won a national competition with entries from every major university in the country. It had been one of her proudest moments.

As the contestant selected a category, the announcer asked, "This number, one of the first twenty, uses only one vowel four times."

"Seventeen," she guessed, beating the contestant by a split second.

"Seventeen," the announcer confirmed.

She smiled happily, waiting for the next question.

"To marry Elizabeth, Prince Philip had to renounce claims to this southern European country's crown."

She thought for a moment, then said aloud, "Greece."

The contestant guessed Italy. The announcer said, "You're wrong. The correct answer was Greece."

"I told you," she said smugly.

"Are you talking to the TV?" Aiden asked.

She hadn't realized he was out of the shower. "Bad habit. I usually play this game alone at home."

"It sounds like you win a lot," he said as he finished

buttoning up his shirt.

For a moment her gaze lingered on his chest. Ruthlessly, she dragged it away, refusing to acknowledge that he smelled really good now, having obviously thrown on a splash of aftershave.

"Around 1542," the announcer continued, "Explorer Juan Rodriguez Cabrillo discovered this island off Los Angeles, and it's believed he's buried there, too."

"Catalina," she said, her answer coming in harmony with both Aiden and the contestant.

"Catalina is correct," the announcer said.

"Hey, I might be able to keep up with you," Aiden said, sitting down on the couch.

"That was an easy one."

"Ouch," he said with a smile.

"Hey, there was only one thing I ever did better than you, so I'm claiming game show questions as my strength."

He laughed. "All right. You can have game shows."

"Thank you."

"But I suspect there are a lot of things you do better than me, Sara."

"I doubt that. I had a ringside seat for a good portion of your life. And it seemed like you got award after award."

"You're thinking of Burke."

"Well, he had a lot, too, but you had your share, and you were more genuinely popular than Burke. He was someone the kids looked up to, but you were the one they really liked." She paused. "By the way, do you know that your television is obscenely large?"

He laughed. "Kyle bought that television when we first moved in together. After he kicked me out and moved Vicky in, I got to keep the TV as compensation for losing my roommate."

"Now, that makes sense, because I can't really picture

you as a couch potato. Although you have a lot of books in this apartment, so you must spend some time reading. And your favorite topic seems to be astronomy."

He tipped his head. "The night sky has always interested me. When I'm up in the mountains, far from civilization, there are a million stars in the sky. I figured I should know what I was looking at. So I got a few books."

"A few?" she echoed raising an eyebrow.

"I went slightly overboard on the online ordering. Then someone in the family found out I liked astronomy, and every Christmas or birthday another book shows up."

"I've never thought much about the stars or seen a night sky like the one you described. In New York, all I can see are the city lights, and San Francisco was the same. My parents didn't like to camp, so we never went anywhere that was far from a city, not that we really went anywhere at all. My dad liked to work. He did not like to vacation."

"It sounds like you're taking after him in that regard."

"You're right," she said. "I do not want to turn into my dad. I'm going to have to change that," she said.

"You should. I'd like to take you camping. I think you'd love it."

"Why on earth would you think that? I'm a city girl."

Aiden smiled. "Only one way to find out."

As he ran his fingers through his damp air, she became very aware of how alone they were and how many hours there were before bedtime. She still didn't know where she was going to sleep, but she didn't want to think about that now. "Should we go out somewhere?"

"Not much open around here on Sunday night after nine," he replied.

"Right. I forgot it was Sunday. The days are all mixed up for me."

Silence followed her words—a tense silence.

"There is one bar that's probably open if you're up for beer and peanuts," he said.

"Sounds great," she said with relief.

"I'll put on my shoes."

While Aiden finished dressing, she went into the bathroom and fixed herself up a little. Her eyes were nowhere near as red or swollen after her crying jag earlier that day, and with a little blush and some lip gloss, she felt immensely better. The pain of deception was still simmering right under the surface, but for the moment she was going to leave it there.

A few minutes later they were on their way to a bar named Gil's.

The bar was dimly lit, lots of western décor, and the music playing was country. They grabbed a table in the corner and ordered two beers from the waitress.

The waitress gave Aiden a sexy smile and said, "Haven't seen you in here in a while."

"Been away," he said.

Her smile dimmed. "Heard the bad news about your friend. So sad."

"Yeah, thanks."

As the waitress left, Sara could see that the tension had returned to Aiden's face. "Maybe this wasn't a good idea," she said.

"It doesn't matter. I had to come back sometime. It's kind of nice not to be here alone."

"So did you and that waitress…"

"No," he said with a shake of his head. "Never."

"She's interested."

"Well, I'm not."

"Okay," she said, wondering why he was suddenly so snappy.

A moment later, the waitress returned with their beers

and a bowl of peanuts.

Sara lifted the mug to her lips and took a sip. It tasted great. She'd never thought of herself as a beer drinker, at least not since college. Most of the parties she went to now involved wine or hard liquor. But the beer was nice, and she liked the warmth and friendly spirit of the bar. People seemed to know each other and care about each other. She was a long way from New York.

"This isn't your usual kind of place, is it?" Aiden asked.

"No, but I like it. It's a nice change of pace. I've been moving so fast for so long, this is the first time in a long time I've really slowed down. It's a dangerous feeling. Makes me wonder if I'll be able to rev myself up again for the seventy-hour work week."

"What else do you do besides work?"

"Nothing."

"Come on. You must have some hobbies."

"Occasionally, I go to the gym, but usually I consider the three-quarter mile walk between my apartment and work to be my exercise. Museums and theaters and nightclubs surround me, and I never go to any of them. I do like Central Park, though. Sometimes I'll take a walk through there on a Sunday, especially in the spring when the flowers are blooming."

He leaned forward, resting his forearms on the table, his gaze solely on her. She'd never had this much attention from Aiden, and she found it both pleasurable and a little unnerving.

"I can see you in the park," he said. "You loved to garden with your mom. Don't you miss having some land of your own?"

"Sometimes," she admitted. "I never thought New York would be forever. I always thought I'd go back to San Francisco."

"You still can."

"Maybe." She sipped her beer and listened to the music. The latest song was typical country, some woman yearning for some man she couldn't have. The story was poetic and emotional, heartfelt. "I like songs that are about something," she said aloud. "Country always tells a story."

"Usually about some man who did some woman wrong," Aiden said dryly.

She smiled. "I was just thinking the same thing."

"At least my gender provides a lot of material for songwriters. But it's not all our fault, you know. Women can be very mysterious. They need to come with instructions."

"As if that would matter. When's the last time you read instructions?" she challenged.

He laughed. "Guilty. Your tongue is sharper than I remember. I like it."

She did not want him talking about her tongue or letting his gaze rest on her lips, because it only reminded her that the few kisses they'd shared had not been nearly enough.

"It's her," Aiden said suddenly, his attention moving across the room.

She turned her head to see a blonde woman talking to the bartender. "Who is that?" she asked, looking back at Aiden. "Is she another one of the women you've had fun with?"

"No," he said, his tone somber, his gaze speculative. "Remember when I told you that I'd seen Kyle with a woman outside of a hotel. That's her."

"You should talk to her. Ask her how she knew Kyle."

He hesitated and then gave a nod as he got to his feet. "I think I will."

Unfortunately, his doubt had cost him valuable time. The woman was already leaving the bar.

Aiden headed after her, but returned far too quickly.

"She got in a cab. I couldn't catch her," he said. "Damn,

why did I wait?"

"Go talk to the bartender, or the waitress. They might know who that woman was. She must have had them call a cab for her."

"You're right." He went to the bar and conversed with the bartender for several minutes, then returned to the table, looking a lot happier with himself. "I've got a name. Sandra Ellingston. Bartender didn't know much about her except that she's divorced and comes in almost every weekend, usually with some other women."

"Well, that's a start. I'm sure Jeanne can find out more about her."

He nodded, pulling out his phone. "I'll text her right now."

While he was composing his message, Sara wondered if Kyle had been having an affair. It could explain why he'd distanced himself from Aiden. He might not have wanted to be judged for his actions. But…

As Aiden finished sending his text, she said, "Even if Kyle was having an affair, how do you think that played into his death?"

Aiden frowned and let out a heavy breath. "I don't know."

"Do you think he was just not paying attention that day because he had other things on his mind?"

Something dark settled in Aiden's eyes.

"No, you don't think that," she said. "Aiden, talk to me."

"It's hard to say out loud." He paused for a long minute and then said, "Every time I close my eyes, I dream that I'm in that forest, and Kyle is walking away from me. I'm yelling at him, and he's ignoring me. It's as if he's deliberately going into the fire."

Her stomach turned over. "It seems too extreme," she said quietly, knowing where his thoughts were going. "An affair isn't worth dying for."

He met her gaze. "I hope not," he said. "But Kyle could be hard on himself. Who knows what guilt could have driven him to do? Let's get out of here."

Seventeen

—➤➤◄◄◄—

Aiden felt unbelievably tense as he drove Sara back to his apartment. He couldn't believe he'd actually acknowledged aloud that Kyle might have killed himself. It was something that had been festering in his mind for weeks, and he felt like he'd just betrayed Kyle by putting words to the thought.

But Sara could be trusted. And he'd needed to say the words because he needed to find out the truth. Hopefully, the investigator would be able to connect Kyle and Sandra Ellingston in a way that made sense.

As he parked in front of his building, a different kind of tension tightened his muscles. He and Sara were about to spend the night together. He couldn't remember a time in his life when he'd had a woman over and they hadn't had sex. It just didn't happen. He didn't have close women friends. He'd always felt he had enough females in his life with three sisters.

Sara was almost like a sister, he tried to tell himself, but that rationalization fell short. He didn't feel like a brother to her at all. He did feel like they were friends, though. And as a friend, he couldn't take advantage of her.

Would it be taking advantage if she wanted it, too?

Of course it would. Because Sara was upset about her parents and feeling angry and reckless. Sleeping with him might make her feel better for a few hours, but in the morning she'd regret it. He wasn't the kind of man for her. She'd grown up with such a cold father that she needed someone to really, really love her, to commit heart and soul.

Love wasn't his thing. It never had been. Love hurt. He could still remember the pain of losing his mother, and that had happened over twenty years ago. The fresh pain that came from losing Kyle had only reinforced his belief that love was an emotion he did not want to embrace; he only wished he didn't want to embrace Sara.

Sara gave him a wary look as she got out of the truck and followed him up the stairs. He wondered if the same kind of thoughts were going through her mind. They'd been dancing around their attraction to each other for a few days now. The kisses they'd shared had only whetted his appetite for more—a lot more.

He opened the door and told himself it wasn't going to happen. He would do the right thing.

"I'll sleep on the couch," he said, as he turned on the light. "You can take the bed."

"No, I'll take the couch. I'm shorter than you. I'll be more comfortable."

"I'm not going to let you do that, so can we save ourselves a long discussion that's only going to end up the same way it started if you just agree to take the bed."

"You Callaways are extremely pigheaded even when you're being generous."

He conceded her point. "I can't argue with that."

"I guess I'll go to bed then," she said, her words a bit hesitant.

"You should," he agreed, knowing that the sooner they had a door between them the better.

"Do you need anything from the bedroom?"

"Yeah, I'll grab some sweats," he said, heading into his

room. His very comfortable king-sized bed looked far more inviting than the couch. He could imagine Sara tangled up in his sheets, her beautiful brown hair spread across the white pillows, her legs intertwined with his, her soft, round breasts perfect for tasting. His groin hardened, and he turned quickly away.

He grabbed some sweats out of a drawer and left the room, deliberately avoiding her gaze as he passed her on the way out. When she shut the door behind him, he felt like he might be able to leave her alone, maybe…

Sara stared at the bedroom door for at least three solid minutes before she finally opened her suitcase and pulled out a T-shirt and pajama bottoms. After changing, she debated the stupidity of going into the hall to use the bathroom and brush her teeth. It wasn't Aiden she didn't trust. He could stay away from her. He'd proven that a long time ago. The question was whether she could stay away from him.

She flopped back on the bed, appreciating the comfort of the soft mattress and the thick blankets. Aiden hadn't slept in the bed in a couple of weeks, but she could still smell his musky scent on the sheets. Or maybe it was just that her senses were acutely aware of every little thing about him—the taste of his mouth, the tenor of his voice, the strength of his stance. He was in the next room, but her nerves were still tingling.

She pressed her fingers to her mouth. It was a crime that he was such a good kisser. He put every other man she'd kissed to shame. In fact, she realized now that she'd been subconsciously comparing every date she'd ever had to Aiden. She'd set the bar with him when she was fourteen years old, and no one had ever come close.

She'd tried to hate him for humiliating and rejecting her, but deep down she'd still had a soft spot for him. Over time, she'd pushed him to the back of her mind. She'd gone out with other men. She'd even come close to falling in love, but she'd always held back. No one had ever felt exactly right.

Aiden felt right.

But he didn't care for her the way she cared for him. He'd been upfront about being a no-commitment guy. And they were opposites in so many ways. There were a million reasons why they didn't work together, the most obvious being that Aiden would probably never feel for her the way she felt for him. He was her friend. There was an attraction, but something more? Was Aiden even capable of more?

He said no, but she'd seen the way he loved his family, his friends. She wished he could let himself love a woman that way. And not just any woman—her.

Maybe she was just lonely. It had been a long time since she'd been attracted to anyone the way she was to Aiden. And it had been a long, emotional day. Her entire sense of identity had been shaken to the core. She was looking for escape, searching for something solid to hang on to. She really shouldn't be thinking of hanging onto him.

She turned onto her side, closed her eyes, and tried to think of something else, but a restless need finally drove her to her feet. She walked to the door, paused one last second, and then entered the hall. She made a quick stop in the bathroom, thinking some cold water on her face might also help. But ten minutes later, face washed, teeth brushed, she felt even more of a need to talk to Aiden.

The living room was dark, but she doubted he was asleep. If he were, that would certainly solve her problem.

She walked down the hall and paused.

"Go to bed, Sara," he said.

His husky voice drew a tingle down her spine. The

caution in his tone was mixed with something else—desire?

She walked into the room, stopping at the end of the couch.

He was stretched out, a light blanket covering him, his head on a pillow, his feet dangling over the edge.

"What do you want?" he asked.

How did she answer that question? A dozen suggestions fled through her brain, but only one stuck. She couldn't give him that answer. It was too bold. Then again, where had being shy ever got her?

"I think you should take the bed," she said. "You can't be comfortable here."

"If I take the bed, you're sharing it with me."

She swallowed hard at his purposeful words. In the dark shadows, she couldn't see his face clearly, but by his tone, she sensed that she was standing on the edge of a precipice.

"Are you sure about that?" she asked. "You're better at starting things than finishing. Every time we've kissed, you've been the one to pull away."

"To protect you."

"Really?" she challenged. "Or were you protecting yourself?"

"You were too young for me, Sara. You didn't know the score."

"That was true back then. I thought I'd gotten over you. But then I came home, and suddenly I was right back where I was before—wanting you." She drew in a much-needed breath. "I'm taking a big chance right now. You could reject me again."

"Then why risk it?" he asked.

"Because I want you." There, she'd finally said it. "It's as simple as that, and you like things simple, so what's the problem?"

He sat up. "You're not at all simple, Sara. You're

complicated, beautiful, smart, and way out of my league. I knew that when I was nineteen, and I know it now."

"That was the past. This is now. You know me, and I know you. You're probably right that we are wrong for each other. Our lives are in different states. We have different priorities, but tonight we're here together, and I don't want to think about tomorrow. I just want to be with you. No strings. No commitment."

"You say that now, but you'll change your mind—"

"Sh-sh," she said, sitting next to him on the side of the couch. "Stop putting walls between us. I know you want me. And that's not a teenage girl with a crush talking. That's a woman who knows when a man wants her. And you want me," she repeated.

His gaze met hers. "I don't want to hurt you," he said, a desperate note in his voice, as if he was getting tired of the fight. "I hurt you before. I didn't handle things well. I don't want to make the same mistake."

"Aiden."

"What?"

"Would you just kiss me already?"

A charged, tense minute followed her words.

Then Aiden slid his hand around the back of her neck. He pressed his mouth to hers in a gentle, tender kiss, almost as if he were afraid he might break her. She didn't want gentleness from him. She didn't want to be the sweet, good girl. She wanted to be bad—with him.

She opened her mouth, inviting him in, his tongue tangling with hers as his hands roamed up and down her back. Urgency and need stripped away the barriers between them. His mouth devoured hers, his kiss touching off the storm that had been brewing for years. It was as if the dam had broken for both of them.

Aiden pulled her T-shirt up over her head. She shook out

her hair as his hands cupped her breasts, as his mouth dipped, and his tongue slid along her collarbone, the light touch teasing her nipples into fine points. She put her arms around him, pulling him closer, sliding her hands up under his shirt, tracing the lines of his rippled muscles with the tips of her fingers.

He groaned and stopped kissing her long enough to shed his shirt. Then his hands moved to her bra. He unhooked the clasp and pulled it off of her shoulders. His mouth sought her nipples, and she gasped at the streak of pleasure that ran through her body.

She ran her hands through the wiry strands of his hair as he kissed her breasts. His fingers slid down her stomach, one hand dipping into the waistband of her loose-fitting pajamas, his fingers seeking the heat that was threatening to consume her.

"Aiden," she whispered as he pushed her back against the pillows of the couch.

"Sara," he muttered. "Beautiful Sara." Then his mouth was on hers again.

She moved her legs restlessly, wanting so many things, and on top of her list was her naked body next to his. She reached down to peel off her pajamas bottoms, grateful when Aiden kicked off his own pants.

He stood up, not at all self-conscious, and why should he be? He was gorgeous and male and, for the moment, all hers.

He held out his hand to her and she took it, getting to her feet.

"Let's go to bed," he said. And then he led her into the bedroom.

He grabbed a condom out of the nightstand, and she swallowed hard, suddenly realizing they were really going to do this. They were going to make love to each other.

He gave her a questioning look.

She answered by stretching out on the bed, happy to see the relief in his eyes when he joined her. For a long minute his gaze ran down her body. She almost covered herself up with her hands, but she didn't want to hide from Aiden. She didn't want him to hide from her. She'd dreamed about this moment for half her life, and she wanted to see it, feel it, live it.

She pulled him down on top of her, loving the weight of his body on hers, the way his hard angles fit so well with her soft curves. He kissed her mouth again, the curve of her neck, the lobe of her ear, his mouth setting off every single nerve ending in her body. He didn't move fast, but there was deliberateness behind every movement, as if he knew exactly how to bring her to a quivering peak of need.

She ran her hands up and down his back, around his waist, cupping the long, hard length of him, hearing his groan of pleasure and feeling an incredible delight that she could make him happy. And she planned on making him even happier.

While a part of her wanted to savor every second, another part of her was urging her on. She wanted to get closer. She wanted Aiden inside her, all around her, so she cupped his buttocks and urged him forward. She was ready, more than ready, and when he slid inside of her, it was absolutely perfect, a feeling better than any she'd imagined.

He picked up the pace, moving inside her with purpose and intensity, the passion between them rising with each breath, each beat of her heart. Her breasts burned from the friction of his chest. And each time his mouth dipped for hers, she felt as if he were taking her to another realm of pleasure. It was too much and not enough all at the same time.

Aiden was right there with her, his husky voice caressing her name the same way he had in her dreams, his hands and body taking everything she had and giving even more in return. They hit the peak at the same time, crying out, holding on to each other, riding the wave back down until they were spent. He collapsed on top of her, and she held onto him, hoping she would never ever have to let him go.

→➤◄←

Aiden didn't move for at least five minutes. He loved the feel of Sara's body under his. He adored the sweet curve of her neck, the swirl of her silky hair against his body, the soft, full swell of her breasts. But he was probably crushing her, so he reluctantly slid onto his side. He propped himself up on one elbow so he could see her better.

Her face glowed in the moonlight, and the smile she gave him made his heart flip over. In that smile, he could see love. That scared him. It also for some strange reason made him feel really, really good.

It was just the great sex, he told himself. He'd seen glimpses of fire in Sara even when she was a shy teenager. Tonight, she hadn't held back a thing, and he'd loved seeing the passion rise in her eyes, feeling the frenzied, demanding movement of her hips. Just thinking about sliding between her legs again made him hard.

He had a feeling he could have her again and again, and it wouldn't be enough.

"Now you're the one who's thinking," Sara teased. "Usually, that's my department." Her smile grew a little wary when he didn't respond. A flash of her old insecurity tightened her expression. "What are you thinking about?"

"You," he said simply.

"In a good way?"

"A very, very good way."

Relief filled her gaze. "I thought it was amazing. Better than any of my fantasies about us."

"You had fantasies about me?"

"Since I was fourteen. You already knew that."

"I knew you had a crush; I didn't know it was X-rated."

"I've always had a big imagination."

He ran his fingers down her bare thigh, smiling into her eyes. "Why did you have a crush on me, Sara?"

"You have a mirror, don't you?" she asked dryly.

"So it was all physical?"

"You were nice to look at, but there was a lot more. I liked the way you stood up to bullies, the way you looked out for Emma and your family. Most of all, I admired your daredevil approach to life. You made me want to push my own boundaries, even though I was never quite brave enough to actually do it."

"That daredevil attitude has gotten me into a lot of trouble." He paused. "I think you saw me as better than I actually was."

"Well, that's what daydreams are for," she said lightly. "But tonight isn't about the past, or the future," she added hastily. "It's just about now—this moment. Tomorrow is another day."

He pushed a strand of hair off her face and smiled. "Tomorrow is still several hours away. You know I don't sleep much these days."

"I don't feel like sleeping either," she said, her hand slipping down the sheet between them. "Oh, my."

He smiled. "I have a few ideas on how we might pass the time. This time we'll go slow."

"You're going to kill me, aren't you?"

"I'm going to give it my best shot."

Eighteen

Sara woke up to the warmth of the sun on her face. She reached for Aiden, but he was gone. She rolled over, staring at the empty side of the bed. She felt a sudden wave of fear. She knew they would eventually go back to their separate lives, but she wasn't ready yet. It was too soon.

She slid out of bed and grabbed Aiden's robe off the back of the door. It was too big for her, but it was warm and cozy, and she felt like Aiden's arms were still around her. They'd made love three times, each time better than the last. She'd had sex before, but not this kind of mind-blowing, life-altering sex. No wonder Aiden was such a hit with the ladies.

She frowned, not wanting to put Aiden, sex and other women all in the same thought.

Walking out of the room, relief washed over her at the smell of coffee and the sound of Aiden's voice on the phone. He'd gotten out of bed, but he hadn't gone far.

He glanced up as she entered the living room, his expression tense. As she sat down on the couch, she wondered who he was talking to. It was obviously a serious conversation."

"Thanks," he said. "I'll wait to hear from you."

"Who was that?" she asked as he ended the call.

"Jeanne. She was able to obtain access to some of Kyle's

financial information—I'm not sure how, and I didn't ask."

"What did she discover?"

"A lot of debt. Kyle was drowning in it. His credit cards were maxed out. And the mortgage has a high interest rate because of their poor credit rating. Apparently, the only way they got the condo was because Vicky's parents came up with a thirty percent down payment. But Kyle was still going to face a stiff mortgage payment not to mention property taxes and homeowner association fees. He never should have agreed to buy that place. But Vicky fell in love with it, and he didn't want to say no to her."

"I wonder if that was because he felt guilty because he was having an affair or if the affair was because he was feeling super-stressed about his marital life."

"Or neither," he said, his mouth turning down in a frown. "I don't know that he was having an affair."

"Just offering a theory, Aiden. You know I'm not trying to paint Kyle in a bad light. I'm just trying to help you work through things."

"I know. I get it. And I can't have blinders on. Kyle wasn't a saint. I wouldn't have liked him if he was."

"The financial issues could be a reason for gambling, not having an affair," she said. "That was another one of your ideas."

"Jeanne hasn't found anything to support that." Aiden got to his feet and paced around the apartment. "I don't know why Kyle didn't tell me about his problems. I would have helped him. I would have loaned him money. I have some saved up, and I think he knew that."

"He might have been too proud to ask for help."

"There was a big life insurance policy," Aiden said a moment later. "Two hundred and fifty thousand dollars. They took out the policy after Robbie was born." He paused again, his gaze meeting hers. "I worry that Kyle was feeling desperate. And in that moment, in the blazing heat of that fire, he thought maybe he was worth more to his family dead than alive."

She sucked in a quick breath, not wanting to believe that any more than Aiden did.

Aiden sank down on the edge of the recliner, his eyes dark and filled with painful shadows. "I just don't want to believe that Kyle might have killed himself. But in my dreams, he heads straight into the fire, as if he knows exactly where he's going. There's no hesitation in his step. He never looks back." He let out a heavy sigh. "I should have seen that he was in trouble."

"You can't see what people don't want you to see," she said. "Kyle knew you were there. He chose not to involve you. We don't know why. Maybe out of respect for your long friendship, he didn't want to burden you with anything, not even perhaps his last decision. And," she added hastily, "we still don't know that's what happened."

"It's sure looking that way."

"What about the woman from the bar? Did Jeanne find out anything about her?"

"Not yet. She said she'd call me later today."

"Okay, so we don't have the whole story yet; let's not jump ahead to the end."

"Too late."

She gave him a compassionate smile, and knowing that he needed something to do, she said, "How about some breakfast? I wouldn't mind another one of your scrambles. I bought all the ingredients yesterday."

"Uh, sure. I could cook something up."

"Good." She checked the clock, realizing it was after nine. "Oh, my goodness. I didn't realize it was so late."

"It's not that late."

"It is in New York. It's noon. And I am not at work." She

was never late and she never took a day off unless she had a fever or was throwing up. People would be wondering where she was. "I need to call in."

"And say what?" he asked curiously. "If you need to get to an airport, I can take you, Sara. I don't want you to feel like you're stranded here."

"I don't feel that way." In fact, she really wasn't in any hurry to leave Redding. She felt relaxed for the first time in a long time. Logically, she knew it was a momentary escape, but that didn't matter. She was going to enjoy it for as long as she could. "I'm entitled to some days off. I'll just tell them I'm taking the time now."

Memories of their night together flashed through her head, and the sexy, intimate look in Aiden's eyes told her he was taking the same trip. There was no way she was saying goodbye to Aiden—not yet anyway.

"What's another day?" she added. "I was thinking you could show me around. We could even go on a hike. It looks like a nice day outside."

"I thought you didn't like nature."

"I said I'd never had the chance to see much of nature," she corrected. "Unless there's something else you need to do."

"I don't think there is. Jeanne seems to be on top of everything. Maybe I'll throw a tent and some sleeping bags into the truck. It's past time for a city girl like you to see some stars."

"I saw a few stars last night."

He grinned. "Baby, you ain't seen nothing yet. I'm going to grab a shower. Then I'll make you breakfast after you make your call."

Sara picked up her phone and punched in her boss's number. Garrett Robbins was in charge of the third-year attorneys, as they were called, and while he'd always been supportive of her career goals, Garrett was a tough taskmaster. He put in long weeks and expected the same from the people who worked for him.

"Sara, where are you?" he asked without bothering with a greeting.

"My father is in the hospital. There was an accident. I need to stay in San Francisco a while longer."

"How much longer?" he asked. "We just took on a big client, and I need you here."

"A week," she said. "At least."

"A week?" he asked, an incredulous note in his voice. "Are you serious?"

"My father is hurt, Garrett." She was annoyed that he hadn't asked her how her dad was doing.

"What happened to him?"

"He broke his leg. He needs help."

"Well, it doesn't sound like he's dying. Hire a nurse."

"That's a little heartless."

"Sorry, Sara, I'm just swamped. I didn't think you were even close to your father."

"That's not the point. I have time coming, Garrett. I'm going to take it."

"If you're not back by Thursday, I'll have no choice but to give this case to Mark."

Mark was her biggest competitor, and Garrett knew that. In fact, he often pitted them against each other.

"Thursday," he repeated. "Don't be late."

He hung up before she could say a word. She stared at the phone for a long minute. She hated the idea of Mark getting a big case over her, but it was difficult to drum up her usual indignation. Did it even matter if he got this case? There would always be another one, always another competition. That's the way the firm worked. The partners didn't want anyone to be comfortable. Comfortable equated lazy in their minds. Everyone had to be at the top of their game at all times.

She was exhausted just thinking about it. She needed the time off—for a lot of reasons, most of which had nothing to do with her father.

She set down the phone and stood up. As she moved toward the hall, she could hear Aiden's voice. He was singing in the shower. She listened to him belting out really bad lyrics in a very sexy voice. He was off key, but who the hell cared? Work was suddenly the furthest thing from her mind. If she was finally going to take some time off, she was going to make the most of it.

She turned the knob on the bathroom door, stripped off the robe, and surprised Aiden in mid-note.

"I want to sing, too," she told him, as she slipped inside the stall.

His soapy hands slid over her breasts, and he leaned in to kiss her, the hot water running over their heads as their bodies sang together in perfect harmony.

———

Two hours later, Sara and Aiden made it out of the apartment. After a long, steamy shower, they'd dressed, eaten breakfast and then packed an overnight bag. Aiden threw some camping gear into the back of the truck, just in case they decided to make a night of it. She hoped they would. Sleeping under the stars with Aiden sounded like something she definitely wanted to experience.

"You never told me what your boss said," Aiden commented as he drove down the highway.

"He gave me three days. If I'm not back by Thursday, he'll start giving my important cases away."

Aiden shot her a thoughtful look. "Are you sure you want to spend one of those three days hiking in the woods?"

"That's pretty much all I'm sure about right now." She turned her gaze out the window. "I can't believe this weather. It feels like summer."

"Nice day for a hike," he agreed.

"Where are we going?"

"To those hills over there. Kyle and I found a great spot to camp a couple of years ago." He let out a sigh. "I can't go anywhere around here without thinking about him."

"So let yourself think about him. You don't have to cut him out of your thoughts. I always hated that I had no one to talk to about my mom after she died. My dad had nothing to say. And after the funeral I was away at college, so most people I was with didn't even know my mom had died."

"That must have been rough. You were very alone, weren't you?"

"Yes, but I was used to it by then." She paused. "When I was talking to Lynda the other day, she mentioned how much she liked Valerie, and I thought it was the first time in a long time that someone actually said my mother's name out loud. It seems wrong that such a vibrant person could just disappear. I feel guilty that I don't talk more about her. I don't want the same thing to happen to you. Tell me about Kyle. You knew him the best of anyone."

"A month ago I would have agreed with you. Now I don't know."

"Don't let the doubts take over. Tell me something funny about him. You must have some great stories."

Aiden thought for a moment and then laughed. He glanced over at her. "Kyle got drunk one night and got a tattoo. It was supposed to be for his girlfriend, Lexy, but he was slurring his words so badly that when he came out of the tattoo parlor he had the word *Sexy* across his biceps. He took a hell of a lot of ribbing over that. We actually called him *Sexy* when we were on the job."

She smiled. "And how did he react?"

"He laughed. Kyle didn't take himself that seriously. At first he thought he'd try to get the tattoo changed, but eventually he got used to being *Sexy*. In fact, he thought it was a good icebreaker with the ladies."

"I'll bet it was. I always liked Kyle."

"But not as much as you liked me," he said with a cocky, sexy grin that reminded her of just how much she'd "liked" him earlier that morning.

"I'm never going to live down my crush, am I?" She tilted her head, giving him a thoughtful look. "Did you ever have a crush on a girl who didn't know you were alive?"

"Andrea Mills," he said immediately.

"Wow, you didn't have to think very long." A pang of foolish jealousy swept through her. She needed to get over that fast. She and Aiden were just having some fun. She could not start feeling like he was her boyfriend.

"I fell for Andrea in the sixth grade," he said. "I sat behind her in class, and most of the day I just stared at her long blonde hair and daydreamed about her."

"You were all about blondes, even from the beginning."

"Brunettes aren't so bad," he said lightly. "But you'll be happy to know that Andrea thought I was an idiot. I asked her to a dance, and she looked down her nose at me and said, 'Are you crazy?' And then she walked away, taking my busted ego with her."

"Aiden Callaway—shot down. So hard to believe."

"Isn't it?" he said with a laugh. "Andrea was a snooty rich girl, and I was not good enough for her. The Callaways were blue collar as far as she was concerned."

"And proud of it," she said.

"You bet."

"Andrea didn't know what she was missing."

"I doubt she gave me another thought. But I have to

admit her rejection stung."

He turned off the main highway, driving down a narrow, winding road into the hills.

"This is a lonely stretch," she commented a few minutes later. "We haven't seen a car in a long time."

"Summer is a more popular time up here, but I'm glad there's no one around. We'll have the woods all to ourselves." He glanced over at her. "I hope you'll have a good time. I know this isn't your usual thing."

"I'm looking forward to camping out. I'm beginning to see the depth of the rut I've been treading the last few years. It's amazing the perspective you get when you step away from your life for a while."

"Sometimes distance adds clarity." He paused. "Have you thought any more about the family secret you stumbled upon?"

She'd been trying really hard not to think about the secret her parents had kept. "Not really. When I think about all the lies, it makes me a little sick."

"Maybe when you speak to your father, his explanation will help you make sense of it all."

"I can't imagine that he'll even give me an explanation. I wish my mom were alive so I could ask her why she never told me about my brother. We were so close, Aiden. I just don't understand how she could keep something so big from me. And she never slipped, not once that I can recall. We had lots of conversations about my being an only child. It was something we had in common, because she was an only child, too. But it was a lie—I wasn't an only child. I had a brother. That feels so weird to say out loud."

"It's going to take some getting used to."

"It's unnatural for a family to hide a death like that. I can't imagine the steps they had to take. Now I know why they didn't have any long-time friends. They had to walk

away from anyone who knew about Stephen Davidson, Jr."
As she thought about their deception, an uneasy feeling crept
over her. "You don't think there was anything sinister about
my brother's death, do you?"

"Like what?"

"Well, I don't know how my brother died. He was four
years old. Was it an illness, an accident? Was someone to
blame? Did someone hurt him on purpose? Why was there a
need for a cover-up?"

"All good questions," he said somberly.

"Too bad I don't have any answers."

"We seem to be in short supply of those these days."

She gasped as the truck hit a big bump and reached out a
hand to the door to steady herself.

"Sorry," he said. "The road isn't paved from here on out."

"How far are we driving in?"

"Just a mile."

"I don't suppose there are any bathrooms out here,
either."

"We're roughing it," he said with a grin. "Trust me; you
will love it."

She'd been trusting him a lot lately; she had no reason to
stop now.

The road ran through some thick redwood forest. The
branches of the tall trees obliterated the sun in some instances
or created eerie rays of light. She felt like they were leaving
civilization behind. She was probably being dramatic. After
all, there was a road, even if it wasn't paved. But she was a
city girl, and she hadn't seen this many trees in a very long
time.

Eventually, Aiden parked the car off the side of the road.
"We hike in from here. I'll get the gear."

Faced with the isolation of their location, Sara felt a little
less sure of her decision to agree to camp overnight. They

were so isolated, and who knew what kind of animals ran through the woods at night? "

"Are there any bears out here?" she asked.

"Oh, yeah, lots of 'em," he said gleefully.

"Great."

He smiled. "Don't worry. I can take care of you."

"You can protect me from a bear?"

"I have wilderness skills, Sara. When we jump into a fire, we pack for at least thirty-six hours. Sometimes we're out in the forest for a week before we can hike our way out or get close enough to find transportation."

She shook her head, the reality of what he did amazing her the more she learned about it. "Isn't the forest on fire when you're in it?"

"We don't jump straight into the fire. We find a nearby location for the drop and then hike in. We try to get in before the fire gets too big to handle, but sometimes that doesn't happen."

"Are you ever scared?"

"All the time."

"But that's part of the fun, isn't it?"

"It's a rush unlike any other. But aside from all that, we protect land like this, and that's important. The world is getting too crowded."

"Having navigated Times Square on a summer day, I can definitely agree that the world can be too crowded."

"You're a long way from home, aren't you, Sara?"

She nodded.

"Are you scared?" he teased, repeating her earlier question.

She gazed into his eyes, a tingle running down her spine. She felt as if she was about to embark on an adventure. "I'm out of my element," she said. "But I'm up for the challenge."

"Good, because we're going to have some fun."

"So far you haven't let me down," she said. She grabbed a bag and they made their way into the forest.

Nineteen

Aiden led Sara through the woods, picking his path with unerring preciseness. He knew exactly where he wanted to take her. They ended up in a clearing next to a winding creek. "We can camp here," he said, setting down the gear.

"This is beautiful. And isolated."

He could hear the nervousness in her voice. "Do we need anybody else?"

"No, but it's very quiet out here, and it's a little spooky."

"I don't think you're listening very well." He moved across the clearing and put his hands on her shoulders. "Close your eyes."

"Why?"

"No questions, Sara. Just do it."

"Fine." She obediently closed her eyes.

"Now, listen for a minute, and then tell me what you hear."

She breathed in and out, her eyes closed, her expression contemplative. Sara liked tests. She liked to pass tests, and he sensed that she would do her best to tune in to the world around her.

"Water running over the rocks like a sweet melody," she said a moment later. "Birds squawking. I can picture them flying across the sky. The wind rustling the branches of the trees." She paused. "And you, breathing."

She opened her eyes, and smiled. "How did I do?"

"Very good."

"Thank you for making me take the time, Aiden."

"You're welcome. Nature has its own soundtrack."

"It's running through me now." She glanced around. "So, do we set up the tents? Take a hike? I hope there's food in that cooler. I forgot to ask what you got at the store."

"All the essentials and some nonessentials. We can set up later. Let's take a walk first."

"Will our stuff be okay here?"

"We're good."

"It's strange to think that there might be no one around us for miles."

"I prefer to think of that as a great possibility."

"In New York, you can't turn around without bumping into someone. I think that's why everyone is so tense all the time. They need more personal space."

"I know I would," he said.

As they walked a trail he'd taken many times before in his life, Aiden found himself appreciating the fact that he wasn't on his own this time. It was fun to share this world with Sara, to introduce her to a new experience, an experience she was embracing with open arms. He liked how she'd blossomed since her teenage years. She was so much brighter now, assertive, confident, adventurous and funny. She had a dry wit, and she didn't take herself as seriously as he would have thought.

His heart twisted a bit more as he watched Sara skip ahead to pick a wildflower. She held it up to her face, inhaling the scent, and something inside of him turned over. It was a sweet yet sensual moment, which was exactly the way he saw her.

Making love to her had been both passionate and tender.

They'd fit together so perfectly. There hadn't been an awkward moment. Everything had seemed exactly right. He could still taste her on his mouth, still feel her body under his and hear the breathy sound of his name on her lips.

It had been a great night, and he was in big trouble…

No matter what she said about casual, no strings, no promises, he knew they were getting too close. He just couldn't bring himself to push her away again. If he did, it would probably save them both some pain. They were very different people, and they were both in a vulnerable place. He didn't know what he was doing with his life, where he'd be working or living next year.

Sara was reeling now because of the secrets she'd learned about her family, but there was probably a good chance that she would go back to New York in the end and return to the life she'd spent so much time building.

Shaking his head, he tried to stop thinking about the future. It would get here soon enough. He picked up his pace, realizing they were almost to his favorite spot, and he wanted to see Sara's face when she saw it.

A moment later, they moved around a bend, and Sara stopped abruptly. Her gaze was full of wonder as she took in the shimmering waterfall, the clear blue pool surrounded by rocks and boulders, the tall trees framing the sweetest picture she'd ever seen.

She turned to him with excitement in her brown eyes. "It's beautiful, Aiden—a secret pool, a secret waterfall. I love it. It's magical."

She was magical, he thought. Because she was stirring up feelings in him that he hadn't thought existed.

"With the sun streaming through the trees, it's like a beacon from heaven pointing right here," she added. "Is the waterfall singing or is it an angel?"

He grinned. "You don't sound much like a hard-headed

lawyer now."

She smiled back at him with joy in her gaze. "How can I be cynical in a place like this?" She knelt down and ran her hand through the water. "It's not as cold as I thought."

"It's pretty shallow. The sun warms it up," he replied, adding, "I'm glad you don't think it's too cold." He kicked off his shoes and slid off his socks, putting them on a nearby rock.

"What are you doing?" she asked warily as he pulled his T-shirt over his head.

"Going swimming."

"It's November," she said, standing up.

"It's California and it's warm. Why don't you join me for a swim?"

"I didn't bring a suit."

He took off his jeans. "So?"

"Oh," she said, a lot of yearning and excitement in that small word.

"If you're going to be in nature, you might as well go native."

"Really, Aiden?" She glanced over her shoulder. "What if someone comes by?"

"We're all alone, Sara."

"You say that now, but I'm afraid I'll strip down and some park ranger is going to show up. That is usually the way my luck goes."

He laughed. "That won't happen, but if it did, you'd have a good story to tell."

"That's true. I've never really had a good story to tell. A couple of weeks ago I was at a bar with some girlfriends, and everyone told their most daring, risqué story. I had nothing to add. It was sad."

"Skinny dipping in broad daylight might be a good start to a story." He stepped out of his boxers and set them on the rock.

She stared at him with lustful appreciation, and his body responded in kind; time for a dip in the cold water.

He jumped into the pool. It was cold but refreshing. "Come on in, the water is fine," he drawled.

"Isn't that what the spider said to the fly?" she asked, hovering on the edge of the pool.

"I have no idea, but I can tell that you want to join me."

"You're such a bad influence."

"Bad or maybe good," he suggested. "Come on, Sara. It's not like I haven't seen everything. And believe me, I have liked everything I've seen."

Even from several yards away, he could see the delightful red flush of her cheeks.

"Okay," she said, finally giving in to temptation. "But don't watch me."

"Sorry, can't agree to that." He enjoyed watching her strip and was even more pleased when she took off her bra and panties. He'd thought she might have left them on.

She waded into the pool, squealing from the cold, her arms wrapped around her breasts. "It's not as warm as I thought."

"Just keep going. It gets better." He paddled across the pool and wrapped his arms around her as they sank down in the water. "Let me warm you up." He lowered his head and kissed her, loving her little sigh of delight, the way she melted into his arms. He was fast becoming addicted to her. The pleasure of holding her was unfortunately followed by a terrifying fear that he might be falling for her. But this wasn't the time for thinking. They were living in the moment. And today in this beautiful pool with the sun shining brightly on his head, he was determined to make the most of this moment.

"This is a first for me," Sara said, lying on the soft grass next to the pool, her head on Aiden's chest, her leg over his, the heat of the sun toasting her skin, making her feel warmer than she had in years. It wasn't just the sunshine heating her blood; it was Aiden. He'd chipped away the layer of ice that had surrounded her heart for a very long time, so long she couldn't remember when the freeze had begun.

Maybe when she was a little girl. Maybe when she first realized that her father didn't like her, much less love her. Maybe it was when Aiden had rejected her.

She raised her head to look at him.

His eyes were closed, and his expression was happy, peaceful. She'd given him that much, she thought. He might not want love from her, but he wouldn't go away empty-handed.

"You're staring at me," he said.

She was staring. She could look at him forever, but she knew that forever wasn't going to happen, so she planned on savoring these very special minutes. She liked the way his thick eyebrows arched over his eyes, the sweep of his long black lashes against his cheek, the slightly crooked turn to his nose, a nose that had been broken by one of his brothers a long time ago. His jaw was strong, his lips and mouth oh, so sensual. Her breath caught in her chest as she realized not only was she back in her mad crush, it was even worse this time around.

She knew him better now. He wasn't just some romantic ideal. She connected with him on a lot of levels, understood his need to prove himself not only as a Callaway but also apart from the rest of them. She admired his loyalty to friends and family. She envied his courage, his zest for adventure… Saying goodbye was going to hurt.

She couldn't think about that now. Maybe later.

Aiden's lids fluttered open. He smiled at her. "What's on your mind?"

"Nothing," she lied.

"Really? You look a little more tense than you did earlier."

"I'm getting chilly. We should get dressed."

"You first," he said. "And take your time getting to your clothes. I like to watch."

She shook her head, a blush crossing her cheeks. "I am nowhere near as uninhibited as you."

"Seeing you now, that's hard to believe."

She sat up, crossing her arms in front of her breasts. "I got caught up in the moment."

"So did I."

"You're a bad influence."

"Or a good one," he suggested. "When is the last time you went skinny dipping?"

"Uh, let's see—never," she said.

"You were missing out."

"Apparently, I was. How many times have you swum here in the buff?"

"About three dozen," he said.

"And here I thought I was special." She felt a little disappointed by his answer.

He rolled onto his side and propped himself up on one elbow. Then he reached out to tuck a strand of hair behind her ear. His gaze was tender when he said, "You are special, Sara. I've never been here with anyone else. I've always been alone."

"I'm sure you could have had company if you wanted it."

"I never felt like sharing this spot—until now."

There was a seriousness in his eyes that made her heart skip a beat, but she didn't want to get ahead of herself, didn't want to read feelings into his words, feelings that might not be real. "I'm glad you shared the pool with me."

"I am, too. Now, go on, get dressed."

She got to her feet and walked across the grass to get her clothes. Aiden followed, and they quickly dressed.

"We should go back and get camp set up before it starts to get dark," Aiden said.

"And maybe open up that cooler. All this fresh air makes me hungry."

He laughed and stole a quick kiss. "You make me hungry, Sara, and I'm not talking about food."

She made a face at him. "Not a good line, Aiden."

"Really? I thought it was one of my better ones." He swung an arm around her shoulders, and they headed down the trail.

When they reached their campsite, Aiden put up a small tent while Sara sliced some cheese and put crackers on a plastic plate. She spread out a blanket and then sat down to enjoy her afternoon picnic. She couldn't remember feeling this relaxed in a very long time. Worries about work and her father nudged at the back of her brain, but she refused to start thinking about her problems now.

They spent the rest of the afternoon being lazy, talking about everything under the sun: movies, books, sports, politics and religion. They'd both gone to Catholic school, both spent time in church in their childhood and teenage years, but neither one of them had really kept up the practice of Sunday Mass.

"I do miss church sometimes," she told him. "Not so much for the formal teachings but for the sense of community, the familiar, reassuring repetitions that cut through the chaos of life. What about you?"

"I like that part of it, too. But the rest—I don't know. I'm not that big on organized religion, but don't tell anyone in my family I said that. I've got an uncle that's a priest and a second cousin that's a nun."

"I remember your uncle, or as we called him—Father Mike," she said with a warm smile. "He was the nicest priest at St. Andrew's. He used to play basketball at recess with you and your brothers."

"I think Uncle Mike was about thirty then," Aiden said. "He's seventeen years younger than my father, so he was almost closer in age to me than to my dad."

"He was kind and funny. When I went to confession, I was always hoping he was the one in the confessional."

"As if you ever had anything to confess," he said dryly.

"True." She paused. "I wonder what Father Mike has heard from your family over the years."

"I can't even imagine."

"It seems like it would be a burden to keep everyone's secrets."

"Probably. I never thought about it like that."

"I wonder if my mom told him her secrets. It seems like she would have had to talk to someone. I can see my father locking it inside and throwing away the key. But my mom must have had moments of pain, flashes of memory, especially after I was born. How could she not relive those early years? Baby's first birthday, baby's first Christmas— wouldn't she have been thinking about little Stephen then?"

"That would be logical," he said.

"Now you sound like my father."

"Please don't ever say that again."

She smiled. "Don't worry. I would never compare the two of you. You're very, very different."

"Thank you."

"So when is the last time you saw Father Mike?"

"A long time ago," he answered.

"Do you think it might be good for you to talk to him

about Kyle?" she asked.

"Possibly," he conceded. "I hadn't considered the idea, but he's a good man."

"A good man who can keep secrets." She paused for a moment. "Maybe he knows what secret your grandmother was talking to you about."

Aiden frowned at the reference to his grandmother. "I'm sure her rambling was just the result of old age and confusion."

"So you don't believe there are any skeletons in the Callaway closet?"

"After what you discovered in your basement the other day, I couldn't possibly make that claim, but as far as I know, there's no big, dark secret."

"I think I'm ready to talk to my father now. Well, not now; tomorrow will be fine."

"Good, I was afraid you were going to ask me to drive you back to San Francisco tonight."

"No way. The sun is going down, and I want to see those amazing stars you promised me." She also wanted to spend another night with Aiden, because it was quite possible it would be their last night together before reality returned to their lives.

While waiting for the stars to come out, they ate sandwiches and drank wine, laughed and talked and enjoyed each other's company. When twilight turned to night, they rolled onto their backs and stared up at the most beautiful starlit sky that Sara had ever seen.

Aiden showed her the constellations, telling her stories that were half fact, half myth. She was astonished by the depth of his knowledge and reminded again how much he appreciated the world around him, a world she'd barely noticed until now.

Just before midnight, they crawled into the tent, made

love, and then fell asleep in each other's arms.

Sara woke up in the middle of the night. Aiden was tossing and turning, his breath coming fast, his legs kicking at the sleeping bag that covered them.

"Stop," he yelled.

"Aiden, it's okay. You're dreaming."

She put her hand on his chest. He shoved her away, his eyes flying open. He stared at her as if he'd never seen her before.

"You were dreaming," she repeated, trying to get him to wake up.

Awareness slowly seeped into his gaze. "Sara?"

She nodded. "It's me. We're camping, remember?"

He shoved a hand through his sweaty hair, his breathing starting to calm. "What did I say?"

"You yelled *stop*. Were you dreaming about the day of the fire again?"

"Yes. It's always the same. I'm running after Kyle, but I can't catch him. I'm yelling after him, but he just keeps going. And then everything goes black." Aiden let out a frustrated breath. "I want to see what's behind the curtain, but I always wake up before I can."

"Maybe there's nothing to see," she said gently. "You fell down a hill. You were knocked out. It's possible you just don't know anything else. And if that's the case, you will have to find a way to live with it. Kyle wouldn't want you to be haunted like this. He would want you to let go, to move forward. He was your best friend, Aiden. He wouldn't want you to be in this pain. And you know that's true, because if the positions were reversed, you wouldn't want him to hurt the way you're hurting now." She brushed the hair off his face and gave him a warm smile. "Life is going to go on. Someday the pain will ease."

Aiden pulled her back into his arms and whispered

against her hair, "I'm glad you're here, Sara."

"Me, too."

She wished they could stay this way forever, but forever was probably only going to last until the morning.

Twenty

Sara poked her head out of the tent just after eight o'clock on Tuesday morning. Aiden was already up. He was fully dressed and sitting on a rock by the creek, staring into the ripples of water. His expression was contemplative, but he didn't look as agitated as he had the night before.

When he saw her, he smiled and said, "Good morning, Sleepyhead."

She scrambled out of the tent and walked over to him. "I didn't hear you leave."

"You were sleeping so peacefully I didn't want to wake you." He paused. "Sorry about last night."

"You're not responsible for your nightmares. Although you could be sorry about that big rock you set up the tent on. It was right in the middle of my back."

"Sorry, Princess. I'll do better next time."

"How are you feeling today?"

"I'm hungry," he grumbled.

"Me, too, but I think we're out of food. And don't try to talk me into any survivalist ideas. I'm not in the mood to eat a grasshopper or pretend ants are a good source of protein."

"They actually can be very nutritious."

"I'll take your word for it."

"Well, I was thinking more about pancakes. There's a

great restaurant on the way back into town. It has the best blueberry pancakes you've ever had in your life."

She raised an eyebrow at his enthusiasm. "Sounds great. I hope it lives up to your hype."

"It will. Let's get packed up."

As Aiden took down the tent, she gathered the rest of their things together, feeling a little sad that their trip was over, but she couldn't hide out in the wilderness forever. Real life was waiting.

"Thanks for bringing me here," she told Aiden as they loaded up the truck. "I had a great time."

"Me, too," he said, smiling into her eyes. "I guess there was a country girl hiding under all that city soot."

"I guess so."

He gave her a kiss that felt a lot like goodbye, but she tried not to take it that way. They still had some time together. Goodbye would come soon enough.

Fifteen minutes after leaving the mountains, Aiden pulled into the parking lot of the pancake house. There was a good crowd, but they managed to snag a table without a wait.

After ordering her meal, Sara headed to the restroom. She hadn't been so happy to see a public restroom in her life. It was nice to wash her hands and face and run a brush through her hair. She didn't have any makeup with her, but she didn't really need it. There was a glow to her skin and a light in her eyes that she didn't recognize. She was used to seeing a weary reflection in the mirror, stressed eyes and mouth, pale skin, and tangles in her hair that came from twisting the strands while she worked out some long, thorny problem.

The woman she saw in the mirror now looked more like the girl she used to be, and that had a lot to do with Aiden. He was bringing back her old self, and she liked the change. Whether or not her old self would be able to survive in New

York was another question.

When she returned to the table, there were coffee and juice waiting, as well as a huge stack of blueberry pancakes. Aiden had added some eggs to his pancake order, and their table was overflowing with food, but somehow they managed to finish it all.

"I just gained five pounds," she said, rubbing her very full stomach as she sat back in her seat. "But the pancakes were worth it."

"I told you they would be."

As the busboy cleared the table, she felt the pressure of the ticking clock. "I need to get back to San Francisco, Aiden."

His smile faded, his expression turning serious. "I know. You need to speak to your dad. Are you ready?"

"Probably not, but it has to be done."

"You'll be okay," he said, a gleam of admiration in his eyes. "You have a core of strength inside of you, Sara. It got you through a cold childhood, your mother's death, your dad's distance, and it will get you through this."

"Thank you, Aiden." His confident words made her eyes tear up, and she lowered her gaze, not wanting him to see how he'd affected her. She couldn't be an emotional girl around him. She'd promised she wouldn't be. It was all supposed to be light, casual, fun.

After paying the bill, they returned to Aiden's apartment. He wanted to grab a few more things to take back to the city. A moment later, his phone rang. "Jeanne," he muttered as he took the call.

While he was talking, he paced around the living room. At one point, he stopped by a side table, pulled out a notepad and jotted something down. Sara hoped he was finally getting some information, but she couldn't tell. His side of the conversation was very abbreviated. She heard him mention a couple of names like Sandra Ellingston and Becky Saunders. Hopefully, Jeanne had discovered what kind of connection the women had had with Kyle.

"Thanks," Aiden said finally, and then closed his phone. His jaw was tight, his eyes a flinty blue. He met her questioning gaze and said, "Sandra Ellingston is a doctor here in town. She's in a long-term relationship with a woman, so there's no way she and Kyle were having an affair."

"Oh, well, I guess that's good news." She wondered why he didn't look happier.

"Is it good? He was seeing a doctor for something."

"It could have been as simple as a flu shot. What's her specialty?"

"She's an ear, nose and throat doctor," he said.

"Well, that doesn't sound so serious. Maybe he had allergies."

"I never heard him mention any. But what's also interesting is that Becky Saunders is a nurse."

She stared at him, her stomach beginning to churn. "That's a coincidence."

"I don't believe in coincidence."

"Do you think Kyle was sick?"

"He never showed a sign of being ill. But he did take a few days off about six weeks ago. He told me he was helping Vicky move into their new place in San Francisco, but Jeanne said that she found credit card charges in the Los Angeles area for that same weekend. Kyle spent time at a place called The Healing Sun. The facility specializes in holistic medicine, acupuncture, massage and stress therapy, as well as osteopathy. No one at the center would provide information as to whether or not Kyle was there or what he was there for."

Silence followed his words as they both pondered the possibilities.

"Aiden, you need to talk to Vicky again," she said. "If

Kyle was sick, she had to know."

"Maybe not. He could have kept it a secret from her, too. There were certainly no outward signs of an illness." He let out a frustrated breath. "Damn. Every time I get an answer, I end up with more questions. I doubt I can even get Vicky to talk to me again."

"What about Becky? She might speak to you. Now that you have more information, you'll be able to ask better questions."

He nodded. "You're right. I'll start with Becky. Jeanne gave me her phone number."

As he reached for his phone, she said, "Can you put on the speaker? I'd like to hear what she has to say, too."

"Sure." He punched in a number.

A woman answered. "Hello?"

"Becky?" he asked. "It's Aiden Callaway."

"Aiden," she said, a resigned note in her voice. "I had a feeling you were going to call me."

"You started to say something the other night, something about Kyle. I need to know what he was talking to you about."

"I'm sorry, Aiden, but my conversations with Kyle were private."

"Was he sick, Becky?" Aiden's blunt words brought a long silence. "Becky?"

"Kyle asked me not to tell anyone," she said finally.

"Tell anyone what? Becky, please. I need to know what was going on with Kyle. He was my best friend. You know that better than anyone."

Sara could hear the anguished plea in Aiden's voice. She thought Becky might cave, but a second later, she apologized again.

"I'm sorry, Aiden. I made a promise to Kyle. I didn't always keep my promises to him, but I'm going to keep this one. Please don't call me again."

Aiden uttered a protest, but the dial tone made it clear that Becky was not going to help them.

"I shouldn't have done this over the phone," he said. "If I saw her in person, I could probably make her talk."

"I don't think so, Aiden. Becky seems determined to keep Kyle's confidence."

"A great time for her to develop a conscience," he said sarcastically. "Becky was breaking promises right and left in high school."

"This isn't high school. You're going to have to talk to Vicky."

"She'll more than likely slam the door in my face."

"Only one way to find out." She got to her feet, aware that they both needed to have difficult conversations. "San Francisco, here we come—ready or not."

On the four-hour drive back to San Francisco, Sara used her phone to search the Internet. Before she spoke to her father, she wanted to see if she could find any more information on her brother or her parents during the time period that they'd been together.

As she typed in her brother's name, it hit her again that he had been named for their father. When little Stephen died, her dad must have felt like he was losing himself.

Was that what had happened? Had her father simply given up, gone through the motions of life with no warmth, no love, no happiness? It made sense. But she couldn't help wondering why her own birth hadn't changed things for him, hadn't brought him out of that depression and made him want to be a father again.

Her mother had found joy in having another child. At

least, it had felt that way. Doubts crept into her mind that anything she'd believed in was actually true.

Tired of her own problems, she started searching for more information on Kyle. She put in his name, wondering what would show up. To her surprise, she found a training video for smokejumpers.

"Look at this," she said, holding up the phone for Aiden. "It's you and your team suiting up for a jump. You're famous."

"That was taken at the beginning of last fire season. I was trying to be professional in front of the rookies, and half the team was heckling me. Kyle was the worst. He never seemed to be paying attention. I'd have to ask him three times to do something. He really pissed me off that day. When I told him how annoying he was, he just laughed and told me to chill out. He said I used to be a lot more fun before I became the boss."

"Was Kyle jealous of your position?"

"Possibly," Aiden admitted. "But once Kyle got married and had a baby, his priorities were split. Mine weren't. I could give the job a hundred and fifty percent all the time. It made sense for me to get the promotion instead of him. It wasn't that I was better than him. I was just more present, more committed."

"That makes sense. I'm always afraid to take time off work because there are people just waiting to take my place if I slip even a little bit."

"I didn't feel that kind of pressure from Kyle. I was just doing the job the only way I knew how, and that's by putting everything I have into it. I've always been that way. It wasn't about titles."

"No, it was about being good, being the best. You were always more of a high achiever than Kyle. I'm not saying anything bad against him. He was great, but he didn't have your intensity. You shouldn't feel guilty for being promoted. You should be proud of yourself. You were good and you were rewarded for it."

"I doubt too many people think I'm good now."

"Because they don't know the whole story. We're still trying to figure that out."

She turned her attention on the video, interested to see Aiden in action, and she was impressed. He spoke clearly and decisively, and he had the attention of everyone on the plane. As she watched the men jump, she felt as if she were right there with them.

Aiden was the last one to step into the open doorway. She caught her breath as he jumped into the sky. Seeing him actually take that leap was incredibly exciting. "Wow," she said. "I can't believe I just watched you jump out of a plane." She set down her phone and looked at him. "What are you going to do, Aiden? It's clear you love your job. You can't quit."

"I love parts of it, Sara. But it's a grueling job, and it's seasonal. To be honest, I've been thinking about making a change for a while now. I thought I'd figure out my next step during the off-season. I didn't foresee that the decision of whether or not to go or stay would be taken out of my hands."

"It hasn't come to that."

"It might. Who knows what the future holds?"

She settled back in her seat, watching the landscape fly by and foolishly wondering if he'd consider firefighting in New York City. But she couldn't picture him there. She wasn't sure she even pictured herself there anymore. All too soon, they ran into the Tuesday afternoon commute through Berkeley and over the Bay Bridge. When they hit the city, it was five o'clock and already starting to get dark.

Aiden gave her a questioning glance. "Where to? The hospital?"

"Not yet," she said.

He raised an eyebrow. "Second thoughts?"

"No. But I want to stop by my house and get the photographs first. I doubt my father will confess without being confronted with proof."

"So, we'll go home then."

"I have a better idea. Let's go to Vicky's. It's almost dinnertime, and you have a good chance of catching her at home."

He sighed. "I need to talk to her, but I don't want to hurt her. She's in a lot of pain right now. I'm not sure this is the best time to press her for information."

"Waiting won't change anything. This pain isn't going away for a long time. But your career is in jeopardy now, and Vicky might be able to answer your questions. Maybe she'll remember that you used to be good friends."

"I'm not going to hold my breath on that."

"If you're worried about me tagging along, don't be. I'm happy to wait in the car."

"You can come with me," he said. "I have no idea how Vicky will react to my presence, and it's quite possible I might need a lawyer."

Twenty-One

Aiden was happy to have Sara's company when he rang Vicky's buzzer. His last visit had not gone well. He hoped this one would go better.

When Vicky answered the intercom, he said, "It's Aiden; I need to speak to you."

"I asked you not to come back, Aiden."

"It's important. Really important."

Silence followed and then finally the sound of a buzzer. They were over the first hurdle.

Vicky stood in the doorway, just as she had done the last time, but today Robbie was in her arms. The little boy was crying, and Vicky looked like she'd been crying as well. Her eyes and nose were red, her skin was pale and she didn't look like she'd brushed her hair in a few days.

"I told you this was a bad time," she said, trying to bounce Robbie into a good mood, but the little boy kept crying. "Who's this?" She tipped her head toward Sara.

"This is Sara," he said. "She's a friend. She went to school with Kyle and me."

Vicky barely glanced at Sara. "I need to feed Robbie. Make it fast."

"It's not going to be fast. Why don't I hold Robbie while you get his bottle?"

She hesitated, but as Robbie screamed louder, she must have decided the offer of help was too good to resist. She handed her son into his arms and then left the room.

Sara closed the door behind them as they moved further into the living room.

He stared down at the little boy who looked so much like Kyle that his heart actually ached. "Hey, buddy," he said in a soothing voice. "Dinner is coming."

Robbie's cries diminished as he stared at Aiden in fascination. His chubby little hands cupped Aiden's face. It was the sweetest touch he'd ever felt. He loved this kid, loved him as much as he'd ever loved Kyle, because Robbie was Kyle's son.

"You have the magic touch," Sara said, watching him with a warm smile.

"I did a lot of babysitting when I was younger." He shifted Robbie in his arms. "He's so big now. He's grown a lot in the last month. I really want to help Vicky take care of him." He paused. "I don't want to get in the way. I just want to be there for her and for Robbie. I owe Kyle that. He was my brother in every sense of the word. I was there when Kyle first fell in love with Vicky. I stood up for him at his wedding. I was the first one he called when he found out Vicky was pregnant. He was so happy, Sara. It was the most amazing joy I'd ever seen on his face. And when Robbie was born, Kyle was in complete and utter awe. I watched my best friend go from being a single guy to a man deeply in love, committed to his family. I feel like Robbie and Vicky are part of my family, too. We spent so much time together. I hate that the friendship we have is over. I can't stand the thought of not being able to watch this little guy grow up."

When he finished speaking, he realized Vicky had returned to the room. She was staring at him, tears streaming down her face. He'd hurt her again.

"I'm sorry," he said, knowing that no number of apologies would probably make a difference, but it was all he had to offer. "I wish I could bring Kyle back to you. I wish he could be here to hold his son, to hold you. I can see how much pain you're in, and I just want to help you."

"I'm sorry, too," she said shakily. "You just reminded me of everything I'd forgotten. I didn't want to see you because I knew it would make the pain worse, because we were like a family and you and Kyle were so damn close. When I see you, I see him. But you're not him, and you're in pain, too. And up until this minute, I just refused to acknowledge that fact. It was easier to blame you, to hate you, but it was wrong." She brought the bottle over and slipped it into Robbie's mouth, but she made no attempt to take her son out of his arms. "Kyle would hate the way I've been treating you. He would be so angry with me if he knew that I'd kept you away from his funeral."

Her eyes pleaded with him for understanding. "I'm angry, too. I lost my best friend. And it's frustrating as hell not to have someone to blame for it."

"When Ray Hawkins said his brother told him you were responsible for Kyle's death, I just snapped. I remembered all the times you promised to bring Kyle home safe. Ray said everyone knew you were pushing too hard, taking too many chances, and it wasn't that difficult to believe, because that's the kind of man you are." She took a breath. "But I shouldn't have listened to Ray, because I know Kyle was not a big fan of Ray's brother, Dave." Her gaze filled with guilt and regret. "Your leadership wasn't a negative for Kyle. He told me many times that you inspired him to be better than he ever thought he could be. When people would criticize you in his presence, he would jump to your defense. He would tell them that nobody was better, and they were lucky to work with you."

His heart ripped apart at her words. The past few months he'd felt a break in his friendship with Kyle, and he'd thought it might have had something to do with Kyle having to work under his command.

"I know that you wouldn't have let Kyle die if you could have prevented it," Vicky continued. "I know how much you loved him. I never should have blamed you. I wish I could take it back. It wasn't fair to you."

Hearing Vicky say the words meant more to him than anything. "Nothing about this situation is fair. Kyle should be alive right now." He gazed down at Robbie, who was drifting asleep. He didn't want just answers for himself but also for Robbie, because some day this little boy would grow up and want to know what happened to his father.

"So you said you had something important to tell me," Vicky said.

"Not to tell you, but to ask you. I have some questions, and I feel like you're the only one who might be able to answer them."

"I'll try."

"I need to know what was going on in Kyle's head the day of the fire," he said, hoping she was more in a mood to help now. "I told you before that he was distracted, that he had been for weeks. I thought it was the fact that you were gone, that he was missing you, but I think there may have been something else going on." He paused, wondering how to ask the question, but this was no time to be vague. He looked her straight in the eye, wanting to see her reaction when he said, "Was Kyle sick?"

Her jaw dropped and he saw nothing but genuine surprise in her expression. "No, he wasn't sick. What are you talking about?"

"He was seeing a doctor in Redding. Her name is Sandra Ellingston. He was also in communication with a woman named Becky Saunders, who is a nurse. In addition, about six weeks ago, he went to L.A. and spent time at a holistic healing center."

"I don't understand," she said in confusion. "Kyle wouldn't have gone to Los Angeles without telling me. And it was fire season. He didn't have that kind of time off."

"He took a long weekend. He told me he was helping you get settled."

"He wasn't here, Aiden."

"And he never mentioned not feeling well?"

"No." She tilted her head, lost in thought for a moment. "There was so much going on, it's possible I wasn't paying close enough attention."

"I wonder if Kyle's computer would be helpful," Sara said.

He turned his head. She'd been so quiet, he'd almost forgotten she was there.

"There might be clues in his email," she added. "Or receipts in his files."

"Do you have Kyle's computer?" he asked Vicky.

"It's in a box in the closet. Our former landlord shipped me Kyle's stuff after his death."

"Would you mind if I took a look, Vicky?"

"I guess not," she said slowly. Her brows knit into a frown. "I don't want to think my husband had any secrets, Aiden. He didn't seem like that kind of a man."

"Not to me either, but things aren't adding up, and I can't stop looking for answers, Vicky. I can't sleep at night. I have dreams of Kyle walking into the fire. I just have to know if I missed something."

"All right. Follow me." She led them into the hall and opened a closet where several boxes were stacked up. "It should be in the top box," she said, taking a now sleepy Robbie out of Aiden's arms. "His email is through Yahoo, his

ID is kdunne and his password is sexyguy12; that damn tattoo strikes again," she said dryly. "I'm going to put Robbie down for a nap."

As Vicky left the room, Aiden opened the box, relieved to see Kyle's laptop computer. He took it into the living room and set it up on the coffee table. Sara sat down next to him and gave him an encouraging look.

"Here goes," he said, as he turned on the computer and opened Kyle's email.

He didn't know what he was looking for, and the first few emails seemed to be nothing important. In fact, there was a lot of junk mail that had come in since Kyle's death. But as he went back a few weeks, he found an email from Becky. "I hope you found the clinic helpful," he read aloud. "If you didn't, I have some other recommendations. I think you should talk to your wife, Kyle. I know you don't want her to know, but this problem isn't going to just go away. And it's going to affect a lot more people than just you."

"What problem?" Sara murmured.

"Whatever he went to the clinic to get help with," Aiden said, his gut churning. He continued down the list of emails. There was nothing else from Becky.

"Look in his search history," Sara suggested. "When people are sick, they often look on the Internet for answers. Let me help," she added, taking over the keyboard. "Here's a list of the most recent websites he visited. One is the clinic." She paused, running her finger down the entries. "Look at these sites, Aiden. They're all on the same topic."

A pain burned in his gut. Every one of the sites had something to do with hearing—hearing loss, hearing aids, diagnosing ear problems, ringing in the ears. It suddenly all made sense. All the times Kyle didn't seem to be paying attention, the times he'd asked Aiden to repeat what he'd just said. And the recurring dream fit, too—Kyle walking away from him, never looking back. Kyle hadn't heard him. He hadn't been ignoring him. He just couldn't hear. The fire had been too damn loud!

Fury followed the realization. Why hadn't Kyle told anyone that he was suffering from hearing loss? Why had he put his life in jeopardy—and not just *his* life but everyone else's, too?

He jerked to his feet. "Damn, Damn, Damn."

"What did you find?" Vicky asked. She entered the room with worried eyes. "Was Kyle sick? Did he…" She stumbled, searching for words that he knew she did not want to say.

"No, he didn't kill himself," he said.

"Are you sure?" she asked, relief in her voice.

"Yes. We'll need to do more research to know everything, but judging from what I've seen here and what I know, I believe Kyle had a hearing problem."

"What? Why would you say that?"

"The doctor he went to see was an ENT, an ear, nose and throat specialist. The nurse was an old friend of Kyle's from high school. She told me that he'd sought her out, and I couldn't think of any reason why he would have done that. She also said that she couldn't tell me what Kyle's medical issues were, but she had told him to tell you about his problem." Aiden pointed to the computer. "And she did that in an email to Kyle. We also went through his search history. Kyle spent the last month of his life researching hearing loss and hearing aids. Why would he do that if he didn't have a problem? It's not definitive, but when you put all the pieces together…"

Vicky sank down on a nearby chair, as if she no longer had the strength to stand up. Surprise in her eyes had been replaced with a more thoughtful gleam. "I went into the bathroom one day a few weeks after Robbie was born. Kyle was staring in the mirror, an odd look in his eyes. He asked me if I ever heard ringing in my ears. I said no. I think I was about to ask him if he had a problem when Robbie started crying. Kyle never mentioned it again." She paused. "If he had a problem, why wouldn't he tell me?"

"You had a newborn, and you were stressed out. I'm guessing he didn't want to worry you. He was very protective of you."

"He was," she said, her eyes watering again. "I dated some real losers before him. Kyle was like a knight in shining armor. I don't think I appreciated him enough while he was alive."

"You did," he reassured her.

"So you think his hearing was a factor in his death?"

The same old flash of memory crossed his mind, Kyle refusing to look back, not answering his calls. "Yes, I do. It's all coming together, all the little things I saw but that didn't register until now."

"I know what you mean. I remember times when I thought Kyle was ignoring me. I thought he was tuning out my complaints, that he was being a typical guy. I didn't realize he might not have heard what I was saying. But that brings me back to why didn't he tell me? Why didn't he tell you, Aiden?"

His lips drew into a tight line.

"I have to believe it's because he didn't want to put me in a difficult position. If I'd known there was a medical issue, I wouldn't have let him jump. I would have suspended him until he could get medical clearance."

"That would have meant less money, right?" Vicky asked. "Kyle was really worried about making the mortgage payments. I pushed him to get this condo. I made him take my parents' money. I put too much pressure on him. He must have felt trapped. If he lost his job, we probably would have lost this place."

The picture was becoming sharper, Aiden realized. Kyle's father had run out on him and his mother when Kyle was a little kid. There was no way Kyle would let Vicky and Robbie down. "He probably thought he could get his hearing fixed without anyone ever knowing there was a problem. All he had to do was make it through a few months."

"But that last day…what happened out there, Aiden? I need to know."

"It was business as usual until the winds changed. We couldn't keep up with the fire. It was jumping our breaks. There was too much fuel. We kept changing positions. The crew split into three teams. We tried attacking from different fronts. Then the fire blew up. Our exit routes were cut off. Communication with the other teams became impossible. The smoke was thick and black. There were four of us in that final group. We went over our directions in case we got separated, and then we set off. Kyle was in the lead. He started going up instead of down. The other men went the right way. I went after Kyle."

Aiden could see the moment so clearly now. "I yelled at him to turn around, but he wasn't listening. He was literally running straight into the fire. I didn't know what the hell he was doing, why he'd veered off our course. And I have to admit that in the weeks since then I wondered if he was trying to kill himself. I knew he was under financial pressure, too, but I just couldn't believe he would do that to you. Now I'm sure that he didn't do that. He just couldn't hear me. I suspect he missed a lot of instructions that day. The fire was so loud he might not have even realized just how much he was missing."

He let out a long breath of relief as he finished the story. "I just wish I'd seen what he was trying to hide."

"I didn't see it, either," Vicky said. "He didn't want us to know. He was going to fix it himself. He often underestimated the difficulty of the tasks he attempted. It took him weeks to admit that he couldn't figure out why the car's *check engine* light was on. I begged him to take it to a mechanic, but he wouldn't do it. He was so stubborn."

"I remember that. I told him he was an idiot, that he should take the car to a mechanic."

Vicky gave him a painful smile. "That's the first time I've been able to remember him without the anger. I guess we should have talked earlier."

"We weren't ready."

"It wasn't your fault, Aiden. If Kyle couldn't hear you, and you couldn't get to him, there was nothing else you could have done." Tears filled her eyes again. "I try to take comfort in the fact that he died doing something he loved, and he loved smokejumping. He did not want to quit, even though I wanted him to. I was selfish. I wanted him to be with me all year long."

"Vicky, if you can believe anything I say—believe this. Kyle loved you more than he loved the job. I have no doubt in my mind about that."

"Thank you, Aiden. I just miss him so much. It's like he took a piece of my heart with him. I don't know if I'll ever be whole again." Her shoulders began to shake as the sobs overtook her.

He crossed the room, dropping to his knees next to her. He put his arms around her and held her while she cried, hoping that the truth would help them both heal. Her storm of tears went on for a long time, but Aiden never let go. Comforting Vicky was the one thing he could do for Kyle, and he would do it.

Finally, her cries turned to sniffs, and she lifted her head from his shoulder, her face ravaged from emotion, but there was a new lightness in her eyes.

"I'm sorry I destroyed your shirt," she said.

"You needed to get it out."

"I didn't realize how much I was holding in. Thanks again."

"No problem." He got to his feet with a grimace, his thigh muscle having cramped from the odd position he'd been in.

"You're hurt, too," Vicky said.

"Not too badly. It will heal." When he turned around, he realized that Sara was no longer sitting on the couch.

Vicky followed his gaze. "I hope she didn't go far."

"I drove, so probably not. But I should find her."

"She's important to you, isn't she?"

"I think so," he admitted.

"You said she knew Kyle?"

"Sara grew up with us. We've only recently reconnected."

"I saw the way you looked at her, Aiden. You never looked at anyone that way. If she's the one, don't wait too long to tell her. We both know life can be way too short."

"I want to help you with Robbie, whatever you need, money, babysitting, anything."

"Thanks." She hesitated. "Are you going to tell people about Kyle's hearing problem?"

He hadn't thought that far ahead. He could clear his name if the truth came out, but at what cost? He'd ruin Kyle's reputation. But Kyle had paid the ultimate price for his silence. Didn't Aiden owe his friend that same silence?

"I don't know," he said finally. "I have to think about it."

When he left the condo, Sara was standing on the sidewalk, leaning against the truck, her questioning gaze meeting his. "Are you all right?" she asked.

"You didn't have to leave."

"It felt like a private moment between you and Vicky. I'm glad that she finally saw you again for the incredible friend that you were and still are."

He smiled at the passion in her voice. "Thanks to you."

"I'm glad I could help."

"You did more than help. You inspired me to find the truth. I might not have done that without you."

"I don't believe that for a second, Aiden. I just had the benefit of a clearer head and a more objective perspective. But there's no way you would have gone through life without trying to make sense of Kyle's death. It's not who you are."

"I wish he would have told me about his hearing problems. I attributed so many other reasons for his distraction—worrying about Vicki or his finances, losing interest in the job, being pissed off that I was now his boss instead of just a coworker. But it was none of those things. He just couldn't hear me."

"How's Vicky doing?" Sara asked.

"Better. I think the truth released some of her anger, made her see that it was an accident. If the fire hadn't blown up the way it did, if we hadn't gotten trapped on that ridge, Kyle's hearing loss wouldn't have affected a damn thing."

"I hope you'll be able to accept that it was an accident, too."

"It's going to take a while."

"What are you going to do—now that you know the truth?"

"Hell if I know." He could see the tension in her eyes and knew she was burning to say something but really trying hard not to. "Do you have an opinion?"

"You should tell the truth."

"It will hurt Kyle. He won't be the hero who died in the fire. He'll be the guy who was hiding a medical issue, who endangered not only himself but everyone on the team." He paused. "Vicky wouldn't want me to say anything."

Sara frowned. "I'm sorry if this sounds harsh, but it's not up to Vicky. You're the one who's being impacted by the rumors. Your career has been tainted, and it's just wrong. Your job is important to you, and if you want to continue smokejumping or move into some other area of firefighting, then you should be able to do it with a clean slate. I don't think Kyle would want you to suffer for his mistake. He was your best friend."

"I can see why you're a good lawyer. You're very persuasive."

"And I hate injustice. Promise me you'll at least think about it."

"I will think about it," he said. "Now it's your turn."

"I'm not ready to see my dad," she said quickly.

"Then get ready, because you're supposed to be on a plane tomorrow." As he said the words, he felt his gut clench at the thought of saying goodbye to her.

He didn't usually have trouble with goodbyes. They were always accompanied by feelings of relief and enthusiasm for moving on. But watching Sara fly away was not something he was looking forward to doing. "Unless you want to postpone your return to New York?"

She stared back at him. "Why would I want to do that?"

He could read between the lines of that question, but what reason could he give her to stay? He was still reeling from what he'd learned about Kyle. He didn't know what he was going to do with his life, where he was going to live or work. How could he suggest that she give up the life she'd built when he had nothing to offer in return?

"Never mind," she said.

He sent her a silent plea for understanding. "It's been a rough day."

"You're right. It's been an emotional time for both of us. It's also been great. I had a wonderful time with you, Aiden. It was my fantasy come true," she said, her eyes watering a little.

"Sara—"

"No, let me finish. I have loved you since I was fourteen years old. But you have never felt the same way about me, and that's all right." She forced a smile on her face. "We had fun—a lot of fun, and I told you that I wasn't looking for promises. I meant what I said. I wanted to be with you, and it was amazing. And now it's over."

"Sara," he started again.

She put her fingers over his mouth. "I don't want you to say anything—except goodbye. That's all that's left."

"That's not all that's left between us."

"Yes, it is. This time it's my decision, Aiden. Not yours. Now, if you'll drive me back to my father's house, I will get the photos, I will confront him, and then I will go back to New York where I belong."

Twenty-Two

Sara didn't say a word during the drive across town. Aiden glanced at her every now and then, looking as if he wanted to say something, but in the end he stayed silent. She was relieved. It took every bit of strength she had to stay strong, because despite her words she was in deep physical and emotional pain. She hadn't just had fun with Aiden, she'd fallen in love with him again. In fact, she'd never stopped loving him, which was probably why she'd never been able to really love any of the other men she'd dated. He'd always been the standard against which all other men were measured.

But Aiden didn't love her. He liked her. He found her desirable. But that wasn't love, and she couldn't settle for anything less, not from him. She was in too deep to be casual.

When he parked the truck in front of his house, she took her bag, looked him straight in the eye and said, "Goodbye, Aiden."

He stared back at her, his blue eyes filled with dark shadows.

She waited for him to say goodbye back, but in the end, the tense silence was too much to bear, so she turned and walked away. She wondered if he'd call her back. He didn't.

She entered the house, set down her suitcase and let out a breath. Tears blurred her eyes, but she wasn't going to let herself cry, not yet anyway. She had to see her father. She had to confront him, and then her time in San Francisco would be over.

She went upstairs. The photos were on her bed where she'd left them. She picked up the picture taken at the park. Staring at the face of her big brother felt strange and awkward, but she could see her father in this child's face. She'd always looked like her mother.

Wishing again that her mother or her grandparents were still alive to answer questions only reminded her that they'd had years to share the truth with her, and they never had. She'd talked to her mother right before her death, and what had she said?

Take care of your father, Sara. He needs you more than you'll ever understand.

Why hadn't her mother taken that moment to explain why her father needed her? Because it certainly wasn't apparent. And why hadn't she taken that chance to tell her about the brother she'd never known and the family unit she'd never been a part of?

Had her father begged her mom to remain silent?

She must have kept the secret because of him.

That secret now made her feel less close to her mom, made her question if there were other things she didn't know.

It was time to face her dad. Gathering the photos together into a neat stack, she put them in her bag, grabbed her car keys and left the house. As she crossed the lawn, she took a quick glance at the Callaway house. Aiden's truck was parked out front, and there were two other cars in the driveway. She could see shadowy figures in the kitchen. She wondered if Aiden would do as she suggested and come clean with his family. It was certainly a risk. Burke and Jack might not be willing to keep quiet. They would want to defend Aiden, just as she did. Not that anyone wanted to hurt Kyle's memory, but no one wanted to protect Kyle at Aiden's expense.

Unfortunately, it wasn't up to her. Aiden would make his own decisions. And she had other things to worry about.

"Here I come, Dad," she muttered. "Ready or not."

———————

It was almost seven when Aiden made his way into the main house. He hadn't expected to find half of his family seated around the kitchen table on a Tuesday night. Not only were Jack and Lynda there, but Burke, Emma, Nicole, and his grandfather were also present. At first he thought the worried, strained expressions were about him, but that didn't ring quite true.

"What's going on?" he asked.

His grandfather, Patrick Callaway, gave him a pained look. "I was just telling the family that I took your grandmother to the doctor today, and they've admitted her to the hospital. They think she has Alzheimer's."

The diagnosis wasn't a total shock after what Aiden had witnessed the day before, but it hurt just the same. He'd been through such an emotional storm the last few hours, he wasn't quite ready for another. "I'm sorry. How long will she be there? I'd like to go see her."

"We're all going over in a bit," Lynda told him.

"As for how long," his grandfather said. "They don't know yet. They don't know whether she'll even be able to come..." His voice cracked. "They don't know yet," he repeated, as if he couldn't bear to look further down the road. He got to his feet. "I need to get back. I don't want her to wake up and not see anyone she recognizes."

"I'll walk you out," Jack said, accompanying his father out of the room.

As they left, Lynda, Burke, Emma and Nicole turned

their questioning eyes on him.

"Where have you been?" Emma asked, breaking the silence first.

"Why don't you ever return calls?" Burke demanded.

"Let him talk," Lynda interrupted.

"Are you all right?" Nicole asked.

"And where's Sara?' Emma said.

He put up a hand to slow down the questions. "First, I didn't return your calls because I needed to figure some things out. Second, Sara is fine. She's at her house now, and then she's headed to the hospital to speak to her dad. Third, I've discovered some new information."

Sara's plea to tell the truth had been going around and around in his head. Kyle had gone to great pains to keep his problem private, but Aiden didn't want to lie to his family. He'd seen the pain on Vicky's face when she'd realized her husband had been keeping his illness from her. And he'd seen the devastation in Sara's eyes when she'd realized her parents had kept something monumentally big away from her. The Callaways had always valued honesty. It was a code they lived by, and he didn't want to be the one to break that code.

"Aiden," Lynda said gently. "Whatever it is, you can tell us."

"I know. But what I have to tell you can't leave this room. And I'm not sure that's fair to ask."

"Of course it is," Emma said. "We'll put it in the Callaway vault."

"Just say what you have to say," Burke said.

He looked into his older brother's eyes, knowing that he was probably the one most likely to understand the position Kyle had been in. "Kyle had an illness that he didn't want anyone to know about. It wasn't life threatening, but it was quite possibly career-ending. Unfortunately, his problem played a part in his death in a way that I'm sure he didn't expect. Vicky would want me to keep his secret, to protect his name. She would want her son's father to be a hero."

"You can't do that," Burke said immediately. "You're putting your career on the line, Aiden. I understand that you want to protect Kyle and his family, but you have to think of your future."

Burke had always been practical, able to cut emotion out of a decision, but it didn't seem nearly as cut and dried to Aiden.

"Kyle wouldn't want you to suffer for what he did," Nicole said quietly. "You have to know that, Aiden."

"It sounds like he kept a secret to protect his job. But as sad as it is, that's not an issue anymore," Emma said. "You have to tell the people he worked with."

"You owe them that," Burke added. "If Kyle's illness was career threatening and it played into his death, then he jeopardized everyone on his team by hiding it. This isn't just about clearing your name, Aiden. Your fellow firefighters need to know the truth, because you're not the only one blaming yourself. I guarantee each and every one of them is asking themselves if they could have done something differently." He paused. "But you already know that, Aiden."

He did know what he needed to do, but Burke's impassioned speech had solidified his decision. He couldn't let anyone else carry the guilt of Kyle's death, not when he knew what had really happened.

"Burke is right," Emma put in. "Everyone who knew Kyle is hurting, and one of the reasons you got the blame was because they needed to point the finger at someone else besides themselves."

"Listen to your sister; she's smart," Burke said.

Emma smiled. "About time one of you big lugs figured that out."

"Hopefully you're being smart when it comes to your

own job," Burke added.

Emma's smile faded. "Of course. Has someone said differently?"

"No, but I know you, and these latest fires are hitting a little too close to home. I heard that Sister Margaret is missing, and her disappearance is suspicious, which might mean that your firebug may have jumped from arson to murder."

"God, I hope not," Emma said. "At least you aren't suggesting that Sister Margaret had something to do with the fire at St. Andrew's like that annoying Inspector Harrison."

"Just be careful."

"I am being careful. I really hope that Sister Margaret is okay and that her disappearance is not connected to the fire, but if it is, that's only going to make me more determined to track this firebug down. You don't need to worry about me, Burke. I can take care of myself."

"I don't know why I try to help any of you," Burke muttered as he stood up. "You're all so damned stubborn and always think you're right."

"Just like you," Emma retorted. "It's the Callaway way."

"I'll see you guys at the hospital later," Burke said. "I have a few things to do first."

As Burke left, Nicole also rose. "I won't get to the hospital tonight, but I'll see Grandma tomorrow." She smiled at Aiden. "Ryan said you came by the other night and played with Brandon. I appreciate that."

"He's my nephew. I plan to spend a lot more time with him in the future."

"Good. He needs as much help as he can get."

"Don't be afraid to ask for help yourself, Nicole," he said. "I'm here."

"For how long?" she asked.

"I don't know, but whatever I do, wherever I go, I plan to

stay in better touch."

Nicole gave him a quick hug. When she left the kitchen, it was just Emma and him. He could see she was itching to ask him a question, and he had a feeling he knew who that question would be about.

"So what's up with you and Sara?" Emma asked. "Is my friend still in one piece?"

"Sara is fine. She's an amazing woman."

"I know that. I've always known that. It's about time you realized it." Emma paused, tilting her head to one side. "Why did you guys run off without a word? I can't believe it was just to hook up away from here. It was too sudden. Something happened.

"You need to ask Sara that question."

Emma frowned. "Why all the secret-keeping, Aiden?"

"Because they're not my secrets to tell. Maybe give Sara a day before you grill her."

"Do I have a day? When is Sara going back to New York?"

"She's supposed to leave tomorrow," he answered, feeling the same stabbing sense of loss that he'd felt earlier that day.

"And you'll just let her go?" Emma queried. "When are you going to realize that you're in love with her, Aiden?"

Emma's words struck home, words he hadn't allowed himself to speak out loud, much less to anyone else. But he didn't do love—did he?

Emma got up from her chair and crossed the room, stopping right in front of him. He towered over her small frame, but he could still feel the force of her personality.

"Sara is my friend," she said. "And I know you hurt her when we were teenagers. She never gave me the details, but she had this crazy crush on you, and while I couldn't imagine why that was, she seemed to have really strong feelings for you. Something tells me you haven't discouraged those feelings on this trip. If you care for her at all, Aiden, you need to be upfront with her."

"I've always been upfront with her. I'm not a relationship guy."

"Aren't you? You care more about your family and friends than most of the guys I know. Those are relationships, too."

"That's different."

"That's true. But you have a tremendous capacity for love, and I hate to see it going to waste. I also do not want to see two people who are perfect for each other giving up without a fight. You have to be the one who goes all in first, Aiden," Emma added. "You owe her that. You broke her heart once. She's not going to be able to put herself out there for you."

Emma was right. It was his turn.

"Don't you dare let her leave without telling her how you really feel," Emma continued.

"This really isn't your business," he said.

"You're my brother, and Sara is my friend. This is totally my business," Emma snapped. "I know you like to play the bachelor, but you have a woman who is worth a long-term commitment, and if you let her go, you are out of your mind. You will not find anyone better than Sara."

—————

Sara walked into her father's hospital room feeling strangely calm and oddly confident. For the first time in her entire life, she felt like they were equals. In fact, to be honest, she felt like she was better than him. He couldn't intimidate her any more. He couldn't manipulate her by withholding love. She no longer cared what he thought about her. She only cared about the truth.

He set down the newspaper, his expression growing wary as she approached.

"I thought you'd gone home," he said.

"I was going to, but before I left I wanted to go through the box I found in the basement a few days ago—the one you were probably trying to get when you ran down the stairs and broke your leg."

Her father's face paled, and his lips tightened. "You had no business going through my personal things."

She ignored his protest. "I was touched at first that you'd kept photos of me, even if you had stored them in the basement. But then I realized that most of the pictures were not of me, but of someone else, a baby I didn't recognize, a toddler I'd never seen before. What was even more odd was that he had your name and your eyes and even your smile. The smile was actually unfamiliar to me, as you never looked at me like that, but after more intense scrutiny I came to the conclusion that it was actually you in the pictures."

"Sara, stop."

At one time the forceful determination in his eyes would have scared her into quiet, but not today. "I'm not going to stop, not until we're done. You and Mom had a baby, a boy, my brother." She took the pictures out of her bag, dropping them in a pile on the bed.

Her father glanced away.

"Look at him," she demanded. "Look at Stephen Davidson, Jr., and tell me why you kept his life a secret from me."

Her father finally turned his head. He stared down at the photos and then lifted his gaze to meet Sara's. There was no longer anger in his eyes, but agony. The raw pain shocked her, but she was also infuriated that almost thirty years later he could have so much emotion for a son he'd only shared four and a half years with and yet feel nothing for her.

"He died," her father said finally.

Two short words that meant so much.

"Why did you keep his life a secret?"

"Because he died."

She stared at him for a long minute. "You have to tell me more. I need more."

For a moment there was a battle of silent will.

Finally, he continued. "We were living in Portola Valley at the time. I was planting a bush in the front yard. I accidentally left the front door unlatched when I went outside. I didn't realize that Stephen had come into the yard until I heard a squeal of brakes and saw my son—" His voice shook with pain. "My son was on the ground."

She put a hand to her mouth, wanting to tell him to stop now. She'd heard enough.

But the dam had been opened. The rush of words continued.

"I ran to him. I could hear your mother screaming behind me. Stephen wasn't breathing. I tried to revive him. I blew into his mouth, but he was so limp in my arms. I could hear the fire engines coming. I prayed they would be in time. I kept telling my boy to hang on, that help was on the way. But it was too late. It had always been too late. He was killed on impact."

"Dad," she breathed. "You can stop."

He cut her off with a glare. "You wanted to know, so you'll know. We moved out of that house two months later. I couldn't stand being there, seeing that damn bush I'd wanted to plant, walking down that street. The blood stain on the street was there for days."

She felt sick at his words.

"We got an apartment in San Francisco. I didn't want a yard. I didn't want to see kids playing in a neighborhood." He paused. "But mostly I didn't want to have another baby."

His gaze met hers, and for the first time in her life he wasn't even trying to pretend that he loved her.

"Why did you have me then?" she asked.

"Because your mom stopped her birth control without telling me. After two years of intense loneliness, she wanted another baby, and she was tired of waiting for me to change my mind."

"So she had me, even though you didn't want me."

"I *couldn't* want you. I didn't have anything left to give you. My heart was destroyed. It died on the street with my son. Your mom said she'd do everything and that she'd love you enough for both of us. And I know she tried. I did my part by providing for you. You had everything you needed to succeed in life. I made sure that you got good grades and could get into a good school and make a career for yourself."

"You wanted to make sure I could be independent so that I wouldn't need you."

"I never wanted to hurt you, Sara."

"You just couldn't love me the way you loved him," she said, the truth finally clear. "You can pretend that you didn't hurt me, but you did. Your constant rejection shaped who I was. You made me feel uncertain about myself. You made me think I wasn't good enough. But I was good enough—for everyone but you. How dare you act like providing for me was enough? You may have put a roof over my head, but I deserved a lot more than that from my father."

"I couldn't let myself care about you. I didn't know how your mother could love you. How she didn't panic every time you weren't where you were supposed to be. How she tucked you in at night, knowing that no matter how tight she made the covers, they still couldn't protect you. How she let you walk outside and cross the street." He shook his head, his lips tight, his face pale, his eyes dark with pain. "I didn't know how she did it. I just knew that I couldn't. So I pushed you away, but you kept coming back."

"What a fool I was," she said, her eyes blurring with tears. "I just don't understand why Mom stayed with you."

"I don't know either. You weren't the only one I couldn't love. That's why I worked all the time. At work I felt right. At home, everything was wrong. I was a terrible parent, not just to you, but also to Stephen. I didn't keep him safe. I wasn't meant to be a father."

"Why did you keep Stephen's life a secret?"

"Because it hurt too much to talk about him. Your mother wanted to, but I wouldn't let her. And I wouldn't let anyone else talk about him either. We moved away. We had new friends. No one knew we had lost a child, and that's the way I wanted to keep it."

"And everyone agreed? Even Grandma and Grandpa?"

"They protested at first. They probably talked to your Mom about Stephen, but it had been a few years by the time you were born, and when I asked them to respect my wishes, they reluctantly agreed. Everyone decided that you would be better off not growing up in the shadow of tragedy."

"I don't believe you kept the secret to protect me," she said. "It was all about you." She paused for a long moment. "Do you ever think about him?"

"More than I want to," he replied. "It's been worse since your Mom died and you moved away. The house is very quiet. I can't hide from my thoughts the way I used to."

"Why keep the photos in the basement? You're the only one in the house now."

"I promised your mother right before she died that I wouldn't throw them away. She wanted me to tell you the truth, but I couldn't make that promise. I didn't move them upstairs because I was afraid you'd stumble upon them."

"But you had to know that one day I'd find the photos."

"I was hoping I'd be gone by then," he said frankly. "Is that it, Sara? Have I answered all your questions?"

She stared at him for a long minute. "When I saw the pictures, it wasn't the child who shocked me the most; it was you—it was your face, your smile. Don't you ever want to feel like that again? Don't you miss feeling good? Having a family? Enjoying your life?"

He shook his head. "I'll never be that man again."

"You could be."

"Why would you care if I'm happy or not? We both know I've treated you badly."

"You have been terrible to me," she agreed. "And I realize now that you wanted to make sure that I hated you. Because my hate was easier to take than my love."

He drew in a ragged breath. "When you were a little girl, before you realized what kind of father you had, you used to look at me with this sweet smile. You wanted to hold my hand. You wanted me to tell you a story. And I knew you were going to break what was left of my heart, and I couldn't let you do that. I just couldn't, Sara. I was holding on by a thread, and you were going to snap that thread. I couldn't let that happen."

His eyes glittered with moisture. Tears, she wondered in amazement. Was it possible this ice cold man could actually cry?

"I'm sorry," he said. "I'm sorry I couldn't be the father you deserved."

His apology brought tears to her eyes. "And I'm sorry about Stephen. I wish I'd known him. I wish you hadn't kept his life from me, because he was my brother. He was four years old when he died. He had a personality. He had a life. And I wish I'd known about it, because he was part of our family."

"Stephen was impulsive and fun-loving, very

imaginative," her father said. "He had to explore. He was so curious. That's why he left the house. He wanted to see what I was doing. It was my fault he was out there."

"You didn't close a door. That's not a crime. It's just a mistake. A tragic mistake."

"You're letting me off too easily."

"I doubt anyone could free you of your guilt. I'm sure my mother tried, and she obviously failed."

"So what now?" he asked.

She let out a breath. "I have no idea. But the relationship we had is over. I'm done with that."

He nodded. "I understand."

"But…" She couldn't believe what she was about to say. "If you want to try to get to know each other as adults, I'm open to it."

A glint of admiration entered his eyes. "You're a strong woman, Sara."

"I am," she said, meeting his gaze. "And ironically some of my strength is due to you."

He met her gaze, and she thought that for the first time he was actually seeing her and not the agonizing pain that he associated with being a father.

"I can hear your mother in my head," he said. "She's telling me not to be a fool. My daughter is giving me a second chance, and I should take it."

"I may not give you another one. I need to move on with my life. Your expectations have weighed me down for far too long."

"I would like to get to know you," he said slowly.

"Okay then," she said.

Silence followed her words. Neither one of them had any idea how to move forward. "Can we start tomorrow?" she asked a moment later. "Or maybe next week?"

"Absolutely," he said with relief. "Whenever you want."

She walked to the door, then paused. She gave him a smug smile. "By the way, Aiden and I drank the wine I brought for your birthday. It was really, really good."

Twenty-Three

Sara left her father's room feeling ten pounds lighter. The painfully honest conversation had been extremely cathartic. She had no idea what the future would hold, but the past was done. She was moving on with a clear head and a free spirit, and it felt good.

When she left the hospital, her spirits improved even more. Aiden was sitting on a bench waiting for her. He got to his feet when he saw her, his gaze dark and unreadable. Had he come to offer support or to finally say goodbye?

She slowly walked over to join him.

"How did it go?" he asked.

"It started out bad, then got worse, and finally ended a little better. I'm kind of shocked of how forthcoming he was. Part of me still wonders if I imagined the entire conversation."

He gave her a compassionate smile. "Did he tell you what happened?"

"Yes. He didn't want to, but I demanded answers. You should have seen me in there. I was very impressive."

"I have no doubt about that."

"It's a sad story," she said, relating the basic facts of what had happened.

"That's horrendous," Aiden said. "I almost feel sorry for

your father."

"I admit to feeling a pang of sympathy, too."

"But he still was an asshole to you. You can't forget that."

"I haven't, and I told him that. I couldn't believe the words that came out of my mouth. I said everything I'd ever dreamed about saying to him. I couldn't stop myself. The words just kept coming."

"I'm proud of you, Sara."

"I'm proud of me, too. I used to be so damn scared of my father. Now I can see him for who he really is, and that's a sad, angry, lonely man."

"You're not thinking of trying to fix him?" Aiden questioned, doubt in his eyes.

"I don't think that's possible, but—"

"I knew there was a but," Aiden said with a nod.

"I did tell him I would be open to getting to know each other as adults," she admitted, hoping that didn't make her sound like a complete fool. "But any new relationship has to be on my terms, and he'd have to treat me a lot better than he has in the past."

"What did he say?"

"He seemed a little stunned, but he was open to the idea. Now that the truth is out, he has nothing left to hide from me. I think the reason he treated me so badly was because he didn't want me to like him. He wanted to push me away. He just couldn't believe I kept coming back."

"Because you don't give up on people," Aiden said, his gaze turning serious. "I hope you haven't given up on me, Sara."

Her heart skipped a beat. She was riding such a wave of emotion she didn't want to let herself think that Aiden had come for any other reason than to make sure she was all right after having spoken to her father. But there was something in his gaze that told her there was more behind his actions. She really hoped she wasn't imagining things.

"I don't want you to go back to New York, Sara," Aiden said, shocking her with the words. "You asked me to give you a reason not to go."

"I remember. You couldn't come up with one."

"I could; I was just afraid to say it, and to be fair, you didn't give me much time."

"You've had more than enough time, Aiden." And she was not referring to their most recent conversation.

"I know that," he said, a small smile playing around his lips. "I've been a little slow, but I hope it's not too late. I love you, Sara."

Her heart stopped. Her breath caught in her chest. She could not have heard him correctly. "Say that again."

"Really? You didn't hear me the first time?"

"I want to hear it again."

He grabbed both of her hands and squeezed them tight. "I love you, Sara."

"No, you don't," she said immediately, shaking her head. "You don't do love. You told me so. You told me so a lot!"

"I was trying to convince myself as much as I was trying to convince you."

"You've had an emotional few weeks, Aiden. You lost your friend. You're in pain. You're lonely. You're not thinking straight. You'll wake up in a week and wonder why the hell you told me such a lie."

"Stop trying to talk me out of it," he said forcefully. "Everything you said is true, but I know what I'm saying. I know what I'm feeling. You're the one I want. And if I have to tell you again in a week or a month or a year or every day for the next fifty years, then I'll do that. I'm not going to change my mind. I've never told a woman I loved her. You're the first and the only."

"Really, Aiden?"

He met her gaze head on. "Really. I'm putting myself on the line for you. It's your turn now, Sara. You can say no. You can walk away. It's your call."

"It just seems unreal," she said. "You've always been this amazing possibility for me, but that possibility has never really been within my reach."

"I'm right here, and you can touch me wherever you want."

She gave him an emotional smile. "I'm starting to believe you."

"Good. I'll admit that my love doesn't go back as far as yours does. But I've always cared about you, Sara. I pushed you away all those years ago not only to protect you, but also to protect myself. Even then, I sensed that you had the potential to turn my life upside down, and I couldn't take that risk. I wasn't ready for you then."

"And you're ready now? You have to be sure, because I can't start something with you, Aiden, if you're not willing to go all the way. I don't just want to be your lover; I want to be your—everything." She laughed and cried at her choice of words. "God, I feel fourteen again. That sounded really stupid."

He grinned. "It sounded wonderful. I can commit, Sara. I just never wanted to before. But I want to commit to you. I love you," he repeated.

Her heart filled with tremendous joy. "I really hope I'm not dreaming right now."

"If you are, then I am, too."

"It's crazy."

"No, it's not crazy. You're an amazing woman. You're smarter than just about everyone I know. You're beautiful, kind, and incredibly generous."

"I like those words better than cute and quirky, but I

think you left something out."

He laughed. "How about you're sexy as hell, and every time I see you I want to rip your clothes off?"

"Much better." She gave him a wicked smile. "And just so you know, I feel exactly the same way every time I see you." She paused. "But it's not just physical attraction for me, either. I've admired you for as long as I can remember. You're one of the most amazing people I've ever met, and the reason I've stayed single all these years is that somewhere in my heart I was hoping we'd run into each other again. Emma is going to think I'm nuts!"

"Probably. She doesn't see me the way you do. But my family will be thrilled to see us together. They love you, too." He lowered his head and gave her a tender kiss that was filled with promise. Then he lifted his gaze to hers. "I want to be your everything, Sara." He paused. "Wait, is that a song title?"

"Probably," she said with a laugh. "I came up with that line when I was writing in my teenage diary. I never imagined I'd actually say it out loud and that you wouldn't run away or burst out laughing. But here you are."

"Here I am," he repeated. "I'm not laughing, and I'm not going anywhere. You're *it* for me. And just so you know, my future is wide open. If you want to live in New York, I'll go back there with you."

She was incredibly touched by his generosity. "You? My nature guy in the urban jungle?"

"As long as I'm in your bed at night, I don't much care where I am during the day. And I'm sure New York has some nature somewhere. It also has a fire department."

"I am tremendously touched by your offer, but I don't want to go back to New York," she said. "I want to start something new. I want to find what's really right for me. And I can do that here in San Francisco. Or maybe even in

Redding."

"I doubt you'll find a big law firm there."

"I can always open my own firm. I like the idea of being the boss. And there's a magical pool in a nearby forest that's just perfect for swimming."

"I don't want you to give up anything for me, Sara."

She squeezed his hands, gave him a loving smile, and said, "I don't want you to give up anything for me, either. We'll figure it out together."

"I like the sound of that. Now would you just kiss me already?" he said.

"Hey, I think that was my line."

He cut off her protest with one kiss and then another, their passion even stronger, because it was backed by love. She'd finally gotten the man of her dreams, and he was more than worth the wait.

The End

Keep reading for an excerpt from

the next book in the Callaway series

SO THIS IS LOVE
(Coming May 2015!)

ONE

Emma Callaway walked quickly down the dark street, wishing she'd arrived at her father's party on time so that she could have gotten a better parking spot, instead of having to hike three blocks up hill. As she passed a lone guy smoking a cigarette in front of a twenty-four hour market, she felt an odd sense of unease. The man's gaze seemed to follow her down the street, and she picked up her pace.

She wasn't normally afraid to walk at night, especially not in the West Portal neighborhood of San Francisco, but the street was filled mostly with retail and commercial buildings, and at nine-o'clock on a Sunday night, they were all closed, making her feel isolated and alone.

She took a quick glance over her shoulder. There was no one following her, but the shadowy street did not ease her nerves. She told herself to stop imagining things. She was just on edge. The last few weeks of work had been challenging, and all she wanted to do was relax and spend a few hours with her family as they celebrated her father's recent promotion to Deputy Chief of Operations for the San Francisco Fire Department.

Emma was enormously proud of her father, but Jack Callaway's latest feat had only set the bar of achievement that much higher for herself and the rest of the Callaway clan. Not that the bar hadn't always been high. Firefighting had been a family tradition for at least four generations, including the current one. Three of her brothers were firefighters, and she'd started out as a firefighter as well, eventually becoming a fire investigator a year earlier.

She loved being an investigator, but it was also frustrating work. Determining whether a fire was arson was one thing, finding the perpetrator and getting justice was another. But she wasn't going to think about her open cases tonight. She just wanted to spend time with her family and friends.

Opening the door to Brady's Bar and Grill, she stepped inside and paused, surprised at the huge crowd. Her father was a popular guy, but it seemed as if half the city had come to toast his latest achievement. A long mahogany bar covered the far wall, and there was a line three deep to get cocktails. The dance floor was packed with people drinking, talking, and laughing, and every table in the main dining room appeared to be full. Gazing to the right side of the restaurant, she saw a cluster of people in the hall by the back room where darts and pool were the games of choice.

Brady's would make a killing tonight, she thought with a smile, not that they didn't do a good business most nights. Brady's was a firefighters' bar. The owner, Harry Brady, had a son, Christian, who was also a firefighter, and it wasn't uncommon for shifts to end with a trip to the bar. Wherever she looked, she saw familiar faces. She was a local girl, and Brady's was a local bar—the kind of place where everyone knew each other's name.

The door opened behind her and a blast of chill November air sent a tingle down her spine. Glancing over her shoulder, that cold quickly turned to heat when she met the deeply intense and penetrating green eyes of Max Harrison, an inspector with the San Francisco Police Department.

Max had transferred from Los Angeles three months earlier, and since then their paths had crossed a few too many times. She'd found Max to be a cocky, territorial detective, whose idea of sharing information was her telling him everything she knew, and him giving nothing in return.

While she didn't like Max's attitude, she couldn't help but appreciate the way he filled out a pair of faded jeans and carried off a brown leather jacket over a cream-colored knit shirt. He was tall and athletically built with a mouth-watering physique, light brown hair that shimmered with gold, and a far too sexy mouth. But she knew trouble when she saw it, and the last thing she needed in her life was man trouble. She'd gotten out of a serious relationship a few months earlier, and she didn't need to dive into another one, especially not with someone who could heat up her body with just one look.

"What are you doing here?" she asked shortly.

Their meetings were always tense, the mix of anger and attraction between them making most of their encounters awkward and uncomfortable. It was bad enough they had to occasionally work together; she didn't want to socialize with him, too.

"Your brother, Burke, invited me. We play basketball together on Wednesday nights."

Of course they did. The police/fire basketball league was hugely popular. As a female firefighter, she'd always felt left out when it came to the basketball games. She could compete in co-ed softball, but the basketball games were all guys, and that was the way they liked it.

Her phone buzzed, and she pulled it out of her bag, hoping it wasn't work calling.

Frowning, she realized she would have preferred a work text than the one she'd just received. "Damn," she muttered.

"Something wrong?" Max asked.

She returned her phone to the outer pocket of her bag. "It's nothing." She'd barely finished speaking when her phone buzzed again.

"Doesn't sound like nothing," he said, a speculative gleam in his eyes. "Aren't you going to answer it?"

"No."

Her phone buzzed again, and she pulled it out of her bag to turn the ring to silent. As she did so, she saw three texts on the screen. Seriously? Jon hadn't talked to her this much when they were sharing an apartment. "I can't believe this," she muttered, then wished she'd kept her mouth shut as Max's interested gaze settled on hers. "Ex-boyfriend," she explained.

"He must want another chance."

"Men always want what they can't have."

He tipped his head in acknowledgement. "The chase can be appealing."

"I'm not good at playing games."

"I doubt that. I've seen your competitive streak."

"Not when it comes to the games of love," she corrected.

Max smiled, and with that smile came sparks, the fluttering of butterflies in her stomach, the sudden dampness on her palms, the tingly feeling of anticipation shooting down her spine. They weren't standing very far apart, only a few inches between them. It wouldn't take more than a step to put her hands on his solid chest, lean in, raise her face to his.

Whoa!

She put the brakes on her runaway thoughts. She was not going to kiss Max Harrison. That would be reckless and stupid. It would probably also be really good, because he looked like the kind of man who knew how to kiss a woman. But she was not going to test out that theory.

She couldn't let a little lust get in the way of her common sense. They had to work together. She needed to keep things professional.

Clearing her throat, she said, "I should find my father."

"Isn't that him over there?" Max tipped his head toward the center of the room.

As the crowd parted, she could see her parents, grandparents and several of her siblings seated at a table in the center of the room. Her father was the focus of attention, which didn't surprise her. Jack Callaway had a larger-than-life personality, and like his Irish ancestors, there was nothing he enjoyed more than telling a good story and sharing a pint or two.

With dark brown hair that was now peppered with gray, wide-set blue eyes, and a big booming laugh, Jack had charisma and presence, which was probably why he'd done so well in his career; he was a natural born leader. He was also a man of high integrity and deep commitment to his job, which made him a great role model. She'd admired him for a very long time, not just as a father but also as a firefighter. She could see that same respect in the eyes of everyone at the table.

"That's him," she murmured, glancing back at Max. "You haven't met yet?"

"No. Is that your mother next to him, the pretty blonde in the red dress?"

"That's her."

"You look more like your mother than your father."

"I do take after my mom, but Jack isn't my biological father. He's my stepfather."

Surprise flashed in Max's eyes. "I didn't know that. You have his name."

"It all happened a long time ago. My mother, Lynda, married Jack when I was four years old. He legally adopted me as well as my older sister, Nicole, three years later. Since we rarely saw my biological father, we were both happy to become Callaways."

"So you and Nicole are biological sisters. What about the rest of your siblings? Who belongs to who?"

"Burke, Aiden, Drew, and Sean are my stepbrothers. Their real mother died. Jack was a widow when he met my mom. After they got married, the twins, Shayla and Colton were born. It's a yours, mine and ours kind of situation, but in reality, we're just one big happy, sometimes crazy, family."

"I can see the pride in your eyes," he commented.

"I love my family. Although, I have to admit that being a Callaway comes with expectations. Jack and his father are hard acts to follow."

"From what I've seen, you're up for the challenge."

She tilted her head, giving him a thoughtful look. "Is that a compliment, Harrison?"

"Don't let it go to your head, Callaway. Who else is at your dad's table?"

"Next to my mother are Jack's parents, Eleanor and Patrick. Then there is my baby sister, Shayla. She's a girl genius, only twenty-three and almost done with medical school. And lastly there's Colton, Shayla's twin. He's a rookie firefighter. I'm not sure where the rest of my siblings are."

"It sounds like your siblings are all very high-achievers."

"Jack told us the Callaways were born to serve and protect, and most of my siblings have followed that tradition, four in firefighting, one in medicine, one in search and rescue, and one in teaching. My brother, Sean, is the only one who didn't follow the plan. He's a musician, a fantastic singer and song writer," she added, not wanting Max to think she wasn't proud of Sean. "He couldn't come tonight, because he's touring the Pacific Northwest."

"How does he get along with your father?"

"They have their moments, but Sean has always moved to a different beat. That's my family. Tell me about yours."

Excerpt from *SO THIS IS LOVE* (Callaways #2)

"Nowhere near as interesting," he said shortly.

"Let me be the judge."

"Maybe another time. Can I get you a drink? It looks like the line for drinks is thinning out."

She wasn't surprised he dodged her question. He'd been remarkably reticent when it came to his private life. She'd been tempted to do a little research on him more than once, but she'd always stopped herself. The less she knew about him the better.

"I'll take a sparkling water if you're going to the bar," she said. "I'm on call this weekend."

"Got it."

As Max turned around, he was almost run down by one of her long-time friends, Tony Moretti.

Tony was an attractive thirty-two-year-old of Italian descent. He and his twin brother, Jarod, had grown up around the corner from her.

"Emma," Tony said, opening his arms wide. "I was hoping you'd be here. I was looking for you at Mass today, but I didn't see you." She gave him a quick hug, aware that Max hadn't actually gone to the bar as he'd proposed. Instead, he lingered a few feet away watching them. She wondered why he was so interested.

"I didn't make it to church this morning," she said, turning her attention to Tony. "I've been really busy at work."

"I couldn't believe someone torched the school at St. Andrew's. Do you have any suspects?"

"Not yet. But I haven't given up."

"Speaking of not giving up, you owe me a date," Tony said. "Remember? I helped you move out of your ex-boyfriend's apartment, and you offered to buy me dinner."

"I do remember. I'm sorry I've been busy."

"So let's make a date."

She saw the determination in Tony's eyes and wondered

where it came from. She'd known him since she was six years old, and while they'd been a part of the same social group for years, they'd never gone out alone together, and she wasn't sure she wanted to change that. She liked Tony a lot, but he was a flirt, and she didn't want them to end up in an awkward situation. Their families were friends.

"I'll take a look at my calendar tomorrow, and we'll find a day that works," she said.

"Good."

"What's good?" another man asked.

She smiled at Tony's brother, Jarod. The Morettis were fraternal twins but looked almost identical with their dark hair and dark eyes.

"Is my brother hitting on you again, Emma?" Jarod asked.

"We're just talking," she said. "How are you doing? How's the construction business?"

"It's picking up." He cocked his head to the right, giving her a thoughtful look. "I don't think I've seen you since you became an arson investigator. How's that going? Are you working the fire at St. Andrew's?"

"Yes, I am." She paused. "I need to say hello to my dad. I'll talk to you guys later, all right?"

"Don't forget to call me," Tony said as she walked away.

As she moved through the crowd, her gaze drifted across the room. Max had gone to the bar, and she felt relieved that he was no longer watching her. She didn't need any more tension in her life, and that's what Max brought with him every time he came around. Hopefully, he wouldn't stay at the party long.

—➤➤◄◄—

As he waited for their drinks, Max felt restless and irritated. Emma Callaway always got under his skin, and tonight was no exception. Usually, he could keep the attraction between them at bay. Usually, he saw her in uniform or in firefighting gear, her blonde hair covered by a helmet, her slender body in thick, shapeless overalls, but tonight, in a short turquoise dress, her sexy legs bare, her feet encased in high heels, her blonde hair styled, and her blue eyes sparkling under thick black lashes, she'd stolen the breath right out of his chest.

Damn! He really shouldn't have followed up on Burke's invitation. But he'd been tired of his own company, and he'd wanted to see Emma outside of work. Now that they'd seen each other, now that his pulse was racing, and his entire body was on edge, he realized his mistake. It was too late to retreat, but he could make this a short night. He'd buy her a drink and then he'd head home. She wouldn't miss him. She had her huge family to keep her company, not to mention all the single guys in the bar.

It would actually be easier if she were dating someone. He didn't poach other men's women. But she was single and so was he. And as much as she annoyed him with her stubbornness and independence, she also impressed him. Besides being beautiful and sexy, she was strong, courageous and smart.

He needed to stay away from her. They couldn't hook up; they had to work together. And they couldn't have a deeper relationship, because he wasn't a relationship guy. So the only option was to take a hands-off approach, which would be a lot of easier if he didn't want to touch her so badly. For a second earlier, he'd had the strangest feeling that she wanted to kiss him. He'd probably imagined it.

Max glanced across the room. Emma had made her way to her father's table and was giving her dad a hug. There was a lot of love in the warm smile they exchanged, and for some reason, that shared look tugged at Max's heart, reminding him of a connection he'd lost a long time ago.

The bartender set down his drinks. He was grateful for the interruption. He handed over cash and then headed across the room feeling oddly nervous. He'd never been good at meeting the parents, and even though this wasn't that kind of moment, he still felt tense.

Emma accepted her drink with a cautious smile. "Thanks."

"No problem." He could see various members of the Callaways giving him curious looks. He had a feeling Emma's family was as protective of her as she was of them.

"Let me introduce you," she said. "Dad, this is Max Harrison. He's an inspector with the SFPD. My father, Jack Callaway."

Jack got to his feet to shake Max's hand. His gaze was sharp and direct. "Nice to meet you. Hank Crowley speaks very highly of you."

"I have the utmost respect for Captain Crowley," he replied, at the same time wondering why his mentor had been talking to Jack Callaway about him. Hank knew he preferred to stay under the radar, and if there was ever a man who wasn't under the radar, it was Jack Callaway.

"How do you know Emma?" Jack asked.

"We worked on an arson/homicide case last month."

"Max is a recent transfer from Los Angeles," Emma added. "But maybe you already knew that if you've been talking to Captain Crowley." Emma shot her father a speculative look.

"Hank mentioned that. How does it feel to be home?"

"Home?" Emma interrupted, glancing from her dad to Max. "You're from San Francisco? You never told me that."

"You never asked," he replied.

"Where did you live?"

"On Noriega Street in the Sunset District."

"I had a place on Noriega Street once," Emma's grandmother said.

Max looked across the table at Eleanor Callaway. She had white hair and blue eyes that seemed a little hazy, dreamy almost, as if she wasn't quite present.

"When did you live on Noriega, Grandma?" Emma asked.

"A long time ago," she said. "When your father was in high school. It was such a pretty house." She turned to her husband. "You painted the wall behind our bed blue, remember?"

"Just like your eyes," Patrick said, his loving gaze on his wife.

There was clearly a strong connection between the two, Max thought, wondering what it would be like to be in love and married to someone for fifty years. He couldn't even imagine it.

Eleanor smiled at her husband. "We had so much fun in that house, big dinners with all the kids around the table. I was happy." She paused, her smile fading. "But then we had to leave. We had to move after that bad, bad day."

"No one wants to hear about that," Patrick told his wife, his tone sharp and purposeful.

"It's going to be okay, isn't it?" she asked, worry in her eyes as she gazed at her husband. "You said it would. You promised."

"It's fine," he assured her. "It was a long time ago."

"What was a long time ago?" Emma asked.

"Don't add to the confusion with questions," Patrick said, giving Emma a harsh look.

Emma quickly apologized. "I'm sorry."

"I'm Patrick Callaway," her grandfather said, his attention turning to Max. "And this is my wife, Eleanor."

"I'm very happy to meet you both." He wondered how he

could extricate himself from a situation that seemed to be turning more awkward by the moment. He had no idea what Emma's grandmother was talking about, but her odd comments seemed to have left everyone at the table speechless.

Eleanor suddenly stiffened, confusion in her expression as she pointed her finger at Max. "You're not Emma's boyfriend. You're not Jon."

"No. I'm Max."

"I like Jon." She gave Emma an annoyed and bewildered look. "Why aren't you with Jon? He always brings me those hard candies."

"Jon and I broke up, Grandma."

"But he loved you. You loved him. You were going to get married and have babies."

Emma cleared her throat. "We decided it wasn't right."

"So this man is your new boyfriend?" Eleanor demanded, not looking at all happy about it.

"No, he's a colleague. We work together sometimes. That's all." She looked relieved when Burke arrived at the table, interrupting their conversation "Burke," she said with relief. "You're here. And Max is here."

"So I see," Burke said, shaking his hand. "Did you meet everyone?"

"Emma was just introducing me," he replied.

Emma waved her hand toward the other members of her family. "My mom, Lynda, sister, Shayla, brother, Colton."

Her mother and siblings said hello. Colton appeared more interested in whatever he was reading on his phone than the conversation at hand. Shayla gave him a very curious look. Fortunately he did not have to talk to anyone as a group of people approached the table to offer Jack congratulations.

To give the newcomers more room, Max moved a few steps away. Emma did the same.

Excerpt from *SO THIS IS LOVE* (Callaways #2)

"Sorry about that," she said. "My grandmother is in the early stages of Alzheimer's, and we never know what is going to come out of her mouth."

"I'm sorry to hear that she's ill."

"It's hard to watch her deteriorate. She was a very sharp woman when I was younger. I couldn't get anything past her." Emma frowned. "I can't believe she remembered Jon. He hasn't been around the family in months."

"Apparently, the candies he brought her stuck in her head."

"I brought the candies for her birthday. He just took the credit." Emma's gaze drifted back to her grandmother. "I don't know what she was referring to when she alluded to some bad, bad day. It was such an odd thing to say."

"It sounded like your grandfather knew what it was about. He was quick to cut her off."

Her gaze swung back to him, her eyes questioning. "I thought so, too. It's the second time in the last few weeks that Grandma has mentioned a secret, and the second time Grandpa has changed the subject. But I can't imagine what secret she would be keeping.

"Have you asked your grandfather about it?"

"No. You don't ask my grandfather things like that. To be honest, I've always been a little scared of him. He's the only one in the family who ever made me feel like a stepchild."

Her comment surprised him. Emma seemed so confident, so sure of her place in the world, but in this moment he could see uncertainty in her eyes, and he wondered if she had to be good, had to be right, in order to prove herself to her family because she wasn't a Callaway by blood. It might explain why she was so determined to win, to succeed, to be the best at everything.

"Anyway," she said, turning her focus back to him. "How come you never told me you grew up here, and don't say it's because I didn't ask. I spoke to you about Los Angeles and your reason for transferring, and you never said anything about the fact that you were actually coming home."

"I haven't thought of this city as home in a very long time. I left when I was eighteen. That was fourteen years ago."

"Is your family still here?"

"Some of them."

"Why did you leave and why did you come back?" she asked, as she took a sip of her water.

"I left to go to college, and I came back because it was time."

"That's deliberately vague, Harrison."

"Maybe you should take a hint and drop the subject, Callaway."

She gave a dramatic sigh. "Another person with a secret. I seem to be surrounded by them tonight."

He smiled. "I don't know about that. Your Italian boys seemed up front and outgoing."

"The Moretti twins? I've known them forever. They're not to be taken seriously."

Her dismissive words made him feel oddly better about the interaction he'd witnessed earlier. "Are you sure about that? The first one looked really into you."

"Tony is a huge flirt. He's that way with everyone."

"If you say so."

"I do say so," she said firmly. "What about you? No date tonight?"

"Not tonight."

"You do like to be the man of mystery, don't you?"

"I've heard it adds to my charm."

"Charm? You think you have charm?" she asked doubtfully.

He couldn't help but grin at her disgruntled expression.

"Apparently, you don't think so."

"Tonight is the first time I've ever seen you smile. So maybe there's more to you than I thought."

"Maybe there is."

She stared at him, then said. "Well, I don't have time for mystery men. I have my hands full at the moment."

He should be relieved by her answer, but he found himself oddly disappointed.

"I should go and mingle," she added.

"You should," he said, downing his drink. "I have to take off."

"So soon?"

"I have an early morning. Have a good night."

"You, too."

He set his empty glass down on a nearby table and moved quickly through the crowded restaurant. When he stepped outside, he was surprised to see a guy peering into the windows of the bar. He wore jeans and a big sweatshirt with the hood pulled up over his head. The man jerked when he realized Max was looking at him. He turned quickly and walked away.

Uneasiness ran down Max's spine. His car was in the opposite direction, but something made him follow the guy down the street. The man picked up his pace when he reached the corner. Max did the same, but when he jogged around the block, the guy was gone.

Max stopped, frustrated that he'd lost him, even though he didn't really know why he was in pursuit. But he'd trusted his instincts for a very long time, and most of the time his gut did not steer him wrong. Maybe this time, however, his instincts were off. He was on edge. His life was about to change in a big way, and he didn't know if he was ready.

Turning, he walked back the way he'd come. When he reached his car, his phone rang. He pulled it out and saw his mother's number. His stomach muscles clenched.

"Mom? What's up?"

"I just want to make sure you're going to pick me up at eight o'clock tomorrow," she said.

"I promised I would," he replied.

"Don't be late. Your brother has waited long enough for this day."

"I won't be late," he promised. He slipped his phone back into his pocket and then opened his car door and slid behind the wheel, his heart racing a little too fast as he thought about the next morning—about the sixty mile drive north to the prison where he would pick up his brother.

Two

⟶⟫⟪⟵

The fire call came in at three o'clock in the morning on Monday, three hours after the Callaway party ended. Emma had been asleep, lost in a crazy dream that involved her ex-boyfriend Jon, the annoying Inspector Harrison and her grandmother when she'd been awoken by the sound of her cell phone.

It had taken a minute for the bad news to sink in. This wasn't just any fire, it was a fire at Brady's Bar and Grill, and first responders on the scene had determined the fire to be suspicious.

She threw on her clothes and drove back to the bar. She had to park a block away; there was a line of fire engines and police cars blocking the street. As she walked toward the fire, she saw flames shooting out of the roof and through the broken windows. She felt sick to her stomach. The warm, cozy neighborhood bar where she'd spent so many hours was totally engulfed with fire. It seemed a bitter irony that a place so special to the firefighting community was now going up in smoke. A few hours ago there had been dozens of firefighters celebrating her father's promotion. Now there were dozens fighting the blaze.

Was that the point? Had someone wanted to make a statement in a place where firefighters gathered?

Her mind whirled with questions as she drew closer to the scene. She scanned the gathering crowd for anyone who looked out of place or appeared a little too interested or too happy about the fire. It wasn't uncommon for arsonists to stay and watch their handiwork. It was part of the thrill. Some even called the fires in so they could watch the fire trucks come roaring down the street and see the terrified residents pouring out of their homes.

Fortunately, this city block was made up of commercial buildings, with only a few second- and third-floor apartments mixed in, so they didn't have many people to worry about. There were a dozen or so individuals wearing pajamas and robes standing across the street. The adjacent buildings had obviously been evacuated. Fighting fires in San Francisco was always a challenge, as many of the structures shared common walls. A fire could spread through an entire block if it wasn't caught early.

As soon as she arrived on scene, she checked in with Incident Commander Grant Holmes, whom she'd worked under in her firefighting days.

He gave her a tense nod. "Callaway. You got here fast."

"I couldn't believe it was Brady's. We were just here celebrating my father's promotion."

"Looks like it will be the last party here for a while."

"How did it start?"

"We found gasoline cans inside the front and back door. The rear portion of the roof collapsed seconds after the first guys in reported a deceased female. We haven't been able to get her out yet.

Emma's stomach turned over. She knew several of the female servers at Brady's. "Do you have an I.D.?"

"No."

"Has the owner been contacted?" she asked, looking around for Harry Brady.

Excerpt from *SO THIS IS LOVE* (Callaways #2)

"He was here with his son, Christian, but Harry started having chest pains, so the paramedics took him to the hospital."

She was sorry to hear that. "I hope he's okay. This bar is his whole life."

"Let's hope he wasn't the one who burned it down," he said cynically.

She couldn't believe Harry would destroy his livelihood, but as the owner, he would be at the top of her interview list.

As Grant moved away to talk to one of the crew captains, she saw Max walking toward her. He wore the same clothes he'd had on earlier, but his hair was tousled, and there was a shadow of beard on his jaw. He looked even sexier, if that was possible.

"What do you know?" he asked abruptly.

"Not much. There's apparently a female victim. I guess that's why you're here. They haven't been able to retrieve her body." She glanced at the building. "I feel like I'm dreaming. We were just here a few hours ago. Everyone was having a great time. Now, this raging blaze…"

"An interesting irony," Max said. "Firefighters' bar goes up in flames."

He'd jumped to the same suspicion she'd had, that someone had wanted to make a statement to the firefighting community. "It could be a coincidence," she felt compelled to say. "But I will find whoever decided to torch this place. This one isn't just business; it's personal."

Max tilted his head, giving her a thoughtful look.

"What?" she challenged.

"Just thinking that the last two fires were also personal to you—the high school and St. Andrew's Elementary School."

"I grew up in this neighborhood, and all three fires have been at buildings important to the community, but that's hardly personal to me. It's a matter of geography. It's not unusual for firebugs to work close to home. It adds to the secret thrill that they know something no one else does."

"A logical point. But you have to admit that you're a common denominator."

"So are a lot of people. Thousands of children have gone through St. Andrew's and the high school in the last twenty years." She paused. "Speaking of St. Andrew's, has there been any progress in locating Sister Margaret?"

Margaret Flannery, one of the teaching nuns at St. Andrew's, had disappeared a little over a week ago, right before the fire at the school that had destroyed two classrooms. Sister Margaret had also been a teacher at the high school a decade earlier, a fact that Max had used to link her as an arson suspect. But Emma didn't believe for a second that Sister Margaret was their firebug.

"Unfortunately, no," Max replied. "What about your fire investigation?"

She hated to admit that she was no further ahead on her case, but there were no witnesses to the school fire and no forensic evidence. Her investigation was basically stalled. "Nothing new. I need to focus on this fire. I'm going to talk to the neighbors."

"I'll go with you," he said.

"If you must," she said unenthusiastically.

Her words brought a small smile to his lips. "I can be helpful, Callaway."

"You can also get in the way," she retorted.

"So can you, but don't forget we're on the same side."

Somehow, it never quite seemed that way. Most of the time they were butting heads and challenging each other's results. They needed to find a better way to work together; she just hadn't come up with one yet.

It didn't take long to speak to the small group of people huddled together. They were shaken up and worried about their apartments. No one had seen anything. They all reported having been woken up by firefighters or cops ordering them to evacuate. By the time they'd gotten outside, the fire was blazing.

Emma jotted down names, addresses and phone numbers. After her first few questions, Max disappeared, and she couldn't help wondering where he'd gone. He usually liked to be right in the middle of the action.

When she'd finished her interviews, she saw Max coming out of an alley between two buildings across the street. She walked over to him. "Where did you go?" she asked suspiciously.

"Just looking around."

"For what?"

He shrugged. "It's probably nothing," he muttered.

"Tell me."

"When I left your father's party, I saw a guy outside of Brady's. He was staring through the windows, and he jumped when I came out, as if he'd been caught doing something he wasn't supposed to be doing. He ran off before I could get a good look at him. He was probably in his twenties. He wore jeans and a gray sweatshirt with a hood up over his head."

She doubted Max would have mentioned the man if he didn't think he was a possible suspect. She didn't like the way Max took over their cases, but she did respect his instincts.

"There's our victim," Max said, moving quickly across the street as two firefighters brought out a body. They set her down on a stretcher.

Emma stepped up next to Max to take a look. The woman's features were shockingly familiar. She gasped, putting a hand to her mouth as waves of nausea ran through her. "It's Sister Margaret," she said.

Max's eyes widened. "Shit!"

It was hard to look at the lifeless body of a woman who

had been a mentor to her, but she forced herself to do just that. Every detail was important.

Sister Margaret had very short, white, thin hair. Her face had not burned, but her skin was very white with tints of blue. She wore black loose-fitting slacks that hung in shreds over her burned, blistering legs. What had once been a white button-down shirt was blackened from smoke and dirt. The long sleeves had also been burned away, and her hands and fingers showed only remnants of flesh over the bones.

Emma had to breathe through the urge to vomit. She saw burn victims a lot, but she never got used to it.

"Her hands are burned," Max commented, as he, too, took a good look at her body.

She wanted to say that there was no way Sister Margaret had set the fire, but she couldn't. Had the woman had a secret fascination with fire? Had she gotten caught up in her own work?

There were no other visible wounds from a knife or a gun or any other type of weapon. Had she died from smoke inhalation, or had something else happened?

"The medical examiner should be able to tell us more," Max said, motioning for the paramedics to take the body away.

"I can't believe this," she muttered, watching them load the body into the ambulance. Her mind ran through the clues they'd already accumulated. "Whoever set this fire killed Sister Margaret."

"That's one theory."

"Stop trying to make Sister Margaret the villain," she said sharply, taking out her anger and pain on Max. "She didn't do this."

"I'm keeping an open mind. Maybe you should do the same instead of letting your personal feelings cloud your judgment."

Excerpt from *SO THIS IS LOVE* (Callaways #2)

"My judgment is not clouded," she snapped. "You do your job, and I'll do mine."

"We need to work together."

"Not tonight we don't. You're not cleared to enter the building until the fire is out, but I can get in now."

"Emma, wait," he said, as she turned to leave.

"What?"

His lips tightened. "Be careful."

She didn't know how to take his words, because it almost sounded like he was worried about her.

"I always am," she said, then strode away. She was relieved when the commander gave her clearance to enter the building. Sister Margaret's death had raised the stakes, and she wanted to find the bastard who'd killed her favorite teacher and torched Brady's Bar.

Max watched Emma enter the still-burning building. He couldn't help but admire her courage. The fire was under control, but it wasn't out, and part of the roof had already collapsed, but there was no hesitation in her step. She was a woman on a mission. He wished he could have gone inside with her, but he would have to wait, and he hated to wait. He also hated the fact that Emma would get first crack at the crime scene, but she knew what she was doing, and her goal was to preserve as much evidence as she possibly could. Hopefully, that evidence would take them both in the right direction.

Glancing down at his watch, he realized it was four-thirty in the morning. There was nothing more for him to do at the moment. He would wait until the medical examiner gave him official identification before notifying Sister Margaret's family. That wouldn't happen before tomorrow. He also wouldn't be able to get inside Brady's for a few more hours. He might as well go home and grab a couple of hours' sleep. He had a big day ahead, and he was nowhere near ready for it.

After returning to his apartment, he tumbled into bed. Unfortunately, his mind was too worked up to let him rest. Whenever he caught a new case, he had a rush of adrenaline, and Sister Margaret's death had sent a million questions racing through his brain. He'd originally taken on the case as a favor to his mentor, Captain Hank Crowley. Hank had known Sister Margaret for years, and he hadn't wanted to dump the case onto an already overloaded missing persons detail, so he'd asked Max to investigate.

He'd spent a lot of time interviewing the nun's friends and family since her disappearance, and he'd been hoping for a different outcome. Now that the worst had come true, his investigation would continue in a new direction. Hopefully they would find some DNA or some clue as to who had killed her if, in fact, someone had killed her.

While he appreciated Emma's staunch defense of her former teacher, he couldn't overlook the fact that she'd disappeared right before a fire at her place of employment and now had turned up dead in yet another suspicious fire. If she wasn't the arsonist, she was tied to him or her in some significant way. He just had to figure out the connection.

After three hours of tossing and turning, he took a shower, grabbed some coffee and headed to his mother's house. He arrived at exactly eight a.m. as promised. The front door was open, and as soon as he pulled up, his mom was out of the house and locking the door behind her. She was eager to get on the road. He didn't feel nearly as enthusiastic.

As she walked down the stairs, he couldn't help thinking that she looked more energetic and put together than she had in a long time. She'd lightened her brown hair with blonde highlights and exchanged her usual jeans and sweaters for black slacks and a gray blazer. As she got into the car there was a sparkle in her brown eyes, making her look younger than her fifty-six years. Susan Harrison had been reborn into someone with optimism and energy. He barely recognized her from the tired, weepy, depressed woman she'd been for most of the last two decades.

"I didn't think this day would ever come," she said, as she fastened her seatbelt. "It feels like a lifetime."

It could have been an actual lifetime, he thought, as he put the car back into drive, but fortunately for his brother, the murder charge had been dropped to manslaughter.

"I bought all your brother's favorite foods," his mom continued. "Dinner tonight will be roast beef, mashed potatoes and mixed vegetables, followed by apple pie and ice cream. I haven't cooked like this in years. It felt strange to go to the supermarket and buy for more than one person."

"I'm sure Spencer will love whatever you put on the table."

"You'll come to dinner, too," she said.

"I don't know if I can."

She shot him a dark look. "Don't be ridiculous, Max. This is the first night in forever that we'll be able to eat as a family again. Of course you're coming to dinner. We have a lot to talk about." She drew in a deep breath and let it out. "I hope Spencer is all right. I hate to think of what he's had to go through in that terrible place. I hope prison hasn't damaged him forever."

He hoped the same thing, but he had his doubts.

"I wish we were there already," his mom said. "I can't wait to get my boy home."

He didn't bother to reply, knowing his mother was lost in anticipation of a happy family reunion. His older brother had always been her favorite. Spencer had been twelve when their father took off, and his mom had turned her oldest son into the man of the family. At eight, he hadn't been able to offer her the kind of support she needed. But Spencer had stepped up to the challenge.

Max had looked up to his older brother, too. Later on, as an adult, he'd come to realize that his hero had a few flaws, but he doubted his mother had ever come to that realization. She'd always seen the best in Spencer.

"You're not saying much, Max." His mother gave him a warning look. "I don't want anything to mar this day, so if you've got something negative to say, say it now, before we pick up Spencer."

"I don't have anything negative to say."

"Good. I know things have been complicated and awkward between us all. But we're family, and we're going to be together again, and that's all that matters."

"You're right." He just hoped Spencer would be able to let go of his anger and move on.

So This Is Love Releases May 2015!

About The Author

Barbara Freethy is a #1 New York Times Bestselling Author of 42 novels ranging from contemporary romance to romantic suspense and women's fiction. Traditionally published for many years, Barbara opened her own publishing company in 2011 and has since sold over 5 million books! Nineteen of her titles have appeared on the New York Times and USA Today Bestseller Lists.

Known for her emotional and compelling stories of love, family, mystery and romance, Barbara enjoys writing about ordinary people caught up in extraordinary adventures. Barbara's books have won numerous awards. She is a six-time finalist for the RITA for best contemporary romance from Romance Writers of America and a two-time winner for DANIEL'S GIFT and THE WAY BACK HOME.

Barbara has lived all over the state of California and currently resides in Northern California where she draws much of her inspiration from the beautiful bay area.

For a complete listing of books, as well as excerpts and contests, and to connect with Barbara:

Visit Barbara's Website:
www.barbarafreethy.com

Join Barbara on Facebook:
www.facebook.com/barbarafreethybooks

Follow Barbara on Twitter:
www.twitter.com/barbarafreethy